INKING EAGLE

Charon MC
Book 1

MaryBeth
Enjoy the ride!
Khloe Wren

KHLOE WREN

Books by Khloe Wren

Charon MC:
Inking Eagle
Fighting Mac
Chasing Taz
Claiming Tiny
Saving Scout

Fire and Snow:
Guardian's Heart
Noble Guardian
Guardian's Shadow
Fierce Guardian
Necessary Alpha
Protective Instincts

Dragon Warriors:
Enchanting Eilagh
Binding Becky
Claiming Carina
Seducing Skye
Believing Binda

Jaguar Secrets:
Jaguar Secrets
FireStarter

Other Titles:
Fireworks
Tigers Are Forever
Bad Alpha Anthology
Scarred Perfection
Scandals: Zeck
Mirror Image Seduction
Deception

ISBN: 978-0-9876275-1-3

Cover Credits:
Model: Brian K Naranjo
Photographer: R + M Photography
Digital Artist: Khloe Wren

Editing Credits:
Editor: Carolyn Depew of Write Right

Acknowledgements

Being the first book in this genre I've written, it was more intense to write than my other books. As always my wonderful husband supported me and my kids put up with me!

I couldn't have written this book without several people who patiently answered all my many questions about Marine life and MC life. Heath, Dawn, Erin, Diana and Shannon (I'm sure there were more and I'm sorry if I missed you by name) I can't thank you enough for all your help. Especially Heath.

To all my friends who helped me get back up each time I stumbled while writing this book. Becky McGraw, Eden Bradley and Tamsin Baker you three especially.

To my editor, Carolyn, no matter what I throw at you, you always come through with a marvelous edit. I appreciate everything you do and thank you for another job well done.

My beta team, Andy, Shannon, Renita and Tracie, thank you for your input that helped Inking Eagle be as realistic as possible.

xo
Khloe Wren

Biography

Khloe Wren grew up in the Adelaide Hills before her parents moved the family to country South Australia when she was a teen. A few years later, Khloe moved to Melbourne which was where she got her first taste of big city living.

After a few years living in the big city, she missed the fresh air and space of country living so returned to rural South Australia. Khloe currently lives in the Murraylands with her incredibly patient husband, two strong willed young daughters, an energetic dog and two curious cats.

As a child Khloe often had temporary tattoos all over her arms. When she got her first job at 19, she was at the local tattooist in the blink of an eye to get her first real tattoo. Khloe now has four, two taking up much of her back.

While Khloe doesn't ride a bike herself, she loves riding pillion behind her husband on the rare occasion they get to go out without their daughters.

Dedication

To Becky McGraw,

Thank you for pushing me to be brave.

Charon:

Char·on \ˈsher-ən, ˈker-ən, -än\

In Greek mythology, the Charon is the ferryman who takes the dead across either the river Styx or Acheron, depending on whether the soul's destination is the Elysian Fields or Hades.

Prologue

Eagle

Pulling up beside my two Marine brothers, I turned my Harley's engine off, but like the others, I stayed seated on my bike. As was habit after so many years on deployment together, I glanced to the man on my right, to follow his lead. Over my fifteen years of active service, I'd been on several missions with Jacob 'Mac' Miller. The last few he'd been my gunnery sergeant. I trusted him with my life, and would follow him just about anywhere.

He sat staring into the front window of the little hole-in-the-wall cafe we were due to meet in, and I figured, like me, he was wondering what the fuck we were all doing here.

"We going in?"

Donovan 'Taz' Lee's Australian accent was still thick, even though he'd been living in the States since he was a teenager. I sincerely hoped the man never lost it. I'd been hearing it regularly since we'd met at boot camp, after we both enlisted in the Marine Corps after the 9/11 attacks. We'd both gone onto further training, him as a sniper and me as his spotter. Fuck, I could barely remember a time when I hadn't heard his Aussie drawl on a daily basis.

"Yeah, let's go see what the fuck this is all about."

Mac was the first to dismount his ride, Taz and I following. Tension coiled in my belly, because we all knew Sergeant Major Johnson wouldn't want to have lunch with us to just shoot the shit. He was up to something.

With quick, efficient movement, I stored my helmet and followed my brothers into the cafe. My instincts didn't pick up any threat, but all three of us still scanned the area, both outside and then the interior. We might have left the Marines eighteen months ago, but our training never left us. *Once a Marine, always a Marine.* Even here in southern Texas, which was a shitload safer than the Middle East, it wasn't without its dangers.

Sgt. Maj. Johnson stood as we entered, not that we didn't already know precisely where he was. The man had a presence about him that made you stand a little taller, no matter whether he was sitting, standing, or lying the fuck down.

"Afternoon men, glad you could make it."

Taz stepped forward to shake his hand first. Even after all the shit we'd seen and done while serving, Taz had never lost his easy smile or friendly demeanor. Of course, those close to him, like myself and Mac, knew it was a well-constructed mask. We also knew the man wasn't ready to confront his demons, so until that time came, we simply acted as though he was fine.

"Hey, it's been a while. How're the wife and kids doing?"

"They're all fine. Britney married last month—some skinny little runt that'll blow over if the wind blows hard enough. He's an investment banker, or some shit. No idea what my girl sees in him, but she appears happy."

Mac and I silently watched on as Taz chuckled. "Good thing you taught your girl how to take care of herself then. Doesn't sound like her man will be much good if something does go down."

A smile spread across the older man's face and a gleam entered his eyes. "Best thing I ever did was teach that girl how to fight. Of course, her brothers didn't think so when they were teenagers and she could hand them their asses when they tried to pick on her." He paused to shake his head. "She'll probably save *his* butt if anything ever happened."

The small talk continued as Mac moved in to shake Sgt. Maj. Johnson's hand and I frowned. The sergeant major seemed overly calm—as though he was putting on a front, but underneath was nervous. Once Mac finished, I moved to take his palm and greet him.

"Sir, why do you need to see us? You know we're not re-enlisting."

Disappointment flashed in his eyes for a moment. I knew he'd been sorry to see the three of us go, especially Taz. He had been one of the best snipers the USMC ever had. I'd been by his side, spotting for him, for over twelve years of missions. That added up to a fuck-load of kills. I tried not to focus on the number. They'd all been our enemies, but they were still human. And I don't care how badass you are, after twelve fucking years of looking down a scope, killing people, you needed, and had earned, a fucking break. The three of us had decided when our last re-enlistment came up that we'd retire—spend some time stateside, seeing the country. Take a breather from war and gunfire and just fucking relax for a while.

"I'm not here to ask you to, not that I'd turn you away if you changed your minds." He looked to each of us, and when he saw we had no intention of changing our minds, he kept talking. "Take a seat and order some food, then I'll explain."

Curiosity had me wasting no time in ordering quickly, as did the others.

"Now, what's going on?"

Mac, who always liked getting straight to the point, didn't wait long to start pushing the sergeant major for an explanation. It was probably one of the reasons Mac made such a good gunnery sergeant. Mac had already served for a few years before Taz and I enlisted. When we were assigned to a platoon with Mac several years ago, the three of us quickly bonded and hadn't hesitated to stick together once we left the service.

The way the sergeant major's jaw flexed before he cleared his throat had me focusing fully on the man. This was going to be something big.

"I've been keeping tabs on you three since you left." He raised a hand, palm toward them. "Don't jump on me. I haven't done it constantly, just every now and then. Enough to make sure you're all doing okay in civilian life. By that, I mean I know you three have been riding around the country on Harleys since shortly after you returned stateside."

"That can't shock you. Plenty of men turn to riding once they return."

Taz almost sounded defensive. I would have been too, if I hadn't sensed the sergeant major was leading up to something. And it wasn't kicking our asses for wasting time touring around.

"True enough, but since you're the only three I know who have, that I trust, and that are living here in Texas, I'm here talking to you."

The waitress arrived with our food and silence descended as she laid our plates out. The air around us was filled with tension as all three of us waited for Sgt. Maj. Johnson to get to the point.

"I've been approached with a request that I think you three are perfect for—if you're interested, that is. Any of you heard of the Charon MC before?"

I stopped eating. Anyone not living under a rock in Texas had heard of the Charon MC. They were known for serving justice when the legal system failed, and keeping their hometown of Bridgewater drug and crime free. They also owned a few local businesses, which were thriving.

Mac's expression hardened as he leaned forward. "Of course we have. They're based down in Bridgewater, near Galveston, but their reputation spreads a hell of a lot further than that."

"The FBI wants to get some undercovers in the club. At this point, they're not considered a one-percenter club and there's nothing going down right now that they're aware of. The issue is the club is growing in numbers and power, and they're skirting the edge of the law more often. It's making them nervous and they'd like to have a man or two on the inside to pass on any information they might require. You three interested in joining a motorcycle club for at least the next couple of years?"

Mac frowned over at the sergeant major. "Once you join one of those clubs, you don't just leave after a couple years, and you know it."

"Okay, so prospect in, and if you really don't like it by the time you're ready to patch in, call it quits and walk away. I'll tell the feds they need to look elsewhere. How does that sound?"

I thought it through for a moment. On the surface, it didn't sound like a bad idea. But Mac was right. If we decided to do this, it was a long-term thing. That meant we needed some time to discuss how to proceed, because if one of us was out, all of us were.

"We need to think and talk about it. When do we need to let you know?"

Sgt. Maj. Johnson pulled out a leaflet and put it on the

table in front of Mac.

"Next Saturday they're having a poker run, open to the public. They do them every so often this way, and it's the perfect way to get their attention and ask the right questions to get in the door. I can't imagine they'll turn away three decorated marines wanting to join their ranks. I'll be watching along the way. Whether I see your bikes in the mix, or not, will give me your answers."

After the sergeant major stood, tossed a couple bills on the table and left, I looked over to my two best friends.

"So, what do you think?"

Chapter 1

Ten Months later
Silk

"I see Eagle's back on guard duty today."

I sprayed and wiped over the skin I was working on before I reloaded my gun to continue Tiny's tattoo. Colt "Eagle" Benally was the bane of my existence. He'd joined the club ten months ago and was still a couple months off getting his top rocker. He had Native American heritage that gave his shoulder-length, jet-black hair a silky sheen. Made my fingers itch to run through it whenever I even thought about it. His dark, brooding eyes were always watching. That man never missed a thing, hence his road name, 'Eagle'. Rumor had it he originally earned the moniker in the marines. I believed it.

From the first time I caught a glimpse of him at that public poker run last October, I'd been hooked. He was one extremely well-put-together package of sex on a stick. And sadly, one I couldn't touch. Prospects could screw around with the club whores all they wanted, but they weren't allowed to touch the Daughters of the Club. Only patched in members could try to romance us, and even then, they'd better be deadly serious about how they felt. Especially with someone like me. My uncle was the vice president, enough to scare any prospect with half a brain. But I'd caught Eagle watching me more than a few times, his dark, sexy gaze following me around the clubhouse whenever I attended a party or barbeque. And he did seem to be my guard here at the shop more often than not these days. I couldn't wait to see what would happen in two months when he got patched in. Would he make a move on me? Or was he just looking to fill his spank bank with someone untouchable? A grin spread over my face—if he did come after me, I wouldn't make it easy—he'd have to work for it. And if he was using me for spank bank material, it would soon get out and my uncle would deal with him.

"I overheard Uncle Clint saying he was Taz's spotter in the marines, or some shit. Apparently he sees things others don't. Guess that means the poor schmuck gets put on guard duty all the damn time."

Tiny stiffened beneath me but stayed silent as I responded to Gabs, my best friend and fellow artist. I ignored Tiny, knowing he wouldn't rat me out to my uncle for talking about Eagle to Gabs. Gabs might not officially be part of the club, but she's hung around enough of us to know who's who in our world. She let out a sigh before she responded to me.

"I have to wonder why anyone would want to be a

prospect. They get all the shit jobs for *so* long."

I shrugged. I've spent most of my life around the club, and there were always plenty of men hanging around, waiting for a chance to prospect in.

"It's shorter than any apprenticeship I've heard off. Hell, mechanics are doing shit jobs for four years before they get their certificate. Prospects normally only take a year before they earn their patch."

Gabs stilled from where she was sorting out the new order of body jewelry. "Huh. Hadn't thought of it like that."

"Your uncle know you go around calling him Clint?"

Tiny's gruff voice was deep and suited his large frame.

"Sorry, Tiny, but 'Uncle Bulldog' just doesn't roll off the tongue."

It was a constant argument between me and my uncle. Everyone in the club used their road names, not their birth ones, and Uncle Clint grumbled every time I called him Clint, not Bulldog. My aunt on the other hand, thought it was hilarious.

Tiny shook his head with a huff, but didn't say anything more. I was well aware no one else would dare try to call the vice president of the Charon MC anything but Bulldog, and around the clubhouse I did call him by his road name. But outside of that building, he was Uncle Clint. The wonderful man, who, along with his wife, took me in when I had no one else in the world left. I preferred to not even think about how the 9/11 attacks on

New York left me an orphan, let alone talk about it. Or how my dad's brother appeared out of nowhere to take me home a week later. Understandably, he'd refused to fly after what happened and drove all the way from Bridgewater, Texas to Boston, Massachusetts, along with his wife—my aunt Rose—as soon as he'd gotten word. I hadn't ever met either of them before that day. When I'd asked my dad years earlier about why I didn't have uncles and aunts like my friends at school, he'd explained that I did have one uncle. That his older brother was a biker and because of that, he'd been cut out of our lives. I really wished my dad hadn't done that. It had been completely unnecessary, and as a scared, grieving, twelve-year-old, I could have used a familiar face.

Once Uncle Clint brought me home to Texas I was instantly surrounded by this huge biker family that, initially, frightened the shit out of me. Especially after what my father had said about bikers. That was only until I got to know them, though. Now, I wouldn't trade them for the world. They were rough, and occasionally did shit the law said was wrong—but they were always there for me. Whenever I've needed anything, they've come through and supplied it. Like this shop. Silky Ink was my baby. The club had loaned me the start-up funds to open it, and I was slowly paying them back, much to my uncle's disapproval. The club would have been happy to put their name to the shop forever, but I wanted it to be mine. I wanted to prove I could make it successful on my own.

I'd opened it three years ago to instant success. Of course, the fact the entire club came to me for their ink helped a great deal. I currently had three other artists working the shop with me, two men and another woman. Because some of the old timers didn't want a woman doing their ink, I'd had to find an older male tattooist pretty damn quick after opening. Even now, I still had to watch that appointments didn't clash. A few of the old timers are old-fashioned enough, they don't want to have to watch some chick getting a tramp stamp tattooed on her while they were getting their 'real' ink done. I rolled my eyes just thinking about it. *Sexist idiots.* But a girl's gotta eat, so I did my best to keep them all happy.

"How much longer you want to spend in the chair tonight, Tiny?"

This piece was huge and covered his entire back. Naturally, the main image was the club colors, a stylized black skull that had cross bones made out of bike pistons behind it, and a feathered angel wing on one side and a dragon wing on the other. It was the perfect mix of light and dark, good and evil. Because that's what the Charons were. They were the kings of skating the edges of the law (and occasionally breaking it) for good reasons.

As a woman, I didn't know much of what they did. Club business wasn't my business, but I'd heard rumors, and saw what mysteriously happened when no one was looking in the dark of night. I was proud to be associated with the club and loved living in the safe town of

Bridgewater, where everybody within a hundred mile radius knew not to mess with anyone in the town unless they wanted the wrath of the Charon MC brought down on them.

Tiny stretched his neck to look up at the clock on the wall.

"Give it another half hour, Silk. I got work to do later."

Yeah, the boys weren't the only ones that earned road names. I'd been called Silky since I was fifteen. One of the old timers at a club barbeque commented that I could talk Bulldog into any damn thing with my silky voice and the way I'd bat my eyelashes. It'd stuck. As an adult, it got shortened to Silk more often than not. Still, it was better than the incredibly old-fashioned Claudine my folks had named me. Focusing back on my task, I eyed off the design, working out how best to finish it off for now.

"When you coming back? If it's not tomorrow, we're going to have to leave it a couple weeks to heal before I can continue."

I knew he was booked in for a session each night this week, but I didn't know what he meant by work. He could have been pulled in to do a run for a couple of days.

"I'll be here tomorrow. I want this piece done."

I grinned. Good. I wanted to get it done too. It was going to look spectacular.

"It's going to look fucking epic, Tiny."

On the feathered wing side of the tatt, there would be a

kickass vengeful angel. On the other side, a wicked looking dragon. I was really proud of the design. Working with Tiny, it had taken me a couple weeks to draw up the final design and seeing him so hell-bent on getting it inked as fast as he could gave me a buzz like you wouldn't believe.

Gabs stayed quiet until after Tiny left. Then she came over to help me clean up so we could both get going.

"Why do we suddenly have guards 24/7 anyhow?"

My breath caught for a moment before I could force myself to act normal. Anything even close to club business, I couldn't talk to Gabs about. Even if it was something I was only guessing at, because I didn't have a fucking clue about it.

"You know, usual shit with the Iron Hammers. The club's just being careful."

It was an educated guess on my part, and told Gabs nothing the entire town didn't already know. The Iron Hammers had always had it in for the Charons.

The Iron Hammer MC was a club based down in Galveston. They wanted to own the entire strip between there and Houston. Unfortunately for them, the Charons didn't agree. The club kept our town's streets clean of drugs and violence. Every night there were at least a half-dozen Charons patrolling.

My shop didn't normally have the door guarded, and when I'd tried to grill Uncle Clint about it, he told me it was 'club business' and to just accept it. He also told me if I tried to lose my guards, I'd end up on lockdown at the clubhouse indefinitely.

A shudder ran through me. The last thing I wanted was to not be able to leave the clubhouse. I needed fresh air and space around me. I also need to be able to head off for a few days before the eleventh of next month, so I'd be a good girl until then. Because no matter what was going on, on the anniversary of 9/11 I wasn't going to be around a ton of people, listening to them all say how tragic the whole thing was.

It had been so long now, only a few of the older club members remembered how I lost my parents that day. I knew the younger guys didn't mean any offense by what was said every year—I just didn't want to hear it. So, for the week surrounding the anniversary, every year I took off on my own. No one knows where I go. I've never even told Gabs where I retreat to, and this year wasn't going to be any different.

As I followed Gabs out the front door and locked up, I got an eyeful of Eagle in all his hot biker glory. *At least my guard was pretty to look at in the meantime.*

Eagle

Something wasn't right with Silk. She didn't look any different, wearing her usual combo of blue jeans and black t-shirt with her shop's logo on it, with her long blonde hair in a braid down her back. But since I'd arrived first thing this morning, my instincts had warned me that there was something brewing under her surface. All day I'd tried to figure out what it might be, but I couldn't work it out.

My appearance made it obvious I had Native American ancestry, but I hadn't been raised immersed in the culture. My mother had abandoned me to the foster care system as a baby, and the system hadn't given a shit what my heritage was. Despite that fact, I'd always sensed things others couldn't, and learned early on to trust in my instincts.

I earned the nickname 'Eagle' within days of starting boot camp, and it had stuck. Most people think the reason I see things they don't is due to extra-sharp eyesight. But truthfully, it's because I've learned to rely on, and trust in, my other senses over the years. Those instincts saved me more times than I could count while in foster homes, and then again on deployment. I winced as I thought of all the insurgents that had lost their lives due to my instincts and Taz's perfect aim. Our last mission had been weeks of sitting in hides, working out distances and lining up shots. I'd seen way too many middle-eastern alleys in that time. And way too many bodies littering them when we pulled out. Taking a deep breath, I pushed it all down. It had happened two years and five months ago. Nothing I could do to change any of it. I needed to focus on the fact my life didn't involve killing people anymore, not get bogged down in the past.

I was grateful when Silk come through the front door of her shop, and in a heartbeat, had my complete focus on the present and her. This sexy as hell, inked-up blonde bombshell had captured my full attention from the moment I first saw her when Mac, Taz and I rode in that public poker run last October. She'd been riding her purple Softail and damn, but she rode that thing with complete confidence. I'd never seen a woman look more comfortable riding a bike solo than she had that day. And it had drawn me to her.

"You two heading home now?"

"Yeah, having a quiet night in. Got a booking first thing so need my head on straight."

I frowned down at her. "What are you playing at, Silk?"

She blinked up at me and Gabs chuckled behind her. Yeah, I'd heard she'd earned her nickname for the way she used to bat those big doe eyes of hers at her uncle and smooth as silk get away with whatever the hell she wanted.

"I ain't Bulldog, honey. Those eyes won't work with me. What you playing at?"

Her jaw clenched as her gaze narrowed.

"I'm not up to anything. I'm worn out after working my ass off all day, and now I'm going home to crash. What's so unusual about that?"

I watched her closely, looking for anything that would give away what she had going on.

"It's the easy way you're accepting having a 24/7 bodyguard that has me nervous. You planning on slipping your leash?"

The slight stiffening in her shoulders told me I was onto something.

"Leash? Just you try to put one on me and we'll see how well that goes for you."

She was standing close and was poking me in the chest with her finger with each word she spoke. Damn, but she was so fucking sexy all fired up. I hoped she couldn't see the bulge in my jeans I was now sporting thanks to her.

"It's a figure of speech, Silk. Don't get your panties in a twist. No one would be crazy enough to try to leash you. Which is why you just accepting your security detail has me wondering about what you're up to."

Silk rested her fists on her hips and glared at me but before she could say anything else, Gabs came up and linked her arm through hers.

"She's not up to anything tonight. We're both going home and we're gonna order a pizza, watch a rom com and go to bed early. Ain't that right, Silk?"

With a huff, she rolled her eyes. "Yeah, Gabs. Killing some brain cells watching you drool over Hugh Grant sounds like my perfect night."

My lips twitched at her sarcasm. I could see Silk drooling over the Rock or maybe Vin Diesel, but not some pretty-boy actor. No way that girl liked rom coms. Gabs, on the other hand, I could totally see planning her fake wedding to Hugh Grant by night's end. Gabs was all light and fluffy to Silk's hardcore. Somehow they meshed together to form an unbreakable friendship that

I'd been told they'd had since high school.

I raised my hands in defeat. "Fine. You're not going to tell me straight. I'll just have to work it out some other way, so I can stop you."

A flash of heat in her eyes had my cock twitching.

"Like hell you will. It has nothing to do with the club, or you, *prospect*. So get the hell out of my face."

I let her storm by me to her bike. I knew she was lashing out because she was pissed I was onto her. But the whole 'you're only a prospect' thing cut deep. I'm ten months in, and at some point in the next couple months would, hopefully, be asked to patch in. Of course, that was a double-edged sword. I wanted my top rocker to be a full member of the club. But as a full member, I wouldn't be on Silk's security detail as often as I currently was. Of course, being patched in also meant she was no longer out of bounds. Would she agree to be mine? I knew without a doubt she'd make one hell of an old lady.

My thoughts kept spinning as first Silk got on her bike, then Gabs climbed on behind her. Watching those two cuddle up, getting ready to go, had me needing to adjust myself before I got on my own ride. As I predicted she would, Silk gunned the throttle and shot out of the parking lot. I followed them home, but stayed sitting on my bike out on the road. Normally I'd try to get them to let me go through the house before they entered. But I wasn't willing to risk it tonight, especially since my instincts told me it was all clear. I was more likely to get shot by Silk than find anyone in their place tonight.

As a prospect, I hadn't been told why Silk suddenly needed around-the-clock guarding. There were always issues with the Iron Hammers, but nothing specific had gone down that I'd heard about. I knew some of the other Daughters of the Club weren't being watched at all. It didn't add up, but as a prospect, my job was to do what I was told, not to question it. And if it meant more time around Silk, I wasn't going to complain.

Once the girls locked themselves in, I left my bike to do a quick boundary check of the house, just to be sure. When nothing looked suspicious, I rang for the night shift to come in. I was due to work a few hours, manning the bar back at the clubhouse once I finished here, and I was hoping to catch one or two of the old-timers. Hopefully, they would have had a few drinks by the time I got there, and would be willing to answer my questions about what the hell might be going on.

Chapter 2

Silk

Two weeks later I sat at the clubhouse bar and glared at the bottles that lined the back wall. Eagle's gaze burned into my back, but I didn't care. That sexy, badass biker got me put on fucking lockdown so I was pointedly ignoring him while I got falling-down drunk.

"Gimme another one, Taz."

The prospect manning the bar was Eagle's buddy. *Naturally*. I couldn't seem to get away from the bastard lately. It had been nearly a year since Eagle and his buddies Mac and Taz became prospects. I couldn't wait for them to get patched in so they didn't have prospect jobs that meant the three of them were constantly in my damn face.

"Here ya go, luv."

I chuckled as I realized Taz's sexy Aussie accent sounded better and better the more I drank. He had light, sandy-colored hair, clipped up the sides and a little longer on the top. *Jarhead*. Taz was the only one of the three that had kept his high and tight cut. His eyes showed he'd been to war. Literally. I often saw the shadows that would pass over his baby blues when I looked into his eyes. He did a good job hiding his pain behind his wicked sense of humor, but I could see he was only showing the world a small part of himself. Hopefully, once he patched in, he'd open up to his club brothers and let himself enjoy life a little more. It was one of the great things about MC life. Everyone here had your back, guaranteed.

I snatched up the shot and threw it back, barely noticing the burn anymore as I slammed the glass back down.

"Again."

"No."

That last shot had my head buzzing, but not so much I missed the growled command from over by the door. I spun on my stool to glare at him, and had to grip the side of the bar so I didn't fall on my ass. Taz's laughter filled the air, but I ignored him.

"You ain't the boss of me, prossspect."

When I slurred the last word, he smirked over at me. Dammit. It was Friday night and the clubhouse was packed. He shouldn't have been able to even hear me from where he stood, let alone keep eyes on me all bloody night to know how much I'd drunk.

"C'mon, Tazzz. Give me one more? Please."

I batted my eyes the way I had with my uncle. It always used to work...

"Sorry, luv. Big man says no."

With a pout, I scowled at him. "Eagle doesn't fuckin' get a say in what I do."

"When Bulldog puts him in charge of you, he does."

My temper flared and burned off some of my buzz. Pushing away from the bar, I started doing the rounds to find my dear uncle. How dare he? It was bad enough they tricked me into coming here tonight, then locked my ass down when I'd tried to leave. Now they wanted to prevent me from having a little fun too? No fucking way. I marched toward the back hallway. If Aunt Rose was still here, they'd be out the back sitting around the fire pit.

By the time I made it to where I could feel the heat of the fire, my alcohol buzz had completely disappeared. Pissed off that I couldn't even be left alone to get drunk—or stay that way—I stormed around the yard, but there was no sign of my uncle or aunt. I couldn't see any of the other old ladies either, so I figured they must have all left already. That was normally how Friday nights went. All the partnered-up members left with their old ladies and kids before the really wild shit started up. The Charons may have gone mostly legal, but they hadn't left the sexual debauchery behind.

With a sigh I moved back inside. I'd have a quick check in the main rooms to see if Uncle Clint had hung back for some reason. As the VP, he sometimes stayed behind for club business. And if I couldn't find him, I was aiming at finding Scout. The club President would deal with my fucking shadow, who I could still feel watching me.

I made it two steps inside the door of the closed room before a low growl came from behind me. Unsure what Eagle was going to do, I quickly looked around the room for anyone who had the power to order my guard dog to heel. I rolled my eyes at some of the club whores who were naked and being fucked by two or three guys each. This was why I'd wanted to go home an hour ago. I knew nothing happened here that wasn't one-hundred-percent consensual, but that didn't mean I wanted to watch the shit go down.

"You don't need to be in here, babe."

I straightened my shoulders, and because I knew it would piss him off, strode deeper into the room. I didn't want to be here, but somehow annoying Eagle was more important than my discomfort at finding myself in the middle of an orgy. I knew no one would try anything with me. I was wearing my cut with my Daughter of the Club patch sewn on front and center. Well, front and to the side, really. That patch screamed loud and clear that if you weren't thinking "I want her for my old lady", then you didn't touch.

A few low curse words were my only warning. Eagle came to stand in front of me, blocking my view, then faster than I could track, he had his shoulder against my stomach and I was over the damn man's shoulder like a fucking sack of potatoes, then he strolled out into the hallway.

"Put. Me. Down!"

"No way. Not until I get your fine ass up to your room. Bulldog will have me castrated if he finds out I even let you step foot in that room. What the fuck, Silk? You know better."

"I was looking for Bulldog or Scout to order you off my ass. I don't need a fucking bodyguard! Especially here inside the damn clubhouse. And *especially* one that won't even let me have a few drinks. Put me down already!"

He had his arm firmly banded around my legs so I couldn't kick him, and my fists thumping his back didn't affect him one bit. Stupid leather cut was protecting him from my blows. Not that I'd be able to do damage to him, even without the leather. He was a former marine for fuck's sake. Unless I had a sledgehammer to hit him with, he wouldn't feel anything I did to him.

A few catcalls and whistles followed us as he calmly strode through the clubhouse and headed upstairs to the private bedrooms. My breath caught in my throat when he stopped in front of my room and proceeded to unlock the damn door.

"How the fuck did you get a key to my room?"

Fury heated my body as he strode into my room like he owned the damn place. After kicking my door shut, he allowed me to slide down his front. I did my best to ignore how good his hard muscles felt as I brushed past them. The second my feet hit the floor I took a big step back.

"Answer me!"

"I slipped it out of your pocket when I grabbed you downstairs."

I growled at him when he shrugged like it was no big deal. I patted my back pocket, and sure enough, it was empty.

"Fuck you. You have no right! Give it back and get out."

I could not believe how this night was going. And if Eagle thought I would even look his way after this, he had another think coming. I'd been waiting for him to patch in and not be off limits anymore. Sure, I'd intended to make him work for it, but I'd intended to give in eventually. Not anymore. If he was going to be all caveman like this, he could just piss off.

He dropped my key into my waiting palm but didn't leave. He stood, returning my glare with one of his own. He also had his jaw clenched tightly and his left eye had this small twitch. Eagle was beyond mad, and that just pushed my temper higher. What the hell did he have to be angry about?

"What are you so pissed about? You can come and go as you please. You're even allowed in all the rooms of this damn place!"

He shook his head. "Not all the rooms. Not yet."

Ah, of course. A prospect wasn't allowed in Church except for special occasions. Suddenly I had an idea as to why he was so mad. Well, aside from the fact he'd just pulled me out of whore central a few minutes ago.

"You don't know why I'm on lockdown either, do

you?"

He clenched his jaw tight enough I started to worry he'd crack a tooth, before he huffed out a breath.

"Just... Stay here in your room for the rest of the night. Okay?"

"Or what? You'll haul me back up here like some naughty kid?"

I don't know why I was pushing him tonight, but I couldn't stop.

"Ain't nothing about you that's child-like, Silk."

I licked my lips at his change in tone and his hard gaze tracked the movement. The air between us all but crackled with tension.

"Fuck it."

Before he finished speaking he had me pressed up against the wall, then his mouth was on mine. His lips were soft, and oh, so fucking smooth. When he pulled back a little, I nipped at his lower lip before licking over it. He growled, and gripping my hips, moved me up the wall. I wrapped my legs around his waist and groaned when my pussy came up against his hard cock. The layers of denim did nothing to stop the heat I felt radiating from him. I drove my hands into his hair and moaned. It was as silky as I'd predicted. He took my mouth again, his tongue dancing with mine as he devoured me, all the anger and fury twisted into something sexual.

So much for playing hard to get...

Eagle

Fuck me. I knew better than this. Knew she was off limits until after I patched in, but I couldn't resist taking at least a small taste. Not when she was all riled up and sexy as fuck. And having her over my shoulder earlier had flipped some switch in me I didn't think I could turn off. I'd hated that she'd been in the room where the whores were doing their thing. She was above that behavior. Hell, I wouldn't be surprised if she was still a virgin, with the way the club, especially Bulldog and Scout, kept a close eye on her, I struggled to see how she could have managed to spend enough time with any man to get kissed, let alone laid.

When she'd been in that room, I could tell she didn't like what was happening in there, and I suspected she only went so far in because she was trying to rile me up. Well, she'd gotten me riled all right.

I pulled away a fraction, and she stayed leaning against the wall. My hands were still holding her hips and I gave her a squeeze as she continued to run her fingers through my hair. Fuck, her touch felt so damn good. I stared down at her flushed face, her lips dark red from my kissing her roughly. Her chest rose and fell with each breath, and it drew my full attention to her breasts. She had perfect tits, and I really wanted to see them naked. Wanted to wrap my mouth around her nipples and bite and lick until she was writhing against me.

One of her hands left my hair and trailed down my chest, lighting a fire in its wake. She had a tight black tank on under her cut so I could see she had ink from her wrist all the way up over her shoulder—huge, detailed, red roses with black and gray curly shit around them. The contrast looked fucking amazing. When she wrapped her fingers over the top of my waistband, shit got real. As much as it pained me to do so, I couldn't let this go further.

Bulldog would kill me. Well, he'd *try* to kill me.

I didn't have my damn top rocker yet.

The patch on her cut stood out like a beacon, sitting next to her luscious tits that I wanted so much. A blood-red heart with barbed wire wrapped around it. A Daughter of the Club patch. It made her untouchable to the likes of me.

"Fuckin' hell."

I pulled her legs from around my waist and forced myself to turn away from her.

"You can't leave me like this."

I glanced down at the large bulge in the front of my jeans. My cock wasn't real happy at being left like this either.

"No choice, sweetheart. Like you keep telling me, I'm nothing but a prospect. Not good enough for a Daughter of the Club. No one can know what we just did. You hear me? You tell Bulldog about this, and I'm gone."

I'd probably get the beat-down of my life on the way out too. I might have all the training and experience the

USMC gave me, but these bikers could play fucking dirty when they needed to, and I didn't doubt they'd find a way to take me down. But I didn't tell her that. As much as I knew Silk had grown up in the club, I didn't want to risk scaring her with something I doubted she knew anything about. Like how the club dealt out justice to one of their own.

"I know when to keep my mouth shut, Eagle."

She looked so fucking fragile standing there in the middle of her room. She'd moved forward from the wall and was finger combing her long blonde curls that I'd messed up. I couldn't just walk out. I knew I should. But that's not what I did. No, like a lovesick fool, I took two long strides and pulled her against me, holding her close as I breathed in against her hair. She felt so right pressed against me. I just needed a little patience to wait for the right time to claim her.

"The second I get my fucking top rocker, I'm coming for you."

I pressed a kiss to her forehead as she frowned up at me, then spun on my heel and stormed out of her room, making sure the door shut behind me. Running my fingers through my hair, I made my way down to the bar.

"Hey, mate. Things not go well?"

Of course, Taz knew how I felt about Silky and the bastard had way too much fun constantly harassing me about it.

"Just give me a couple beers so I can get back up there."

He grinned, but thankfully stayed silent as he passed over a couple of bottles. I stomped my way back up and made myself comfortable on the floor beside her door. It was going to be a long fucking night, but I needed to make sure she didn't try to slip away before morning. I was grateful the rooms were upstairs and too high for her to make a jump from her window safely. Otherwise, I would have had to find someone to stay on guard out there too.

I scrubbed a hand over my face before I popped the top off one of the bottles. Taking a deep drink, I stared up at the wall in front of me. I was fairly certain her uncle knew I was feeling Silk. I hadn't exactly hidden my interest, but I had been a good boy and kept my hands to myself. At least until tonight.

For the last two weeks I'd been asking around, trying to work out why Silk needed such close guarding but no one would talk. It was beginning to really piss me off. All I'd discovered from my questions was that every year at this time Silk would disappear for a week or so, alone. Apparently, this year Bulldog didn't want her going for some reason, hence the lockdown. I knew Silk thought I'd caused this, but it was all her uncle's doing. Once she was at work tomorrow, I was planning on calling Bulldog, and if he refused to answer me I'd put a call into Scout.

It made it near impossible to keep her protected when I didn't know what the fuck I was protecting her from.

Chapter 3

Eagle

By the time Silk had settled in to work on her first tattoo of the day I was about ready to explode. I'd only managed to get a couple of hours sleep the night before on the floor outside her room. Sure, I'd slept in worse places and at least no bastards were shooting at me at the clubhouse, but still. In the time I'd been back stateside, I'd kind of gotten used to sleeping lying down on a fucking bed.

At least when she'd come out and seen me sitting there she didn't sass me. In fact, I'm sure I'd seen her face soften a moment before she put her pissed off mask back on and stomped downstairs to the kitchen. Scout was eating breakfast when she stormed in, and she'd done her best to smooth talk the club president. Pity for her, Scout knew her too well to fall for it. Instead, he'd demanded her bike keys and told her she'd be traveling with me until further notice. She could choose the back of my bike or a cage, but those were her only two options if she wanted to leave the compound. To say she was unhappy was an understatement. I could understand her anger. She knew as much as me about why she was being locked down. I'd be furious in her place.

Even with her hissing and spitting like an alley cat, I couldn't help but grin as I rode over with her earlier. Having Silk on the back of my bike, with her arms wrapped around me, was a dream come true. As lame as that sounded, I'd had many dreams about it. Of course, my dreams never ended with me horny as fuck while she stormed off in a fury.

I pulled my phone out and shot a text off to Scout to let him know I could talk, like he'd asked me to do earlier. Minutes later, I watched the president walk up the path toward me. Clearly he'd been waiting on my text.

I nodded in greeting. "Prez."

He glanced in the shop before he stood to the side, where, if Silk looked out the front window, she wouldn't see him.

"Eagle. Thanks for staying tight with her. I know she's a handful."

"Wouldn't mind knowing what I'm protecting her from. Make it easier to notice it coming our way."

The older man sighed and stroked his beard. Scout was the stereotypical biker, complete with a scruffy beard, that was more gray than not.

"We're not a hundred-percent on what's coming. But we've heard whispers that something is. Fucking 9/11 bullshit. It never ends."

That caught my attention. This year was the fifteenth

anniversary of the terrorist attacks that brought down the twin towers in New York and tried to take out the Pentagon in Washington. Thousands died so it didn't surprise me in the least that every year the anniversary was marked with celebrations and memorials for those lost. It was the 9/11 attacks that had a lot of people enlisting to go fight, myself included. I was seventeen when those planes hit the towers, but in early 2002, I turned eighteen and signed up to go get those bastards before they could strike us on US soil again.

"What does 9/11 have to do with Silk?"

Scout jerked back a little. "Fuck. You don't know? Shit, I assumed you'd heard. Guess it's been so long now we don't talk about it these days."

I scanned the street again before I focused back on Scout.

"No one's told me a damn thing. It's driving me fucking nuts, to tell you the truth."

I figured the man knew how I felt about Silk, so being honest with the guy wasn't going to hurt my chances of getting info. In fact, I hoped it would get me a little extra.

"Silk came to live with Bulldog and his old lady not long after 9/11. Before that, she lived up in Boston. She didn't have siblings, it was just her and her folks. Then the evening of the tenth of September 2001, John and Claire dropped their daughter off with a friend—told her they'd be back before the weekend, then left. Her parents were on the flight that hit the south tower."

"Fuck. Well, no wonder she takes off every year."

The media talked about nothing but 9/11 for weeks around the anniversary, and this being the fifteenth was going to be bigger than usual.

"That's why we've locked her down so hard. She's planning on slipping her leash to run off to wherever the fuck she goes every year."

"I still don't get why she's locked down. I've heard she does this every year, but I've never heard of anyone trying to stop her before."

"We've had a reporter sniffing around. Doing some fucking story on the orphans of 9/11, or some shit. Silk's parents were up to something. We're still working out what, but their last minute trip to L.A. wasn't just for fun. Someone was chasing them. And you know how quick shit spreads on the internet these days? All it takes is that reporter to mention Silk's name once on some fucking bullshit online gossip site and boom—her location is up in fucking lights for anyone to find with a click of a button. Then, whoever was after them will come for her in no time. Bulldog's been keeping an ear to the ground in L.A. all these years and the word from one of his mob contacts is there is a bounty out for John's daughter. Again, no fucking idea why. All we know is they want her alive."

I took a deep breath as rage flowed through my system. I scanned the street again, this time taking in every building, vehicle and person carefully.

"No way of keeping that reporter quiet?"

"Nah, bitch is from L.A. and we've sent her on her

way, but not before she worked out Silk is Claudine. I don't doubt the mob knows exactly where she is by now."

"What's the plan then? I'm good, but up against the mob? This shit could get heavy fast."

The older man nodded. "That's why I'm here telling you shit no prospect should know. Listen, I've seen how you watch our girl. We all have. Bulldog might not like it, but fuck. We knew she'd end up with a brother. That girl is way too tough for some civilian to handle. This isn't me giving you permission to fuck with her. It's me letting you know I see what you're feeling for her. It's why you were put on her ass. I knew you wouldn't slack off and chase some whore's tail instead of guarding hers. I heard what you did last night. You did good, getting her out of that fucking room and up to hers. You didn't have to sleep in the damn hallway, but I appreciate the lengths you're willing to go to, to keep our girl safe."

"I've slept in worse places, and I had a feeling she would have snuck out if I didn't."

Scout snorted. "She sure as fuck would have. I had Mac on the main door and her bike stashed in the back of the garage. She wouldn't have gotten far." He paused to clear his throat. "We need to work out what the mob wants from Silk. She was only twelve when it all went down so I doubt it's something she knows. Probably something John left behind. Bulldog told me he had all their stuff packed up and moved down to a unit in our storage yard here. He gave Silk the key and hasn't bothered her about it since."

"You want me to get into that unit?"

He shook his head. "It's in our fucking yard, man. We can get into it. And we have. But none of us could find a damn thing that the mob could possibly want. It's got to be something Silk took from there. We need you to talk to her, get her to tell you about anything she might keep close by that's from her folks."

"Can I tell her why? She's hating this lockdown, but if I can explain why she might be more helpful."

That, and I had no idea how I was going to be able to go through all her stuff without her catching me.

Scout reached up and adjusted the bandanna he had wrapped around his head.

"Bulldog don't want her knowing, but you're going to have to tell her. She thinks her daddy moved away and cut his brother out of their lives because he didn't like the fact he was a fucking biker. That ain't the truth, but Bulldog wants her to keep believing the best about her folks."

I shrugged. "Can't blame the man for that. He wants Silk to have a good life, with her belief in her parents intact, I get that. I want that for her too. But she won't have that if this shit catches up with her. Is she still on lockdown at the clubhouse when she's not here?"

"Nah, that was me getting her separated from her wheels. Take her home to her place tonight. I'll have Mac and Taz meet you there. I know you'll want your boys on this with you. Gabs doesn't need to know what's going on. She's got her own tail but we're keeping it so she doesn't know about it unless she needs saving."

"Speaking of my boys, you know Mac has contacts in L.A. that might help us out? I'll ask him about it tonight. He might have heard something your guy hasn't."

Scout stopped talking to pull his packet of smokes out. He pulled one free but didn't light it right away.

"Good deal. You three keep our girl safe through this shit, you'll all get your top rockers. You'll need to deal with Bulldog after that about taking on Silky. So long as you're looking for an old lady, not just some fun, you'll survive him, I'm sure."

The bastard smirked at me before he lit up.

"If all I wanted was some tail, I'd have used the club whores to get it."

Scout's eyes turned serious. "Yeah, we'd noticed you hadn't made use of the entertainment offered. Take care of our girl, Eagle."

With that he turned and walked away, leaving me to go back to scanning the street and trying to work out how the fuck I could tell Silk about all this. Finding out her dad was up to something dirty was going to break her heart.

Silk

I was grateful for the full morning of appointments I had booked for today. Meant I didn't have time to focus on what I was going to have to deal with again tonight. I really didn't want to spend the next couple of weeks cooped up in my tiny room at the clubhouse, especially when I had a perfectly comfortable house available for my use. If I really couldn't get out of town, I at least wanted to be able to be alone.

"You stopping for lunch soon?"

I jerked out of my thoughts and looked up from the appointment book to see Eagle smirking at me from the door way. Bastard knew he'd caught me daydreaming.

"Ah, yeah. I can go now. I've got about an hour before my next appointment."

He didn't respond, but held the door open until I grabbed my bag and headed towards him. *Guess I'm having lunch with Eagle today.* In what I'd dubbed his stealth mode, he had me ushered down the street to a small cafe within minutes. It all seemed a little excessive to me. But I guess as much as you could take a man out of the military easily enough, taking the military out of the man was a completely different story. Not that I'd want to. I rather liked Marine Eagle. The way he prowled around was sexy as fuck.

Once we settled at a rear table and our food had been delivered, Eagle frowned at me with a serious gaze that had my stomach tightening—and not in a good way.

"What the hell is going on now?"

"Scout dropped by to speak with me this morning. I don't want to lay it all on you here, out in public. I promise I'll explain it all tonight. But, I can tell you,

you're not on lockdown at the clubhouse anymore, so I'll be taking you back to your place tonight."

"So whatever the fuck the threat was, has passed then?"

He shook his head. "It's only just started, babe."

"Can you at least give me a clue to what it's all about?"

I hadn't noticed anything. No strangers hanging around—well, except for that damn reporter a couple weeks back. No nasty letters or phone calls. Nothing.

"Word is the mob up in Los Angeles has a bounty on your head, sweetheart."

I froze with my sandwich halfway to my mouth. "Sorry, what?"

I couldn't have heard right. No way had I ever done anything to garner the attention of the mob!

"Seems they want you alive, so there is that."

"Oh, well. I guess that's okay then."

My sarcastic response earned me a low growl.

"It's far from okay. That's why you've had me guarding your ass. The club won't let anything happen to you."

I winced a little at his words. The club. Not him. Maybe I'd been dreaming that he was interested in more than a bit of fun with me. Although that kiss last night sure as fuck hadn't felt like a man who only wanted a good time before moving on.

"I've never been to California, let alone Los Angeles. How do these people even know who I am?"

"I really think you'd prefer have this conversation in private, babe."

"Like it matters? You know full well it's all I'm going to be thinking about all damn afternoon. You might as well lay it out for me so I don't spend my time coming up with shit worse than what is actually going on. I have a very vivid imagination."

He sat back and folded his arms over his chest. "Okay, then. The contract isn't on you by name. It's on John Bennett's daughter."

I dropped the rest of my lunch and pushed the plate away. My stomach rolled and I grabbed my glass of water to take a few gulps.

"This is about my dad? He's been dead for fifteen years!"

Eagle watched me calmly as I sat there feeling like the ground just blew out from underneath me.

"Someone wants something your father had. Scout doesn't know what, but he's guessing it's something illegal. We're going to have to go through anything you have from your parents. Bulldog's already gone through the storage unit and couldn't find anything. But if you think it will help, we can head out there and have a look, too."

I slumped back in my seat. Uncle Clint had told me the same reason my dad had about why I'd not met him before he'd taken custody of me. That my dad hated that his brother was in a biker club. He couldn't possibly have been involved in something against the law. Taking a deep breath, I covered my face with my palms. Closing my eyes, I tried to wrap my mind around what Eagle was telling me.

"Bulldog didn't want you to know about your dad, and I wish you didn't have to find out. I fucking hate having to tear your heart apart by damaging how you remember your father. But this is your life at stake, and I refuse to let anything happen to you, Silk. I know you were young when it happened, but do you remember anything about the day they left to fly to L.A.?"

I rubbed my temples before I dropped my hands down to the table and stared at my sandwich as I began to pick at the thing.

"It's been so long. I can't think of anything off the top of my head. Give me the afternoon. Tonight we'll talk more about it. Gabs has a family dinner she's going to, then she's spending the night at her parents' place, so we'll have all the privacy we'll need."

"Scout's assigned Taz and Mac to help keep you safe. You okay with that?"

I laughed, but there was no humor in it. "No, Eagle. I'm not okay with any of this. But I don't have a fucking choice do I? I've got to put my big girl panties on and deal with this shit before it comes for me and I wind up dead—or worse."

A shudder ran through me as some possibilities of what could be done to me by the fucking mob played in my head like a movie. Eagle's warm palm covered my hand and it was too much. I jerked my hand away and stood quickly.

"You know the three of us were Leathernecks for over a decade? We'll keep you safe, Silk. I promise."

"I need to get back to the shop. Got prep to do for a new piercing client."

I knew I was being a coward, but I was struggling to wrap my mind around this new version of my dad I'd never known existed before today. I didn't need to add in the fucked-up chemistry between us to the mix. He was still a prospect and off limits. I knew the three of them had been Marines. Knew my best chance at surviving a freakin' mob attack would be with them. So, I needed to not ruin it by having my uncle send them on their way because he found out we'd gotten involved when we shouldn't have.

Once all this shit passed and he got patched in, then I'd worry about what was between us.

If I survived that long.

A chill ran down my spine as I walked back to my shop with Eagle beside me, watching everything and everyone. *This can't be real.* Maybe I'd wake up and this past week would turn out to be nothing but a shitty bad dream.

Chapter 4

Silk

I stayed silent on our walk back to Silky Ink. I'd told Eagle I needed to prep for a new client, but I'd lied. The piercing room was always left clean and ready to go. It takes moments to grab the right jewelry and equipment. No, I intended to spend the twenty minutes I had before the appointment on the phone with my uncle. I needed some answers, and didn't want to wait for tonight for them. I didn't want to get them while others watched, either.

Not even glancing to see where Eagle stopped to take his guard duty post, I headed straight back to the break room at the rear of the shop. Grateful to find it empty, I made myself a coffee before I sat at the table and pulled my phone out. Hitting speed dial, I barely got the thing to my ear before Uncle Clint answered. *Typical.*

"Hey there, Silky girl. What's going on?"

Not wanting to drag things out, I got straight to the point.

"Just had an interesting lunch with Eagle. He passed

on some things Scout told him this morning."

A string of growled curses had my lips twitching with a smile. "I didn't want you told dammit."

"Yeah, well, tough shit. I've been told. Now *you* need to tell me what really happened between you and Dad before he left Texas. I need to know everything you do, so I can try to work out what, whoever is after me, wants."

He let fly with a few more curses before he sighed heavily.

"Fine. I suppose it's too much to ask that you wait till tonight so I can tell you in person?"

"My place is going to be a little crowded tonight as it is, what with Eagle, Mac and Taz all playing guard dog. I don't want this shit aired to everyone."

Honestly, it had less to do with people knowing, and more to do with the fact I didn't want to fucking cry in front of anyone, especially Eagle. I hated being seen as all girly and weak, and I was pretty sure if I had to look Uncle Clint in the eye while he told me how my father wasn't the good man I'd always believed he was, I wouldn't be able to hold it together.

"I can understand that. I don't really want this shit aired publicly either. There were only two years between me and your dad. Growing up he always resented being the youngest. He was forever trying to out-do anything I did. It was so stupid and I kept hoping he'd grow out of it. Our folks never treated him as less than me, but somehow he got it in his head he needed to prove he was better than me. When I prospected into the Charons, he—well, he decided it wasn't hardcore enough for him."

A tingle ran up my spine as I put together where he was going with this. "He joined the Iron Hammers, didn't he?"

The Charon MC wasn't officially a one-percenter club, but the Iron Hammers MC sure as fuck was.

"Yeah, honey. He did. Well, he tried. As far as I know, he never patched in. He lived it up at their parties, enjoyed more than his share of freely offered drugs and women." I winced and was really grateful I was alone hearing all this shit. My dad had been an asshole. "Not sure how he hooked up with your mom. Rumor had it she was a runaway looking for someplace to belong when she latched onto him. I guess she was looking for club protection as an old lady."

"If all this happened down here, how the hell did they end up in Boston?"

"No idea what made him run in the end. About a week after we heard about your mom being knocked up, they were gone. Your grandparents used to ring every couple of days when they first left, but after a couple weeks, your dad told them it was too dangerous to keep in contact and he changed his number. Of course, he never shared why, so I'm afraid it's not much help to you. I did track him down when you were a couple of years old. By then your grandparents had both passed, so it was just me and your Aunt Rose who went up. He actually let us both play with you that day. Then he moved and I couldn't get hold of him again. Seeing as you looked healthy and taken care of, I didn't push to find him. Because I didn't know what he was running from, I didn't want to risk bringing down shit that would have landed on your head, Silk."

Everything I thought I knew was being tilted so it now looked different. Every word my uncle spoke had me looking back over my childhood, seeing things in a new light.

"When I once asked him why we didn't have any extended family, he told me I had an uncle. Just like you've told me before, he said it was your connection to the Charons that led to him cutting you from our lives. You both lied to me. Why?"

"I have no idea why he told you that. I simply agreed with what he'd said. Not sure if you remember, but when we came to get you, when I told you I was your daddy's brother. You asked me if I was the bad biker your father had told you about. I could guess what he'd told you, and with him dead, I didn't have the heart to tell you he wasn't as good as you believed. I didn't see the point. I'm sorry I lied to you, Silk, but the last thing either me or your Aunt Rose wanted was to add to your pain. You clearly thought the sun shone out of your dad, I didn't have the heart to take that from you. I still wish it I could have left you with that image of him."

"Yeah well, the rose colored glasses are definitely gone now."

He roughly cleared his throat. "I always wanted to ask, but wasn't sure I could handle the answer. Did he ever hurt you or your mom?"

I took a moment to think back. It had been so long ago now, and straight after they died, I pushed the memories down whenever they popped into my mind so I wouldn't miss them so much. I'd been just a kid, and having my parents ripped away like that devastated me.

"I vaguely remember him slapping Mom, but no idea how old I would have been. I do remember he was so angry. I'd never seen him so mad." I shook my head, even though he couldn't see me. "He never raised a hand against me. He wasn't always around, and he was often drunk, or high, but no matter how out of it he was, he was always protective of me. I don't actually have any memory of him doing drugs, but from what I've seen as an adult I know he must have been taking something fairly regularly."

"Silk, do you remember him, or your mom, saying anything that might help us, the day you last saw them?"

I huffed a breath out. "I remember overhearing Mom tell Dad that this was it, the last time. I didn't hear his response. Then about an hour later, they dropped me off at Marie's house." I frowned as a thought occurred to me. "How did you find me after? If Dad cut you out completely, how did you know I needed you?"

"I guess he wasn't so certain he was going to survive whatever he was going to L.A. for. He left a sealed envelope with Marie that she was only to open if he didn't return. As soon as she discovered their flight was one of the ones that took down the towers, she opened it and found my contact details. Me and your Aunt Rose dropped everything and drove up there to get you the moment she rang us."

My phone dinged, letting me know I had five minutes before my next appointment.

"Thanks, Uncle Clint. I've got to get back to work. I'll talk to you later."

"I think I'll still come over tonight, make sure those boys behave themselves."

I scoffed. "You know full well they will. Bye."

I hung up and stared at the now-dark screen. There was so much I hadn't known, wouldn't have ever even guessed at.

"Ah, Claudine Bennett. Finally I've tracked you down when you're all alone."

Instantly on alert, I stood and spun toward the door as I slipped my phone into my back pocket. A man who I'd guess was in his mid-forties stood just inside the doorway.

"What the fuck? This is staff only, you need to go back out the front."

I didn't think he was here for a tattoo, but you never know. I'd certainly prefer he was nothing but a client who'd strayed, not some asshole out to hurt me.

"Such language for a lady. I guess you truly are your father's daughter."

Icy fingers ran down my spine. I needed to get away

from this man, and fast. I moved to the side of the room, hoping to draw him away from the door so I could make a run for it. He was a big bastard, looked like a boxer that had been jammed into suit pants and a white shirt. Hopefully that meant he was slower than me.

As fast as I could, I picked up a chair and threw it at him, but he ducked out of its way as I dashed toward the door. I had a hand on the door frame when his thick arm wrapped around my waist and jerked me backward.

"Always the hard way."

Something hard pressed against my shoulder a moment before my body lit up with pure agony. *Fuck!* That hurt like a motherfucker. I slumped against the man, unable to move, and he quickly scooped me up in his arms, before he headed toward the back door. I thought I heard my name being yelled, but the darkness invading my mind took over and I passed out.

Eagle

After making sure Silk had made her way to the back room of her shop, I headed to my post next to the entrance. Silky Ink wasn't on a busy street, and there wasn't much foot traffic around either. Made it an easy place to guard, and to make private phone calls. Pulling out my phone, I dialed Mac, my gaze scanning the street as I waited for him to answer his phone.

"What's up?"

"Scout spoke to you yet?"

"Told me to get to Silk's tonight and to follow your lead. You know what's going on yet?"

I'd spoken to Mac and Taz a few times about what could be behind the sudden need the club had to have Silky under guard 24/7 while none of the other old ladies or daughters of the club were.

"Turns out Silk's dad was into something before he died that's coming back to bite her. Word is the mob from L.A. is after her." I frowned and shook my head, even though Mac couldn't see me. "I thought those boys were all but gone now."

"Nah, I doubt they'll ever fucking disappear completely. They're smaller than they were back in the day, but just because they're keeping out of the media spotlight, don't think they aren't as dangerous as they've always been."

I'd heard that a few of Mac's more distant relatives had been involved with the mob somehow, never thought those ties would come in useful before now.

"Any chance you can ask around, see if you can find out what they want? Scout's certain they want her alive, so he's thinking they want something her dad left behind."

"I can ask. How long ago did her dad die?"

"He was on the plane that hit the south tower."

"You talking 9/11? That's fifteen years ago. Why now? I can guarantee it wouldn't have taken them this long to locate Silk. Something new must have happened."

"Scout mentioned a reporter hanging around a few weeks back. I'm guessing that happened just before I got put on permanent guard duty."

"I'll get Taz on finding the fucking reporter, I'll reach out to a few people who might know what's going on. We'll report in at Silk's tonight."

"Thanks, man. See you both then."

I knew Mac would also get Taz to contact our FBI handler to see if he had any information on this whole thing. I stilled, keeping my phone in my hand when I noticed a big bastard heading for the shop. Something about him had me standing straighter. He wore dark dress pants and a white business shirt. I could see the edge of a tatt above his collar so it wasn't like he was out of place entering a tattoo shop, but my instincts were flaring. Making the most of his attention being focused on the shop window, I quickly snapped a couple of photos before I pocketed my phone. He looked over at me, gave me a chin lift, then entered the store.

Once he was out of my view, I pulled my phone back out and texted the images to Scout.

U no who this is?

Seconds after hitting send, I heard a crash from inside the shop.

"Fuck."

I rushed inside and headed down the hallway, just in time to see the bastard who'd just entered the place push open the back door with a limp Silk cradled against his chest.

"Stop right there, asshole!"

I pulled my gun and sprinted after him when he didn't stop. I didn't have time to shoot before he was behind the door, but it wouldn't stay that way. The moment I had a clear shot, I intended to take it. I hit the door seconds behind him, shoving it open hard enough it banged loudly against the wall.

"I said stop."

He was moving fast, which made locking onto him difficult, especially with a handgun. *Fuck!* I wished Taz were sitting up on the roof with his sniper rifle. He'd nail this bastard in less than a heartbeat. When he leaned over to shove Silk into the back seat of a car, I saw my chance. I aimed and popped off two rounds at the bastard. Both went true and entered his thigh, I saw the blood splatter from the wounds. After firing, I took off for the car. I'd hoped in slowing down the bastard, I'd have time to reach them, but it didn't work out like I wanted. Before I could reach them, he'd followed Silk into the car and the vehicle fucking took off, tires squealing as it left black marks in its wake.

Knowing I couldn't run and catch the damn thing, I focused on the license plate, repeating the number over and over in my head as I turned and sprinted back through the shop to my bike. Within minutes, I was on my bike and roaring down the road but I knew I was already too late. I'd broken my promise to keep her safe, not even an hour after making it, and Silk was gone.

With my mind spinning over what the fuck I could do to find her. I pulled over when my phone rang, and answered it without looking at the caller.

"What?"

"Where is that man right now?"

Scout's voice was harsh and sounded raw.

"No fucking clue. In the time it took me to send you that image, he snatched Silk."

Scout's voice was a roar over the line. "What the fuck do you mean he snatched her?"

"I mean I fucking busted him leaving out the back of the shop with Silk out cold in his fucking arms. I put two bullets in the son of a bitch and winged him, but not enough to stop him. Fuck! I've been searching around town for the car but can't find the fucking thing."

I slammed my palm against the fuel tank of my bike, beyond frustrated. I should have gone for a fucking head shot. Silk would have landed heavily onto the road, no doubt getting hurt. And the fallout from killing a man on US soil would have no doubt been fucking epic, but at least she would have been safe.

"You get the plate?"

"Yeah, fucking black Escalade with California plates." As I told him the plate number, the loud roar of another Harley came up behind me. I twisted around to see Bulldog pull up. "You send Bulldog after me?"

"Nope. He came to see me after a phone call from Silk, then he took off for a ride. Listen, that photo you sent me is of an enforcer for the L.A. mob. I want you at the clubhouse right fucking now. Emergency meeting. Tell Bulldog."

"Done."

Shoving my phone away I stepped free from my bike. I had no idea how Bulldog would react to his niece having been snatched but I didn't want him damaging my bike if he decided to throw a fucking punch at me.

"Wanna tell me what the fuck's going on?"

"Scout's called an emergency meeting, we need to get to the clubhouse now."

In seconds, Bulldog was off his bike and in my face. "Why aren't you guarding the shop?"

"Because the mob has Silk and I was trying to chase the bastards down."

As I predicted, Bulldog took a swing at me, but I blocked his punch and spun his arm up behind him to stop any shit before it got started.

"Do *not* come at me like that ever again, or I will put you on your ass. I don't give a fuck who you are."

"You let them take my girl. I'll do more than put you on your ass, boy."

I shoved him away from me and stood in a fighter's stance, ready to defend myself again.

"I didn't let them do shit. And the longer you piss around trying to pound on me, the longer those bastards have her. I gave Scout the license plate of the vehicle, so how about we quit this pissing match and go back to the clubhouse? I'd like to know if we have eyes on them leaving town, or if they're staying local for the moment."

He pointed straight at me. "You better hope we get her back safely, and soon."

The rest of his threat went unspoken, but he didn't need to waste his breath. I'd give my life for Silk, and the fact she was snatched out from under my fucking nose was eating me up. But I pushed it all down. I needed to find and save her first. Then I could worry about dealing with the fallout.

Jumping back on my bike, I revved it hard, then took off after Bulldog, who was already heading to the clubhouse.

Chapter 5

Eagle

Even distracted with worry for Silk, I still felt a jolt roll through me as I walked into Church for the first time. Normally only patched in members were allowed in this sacred room. I glanced around as others came in and settled into seats. The club insignia was carved into a huge hunk of wood that hung on the back wall. A short table with five seats sat below it. The president, vice president, secretary, treasurer all sat in their seats. The sergeant in arms wasn't here yet. I sat silently waiting as the rest of the club sat their asses down.

Taz and Mac came in together and sat on either side of me. I looked to Taz first.

"Any news?"

He shook his head. "Not yet, but they're definitely interested."

Fuck, I hoped that meant the FBI was going to help us take these bastards down. I knew we were supposed to be the ones helping them out, but I could really use their expertise on this one.

"Mac?"

"Yeah, I got something, but how about I wait five and tell everyone together?"

I wasn't waiting five minutes. "Go tell Scout you got information. He'll sort this shit out so we can get started in less than five."

Mac rose and made his way up to the front, then leaned in to speak with Scout. The president's eyes narrowed a moment before he nodded. Then he rose and hit his hammer down on the table.

"Everyone, sit down and shut the fuck up. We don't have time to fuck around today." He gave the club less than thirty seconds to sit. "Silk's been taken. Went down less than half hour ago. Eagle was guarding her shop and put a couple bullets in the bastard, but they still got away. Most of you know, Eagle, Taz and Mac were marines, and that's why, even though they're still prospects, they're in on this. Right. Mac? What have you got for us?"

Mac stood in front of the club looking as confident as ever. He stood at six-feet-three, with his clean shaven head, a closely cropped beard, and two half sleeve tattoos, he looked like what he was, a deadly fighter you didn't want to fucking mess with.

"After I heard the mob up in L.A. was sniffing around looking for Silk, I put out some feelers to see if I could figure out why they wanted her. I haven't found out a whole lot yet since I only started looking into things about an hour ago, but they definitely want her alive and unharmed."

Before Mac could continue, the door slammed open and Nitro, the sergeant in arms came in behind a woman who looked like she was about to pee herself. He casually led the woman to the front of the room and pulled a spare seat forward and placed it in front of the table facing sideways, so everyone could see her face.

"Sit."

At Nitro's growled command, she dropped into the chair without wasting a second. Her wide eyes focusing on Scout.

"Wanna tell us the truth about why you've been sniffing around Silk?"

The woman frowned. "Silk is Claudine, yes?"

"Do not fuck with me, woman. You're a reporter. I'm sure you had that worked out long ago. What did you come after her for?"

Ah, so this was the reporter that set all this shit in motion.

"Like I told your colleague here, I had nothing to do with her being kidnapped. I only wanted to interview her."

"As a club, we generally stick with a rule of not ever hurting women. But with one of ours gone God knows where, we may rethink that rule if you don't start fucking telling me something useful right now."

"I'm trying to explain! Look, with the fifteenth anniversary of 9/11, I wanted to find a new angle to report on. I found it last month. Turns out Claudine's father's bag missed his flight. He tried to take it as a carry on, but it was too heavy so they forced him to check it." She shrugged. "Typically, it missed the flight as they didn't get it checked and out to the plane in time. It was put in with the next flight's baggage. In the aftermath of the attacks, no one gave it any attention. It was tossed into the lost baggage room at LAX. I figured doing a story on Claudine getting her father's personal effects back after all this time would make a good article. Of course, when you wouldn't let me near her, I had to rethink how I was going to write it. But I managed to come up with something. Clearly, the mob still has people in the media on their payroll because not an hour after I emailed my proposed article to my boss, I had a visitor who told me my life depended on getting Claudine back to L.A., to them. Apparently they really want whatever is in that bag.

"And you knew nothing about them snatching her this afternoon?"

She shook her head. "I didn't. Not until your man here came and grabbed me. They've been calling me daily, and I keep telling them that she's under your club's protection and I can't get anywhere near her."

Bulldog thumped the table. "Fuck."

Scout squeezed his VP's shoulder before turning back to the reporter. "What are you expected to do now?"

"I go back to L.A. and hope I wake up breathing tomorrow morning. I somehow doubt they'll want any media present when she goes to get that bag."

I stood and moved to stand near Mac at the front of the room. Scout raised an eyebrow at me before he turned to Nitro and told him to take the reporter back to wherever the hell he'd found her. I waited for her to be out of the room before I spoke.

"That's the best chance we have at getting her back. At the airport."

Mac shook his head. "It won't be that simple. LAX is fucking huge and there's cops and security all over the damn place. Especially this close to the 9/11 anniversary."

I frowned. "That's the only place we know where she'll be. We need to grab her either before she gets the bag for them, or straight after. If they want her to get this bag, they won't touch her until they have it. No way will it not raise flags if some woman beat to shit is trying to pick up a bag that's been sitting there for fifteen years. But there's no saying what the fuck they'll do after they have what they want from her."

Scout frowned at me and Mac for a moment before he turned to Keys, the club secretary who earned his road name thanks to his hobby of hacking into shit.

"You got any video feed on that car? Plate number?"

"It's owned by a rental company in L.A., and the details on the rental agreement are fake. The vehicle stopped briefly at a pharmacy on the outskirts of town, then headed straight for the highway. They're not wasting time getting her to L.A."

"Right, let's get this shit planned out now, then we

move out. Tonight."

I folded my arms over my chest and focused in on the discussion. I might have failed to prevent Silk from being taken, but I vowed to be the one that saved her. It would be by my fucking hands that made sure the bastard who took her paid dearly for it.

Silk

With a groan I blinked open my eyes and wished I hadn't bothered. Pushing past the ache in my head and my dry mouth, I rolled over on a lumpy mattress that stunk bad enough I was fighting to not throw up. Needing to get away from the stench, I shuffled toward the edge and sat with my feet on the floor. I was a little surprised to discover I wasn't tied up, until I glanced around my cell. Bars covered a small window high up the wall. They also filled the doorway. I wasn't going anywhere. There was a small sink in the corner next to a stainless steel toilet bowl. *The full jail experience. Charming.*

My lower belly cramped in demand, as though I hadn't peed in a week. I rose on shaky legs, and stumbled a few steps before my muscles got with the program. Keeping an eye on the door, I used the toilet quickly, then washed my hands and splashed some water on my face before drinking a few mouthfuls from my cupped palms. Thankfully the sink, toilet and water were all clean.

With my dry throat eased and my full bladder relieved, I took in the room once more. Not that I honestly expected to find an escape had magically appeared in the last few minutes, but it would have been nice, and worth a try. With a wince, I made my way back to the mattress. I didn't want to sit on the cold concrete floor, and my muscles still weren't working one-hundred percent. Guess they didn't appreciate having electricity jolted through them. I hoped that if I kept my head up, away from the mattress, the smell wouldn't be too bad. With that in mind, I sat against the wall, brought my knees up in front of me and rested my head on them, closing my eyes.

Fear crept up my spine as images of what could happen to me filled my mind. A moan slipped free as a shudder racked my body when I heard movement at the doorway. Turning my face, I watched as a different man than the one that kidnapped me entered and shut the door behind him with a metallic clunk sound. There went the idea of rushing past him. *Not that it would have worked any better this time, than the last time I tried to do it.*

"I've brought you some food."

His Italian accent was heavy, as though he either hadn't been out of Italy for long, or he spoke his native language enough that his accent had stuck. I suspected the latter was the case. I lifted my head and cocked an eyebrow at him. Like I'd trust it wasn't drugged or something? Between how empty my stomach was and the headache I was currently sporting, I'd guessed they'd already drugged me at least once, to keep me out longer than the Taser would have on its own.

Sensing my question, he lowered the tray to the end of the bed. "It's all in sealed packets so you know it's not been tampered with. We have no desire to hurt you, Claudine."

"Sorry, but I find that hard to believe after you've already had me Tasered and drugged."

I bit my tongue to stop myself from sassing him any further. I really didn't want to piss him off but I was scared, and when I was uncomfortable in any way, I tended to lash out.

"I apologize for that. We'd sent a reporter to speak to you about coming to L.A. with her, but that club of yours wouldn't let her anywhere near you and my patience ran out. Keeping you unconscious was the safest way to bring you to where we needed you to be."

Lifting my head, I frowned up at him in confusion. He was being extremely polite and wasn't trying to intimidate or threaten me at all.

"I don't understand why I'm here."

He glanced at the mattress, curled his lip, then strode over to the door and left for a moment. He returned with a folding chair that he placed across from me before sitting on it.

"My name is Antonio Sabella. Perhaps your father mentioned my family on occasion?"

I shook my head. "I was twelve when he died, still a child. He didn't tell me anything about what he did for work. In fact, I didn't even know what his occupation was, let alone what it involved."

Antonio nodded. "He did lots of things. Mostly illegal. He took something from my family and we require it to be returned. We'd thought it lost in the crash but we've recently come to learn his bag missed his flight."

I stilled. "I'm sorry but that can't be right. He only ever took a carry-on bag when he flew. I know that much because he used to rant over how often bags got lost or people behind the scenes at the airport went through and took things they shouldn't."

He smiled at me. "The reporter who found this information for us was told his bag was too heavy for him to take on board so he was forced to check it in. And as he told you, baggage regularly gets misplaced. As his bag was that day."

"It's been fifteen years. Surely it's been thrown out by now?"

"LAX is a big airport and things get pushed to the side and forgotten about. I assure you, it's safely stored in the baggage claim room at LAX. Once they worked out what flight it was from, they contacted the media to assist in finding its owner. Normally, they would send it to auction, but some kind soul thought a next of kin would like the bag."

My eyes stung with emotion. What would be in that bag? I knew Antonio thought it contained something belonging to him, but I wanted to know what else it contained. Seeing those things he took everywhere with him would hurt, but to have those small parts of his life in my possession—it was a temptation I couldn't resist. I wanted that bag.

"If I go with you to get this bag, you'll take what you believe is yours and the rest is mine to keep? You'll let me go?"

He shrugged one shoulder in an elegant manner. "That depends on what we find. We may need your help for a little longer. We suspect he put our belongings in a safe deposit box and we hope the key will be in the bag. If that's the case, we'll have need of your services to retrieve that box. Then, you will be free to go with the remainder of your father's belongings."

I frowned at him. "How can I trust you?"

"If I meant you harm, I would have done so already, my dear. I have no desire to hurt you. Your father is dead, he paid for his crimes against my family. My family is not seeking further payment for what he did, I simply want what is mine, returned to me. That is all."

I spoke softly, not sure whether I truly believed him that I would walk away unharmed from all this. "If you really want this to end peacefully, you need to let me call my uncle. The club will come for me and it won't end well if they believe I'm going to be harmed."

He stood and folded the chair. "I've already contacted your uncle. How he chooses to proceed is his choice, but some pissant southern MC is no threat to us. If they come, we will deal with them appropriately. I'll leave you to eat in peace. We'll be heading to the airport in about thirty minutes."

With that parting statement he left me alone to ponder what the hell was going to happen with the rest of my day. The fact rape and torture didn't look like it was going to be a part of it was certainly a huge relief. But I still had my doubts if I'd remain unharmed once Antonio had whatever he wanted out of that bag.

Chapter 6

Eagle

I was standing at the counter of the little truck stop we'd stopped off at to fill up, waiting to pay when Bulldog came storming in, cursing and growling before he called me over. I handed Mac some cash to pay for my fuel before I headed after Bulldog.

"What's happened?"

"See for yourself."

He handed me his phone and I swiped the screen to bring up an image I was certain I'd never forget.

"Fuckin' hell."

Silk lay unconscious on a hotel bed. I zoomed in on her fully clothed form, and couldn't see any injuries.

"She looks physically unharmed."

"Read the message."

I closed the image and focused on the text of the email.

I will return her unharmed in thirty-six hours. She was given a sedative, and is safe. I vow she will remain that way. Her father paid for his sins. I have no need to extract payment from his daughter. I will email again with an address for you to collect her from when she is ready to go.

It was signed off by Antonio Sabella. Mac came out and stood beside me, I handed the phone over for him to have a look.

"You know who this fucker is, Mac?"

Bulldog was pacing back and forth like a caged tiger. He looked on edge and I worried he was going to blow our chances of getting Silk back by doing something stupid.

"Yeah, he's high up in the family. One of the few left with some real power behind him. He's also old school. If he says Silk won't come to harm, then she won't. At least for so long as he's in charge."

Scout, Nitro and Taz all came over to join our little meeting. It was just the six of us that had headed out to get Silk back. The whole club was on alert to be called in, but I agreed with Scout when he decided to go with a stealth plan to slip in and take her back. Taking an entire MC all riding loud Harleys into any situation was anything but quiet.

Bulldog moved to stand in front of Mac. "You got any idea on where this fucker would be holding her?"

Mac shook his head. "I got a couple distant relatives involved on the fringes of the mob, no one in the inner circle that would know where Sabella lives. I can put money on her not still being in the room in that photo. Did you look at the window over the bed? The landscape is rural Texas. Not L.A. I'd say he took this photo when they stopped to rest for a few hours. Even if we did, by some fluke, know where this hotel was, they'd be long gone by the time we got to it. Our best bet is still at the airport."

Scout nodded and looked to me then Bulldog. "We're nearly in Palm Springs. We'll find a hotel and crash there for a few hours before we continue on to L.A. The photo shows they've stopped somewhere for at least a few hours."

It was a twenty-three hour drive between Bridgewater and Los Angeles. No matter how comfortable your car or bike was, you had to stop for a few hours at least once, on top of shorter breaks to stretch your legs. Palm Springs was only about one and a half hours away from LAX, so with an early start, we'd be at the airport before breakfast. *Hopefully before Antonio got there with his crew.*

"I'll make some calls when we stop, see if anyone has heard anything new."

As Mac spoke, I held my palm out for the phone. As soon as I had it, I went looking for the time stamp on the email.

"This came in eight hours ago. They either stopped somewhere for the night, and aren't in L.A. yet, or they did what we're doing. Crashed for a couple of hours, then kept moving. In which case they'd already be there."

Mac gripped my shoulder. "TSA shuts down the lost and found at four-thirty. It won't reopen until eight in the morning. We've got time for a short nap. Plus, if we're all riding on no sleep we're more likely to fuck up this rescue."

I clenched my jaw, knowing he was right but not liking it one fucking bit.

"Yeah, I hear you."

No one said another word as we headed back to our bikes and took off towards Palm Springs. The entire way my mind couldn't shake that photo of Silk out cold on some fucking hotel bed. If those bastards hurt her, I was going to use every skill I'd learned in the military to rain down hell on all their asses.

By the time we arrived and Scout arranged some rooms for us, I was ready to climb the fucking walls. I had no idea how I going to try to get any sleep. Silk was in trouble, which made this personal. Not like over in the Middle East. That was fighting for our country and our freedom. Getting Silk back was me fighting for my own future, my fucking heart and soul were on the line this time. For the first time.

My phone buzzing had me pausing my pacing to pull it free. Mac and Taz, who were sharing this piece of shit hotel room with me went silent. There were limited people who had my number, all but a few were here with me. 'Private Number' flashed on the screen and I figured it could be one of two people—either the FBI or Silk's captors. Although, considering they'd already contacted Bulldog, it was a safer bet to assume it was the FBI.

With a deep breath I answered the call.

"Who is this?"

"You alone?"

Yep, their current handler at the FBI. Mr. Smith, which was so not the man's real fucking name, not that I gave a shit what his real one was.

"Just me, Jacob and Donovan. You got anything for us?"

The FBI didn't do road names. They liked to use peoples real ones, which was a fucking joke since none of them went by their birth names.

I knew Taz had contacted him earlier before Silk had been taken, but I wasn't sure if he'd contacted him again afterward.

"We need you to let this play out."

Fury roared through me. "No fucking way will I leave her to the mob's mercy any longer than I have to."

Mr. Smith sighed like he was dealing with a stubborn toddler, which only served to raise my temper further.

"Listen, Colt, we've got eyes on her. If it gets too hot we'll pull her out, but it's important we get whatever it is her father had. This is bigger than the Charons. The mob has been laying low in L.A. for over a decade but we all know shit's going on behind the scenes. Getting our hands on leverage against Sabella and his boys is a higher priority than keeping your latest favorite toy protected."

"Claudine is no toy, and if she gets hurt and I find out you bastards could have prevented it, it'll be the last time any of us help your sorry asses. Are we clear?"

I wanted to threaten I'd come after him, but only a fool said shit like that to a government agent. Didn't change the fact that I would, in fact, hunt him down if Silk got hurt. He just didn't need to be told about it.

Silk

I nervously sat in the rear of a completely clichéd black stretch limo flicking my thumbnail against the underside of the tip of my forefinger. The small noise it made helped keep me from panicking. So far Antonio had stayed true to his word, and I'd not been harmed in any way. In fact, after I ate, he'd returned and showed me to a fancy bathroom. There was a clean change of clothes for me and I was able to lock myself in and freshen up. There had been blood streaked down the lower part of my jeans on one side. I had no clue where it had come from—the fact it wasn't mine was all I'd cared about.

Logically, I understood Antonio couldn't drag a bleeding, broken woman through LAX to get a bag from lost and found. Especially one that was fifteen years old. That meant I trusted him to not hurt me until after I retrieved that damn bag of my father's. But then what? He was a fucking gangster, for crying out loud. My only knowledge about the mob was from the news and movies, so it wasn't a whole hell of a lot, but I don't recall mobsters ever leaving people behind to testify against them.

Feeling a gaze on me, I looked toward the front of the vehicle and found the man who'd grabbed me was now driving. I tensed with a wince under his hate filled glare. Yeah, that one meant me harm in a big way. I risked a glance at Antonio who was seated beside me.

"Don't worry about him. He's pissed off that your boy shot him. Twice."

He didn't look like he'd been shot, but I wasn't exactly an expert since I'd never had a bullet wound. "Should he be driving then?"

Antonio's laughter was deep and rich. It actually sounded sexy, despite the fact the man had to be nearly sixty. But I refused to entertain those thoughts for even a moment.

"That is the reason he's driving. And we're in the limo, which is automatic. His left calf and thigh both took a bullet." He waved a hand through the air. "Only flesh wounds, but he doesn't look all that threatening by my side hobbling around with a crutch. You see, my dear girl, most of this life is an illusion. You look tough, people leave you alone. Of course, it also helps if people also know that you can, and will, take out your enemies. But if you look like a scared rabbit, you'll attract the wrong kind of attention. Every time."

I winced again. I'd thought I'd been doing an okay job at hiding my fear. "Sorry if I can't look all cool and collected for you, but it's not every day I get kidnapped and shipped halfway across the country to have who knows what done to me."

"I've promised you will not be harmed, I've shown you nothing but kindness. What can I do to put you at ease before we arrive at the airport? Police will be called if you look like a frightened mouse being chased by a tom-cat when we arrive at the unclaimed baggage desk. I imagine it's going to cause a stir that you've arrived to claim so close to the anniversary of his death at any rate. However, I am hopeful we can be gone before reporters have time to arrive."

I tried to think of something, but couldn't. "Aside from finding myself safely back home, alone, I can't think of anything you can do or say that will make me believe I'm going to walk away from this."

He huffed a breath and ran a hand carefully over his slicked-back hair, the sun coming in from the window catching on the huge hunk of gold resting on his ring finger.

"How about some logic, then? Dead bodies are a pain in the ass to deal with. Back in the day, it wasn't a problem because we had the contacts to cover that shit up. Now? We share those contacts with the Russians and the Triads. Either of those groups would love to have something over us, like the location of a dead girl that can be pinned on us. And those contacts are fueled by money—no fucking loyalty anymore. It's all about who pays better. Thanks to your father, that hasn't been us for some time now."

"And if whatever we find in this bag makes it so you are the highest bidder? What then? I find myself at the bottom of the ocean with concrete shoes?"

He laughed again, but this time my fear didn't allow it to affect me at all.

"You watch too much TV, my dear. Your father wronged us, and if he were still alive, it is true that we would make him pay for it. But he died, in a nasty way, where he no doubt knew what was coming but could do nothing to stop it. He got what he deserved. You, on the other hand, were a child and had no hand in what he did. I regret we've had to involve you at all, but the TSA would not release the bag to us without your help."

The thought of my parents sitting on that plane watching it head straight for the south tower, knowing they would die, had my stomach roiling. Bile began to rise up my throat.

"Stop the car!"

Antonio nodded to the driver and the moment the car stopped, I shoved the door open. Falling to my knees I threw up my breakfast on the side of the road while grief tore at my heart and tears burned my eyes. Would it ever get better? Stop hurting so fucking much? This was why I ran away every year. Even fifteen years later, the country was obsessed with that one fucking terror attack. I just wanted it to go away, to not be harshly reminded every fucking twelve months how brutally my family was ripped away from me.

Feeling empty and broken, I slumped back away from the mess I'd made, leaning against the car. Somewhere deep inside I considered I'd just wasted a perfectly good chance to try to escape. Wiping my eyes clear I looked around and saw that we'd stopped on the side of the highway. There was nowhere for me to run that they wouldn't have caught me, or shot me. Even if my legs hadn't turned to rubber with all my churning emotions.

"I am sorry to have upset you. It wasn't my intention."

I grabbed the bottle of water Antonio held in front of me. Took a gulp to swish around my mouth before I spat it out, then took a long drink that eased my sore throat.

"I don't like talking about it. I normally go off the grid for a week or so around the anniversary each year. So, you may not wish to physically harm me, but trust me, you're hurting me plenty by preventing me from doing that this year."

I dragged myself up off the ground and turned to the open car door. "Let's just go get this fucking bag so I can get the hell out of here."

Antonio didn't say a word but I could feel the heavy weight of his stare as I climbed in the limo and settled back in my seat. Silently, I continued to sip at my bottle of water. All my energy and will to fight left me with my breakfast, and now I just wanted this whole ordeal done with. I didn't care if I lived or died at the end of it. Not anymore. All I wanted was it to be over.

Closing my eyes, I rested my forehead against the cool glass of the window. I didn't want to talk or think about anything. Antonio seemed to get that and he didn't say another word until we arrived at the airport.

When the car slid to a stop and Antonio got out, I

waited for him to motion toward me before I moved. He handed me my handbag and I slung the strap over my head so it hung against my hip with the strap across my body.

"We're looking after your phone, but all your other things are in there. You'll need your ID to get the bag."

I nodded silently, figuring the best way to help this all be over quickly was to do what I was told without making a fuss. I was blissfully numb inside as I walked beside Antonio, with three of his goons surrounding us as we crossed the interior of the airport, heading past all the baggage carousels. I was scanning over all the tired people waiting for their stuff when I saw him. At the end of a turning carousel, Mac stood calm as could be, staring at the passing bags casually, like all of the other people around him. My heart rate kicked up when he lifted his gaze to me briefly. To a bystander, it would look like he was just another bored traveler looking around. But I could see the hard glint in his eye—he was here for me. It took everything in me to keep my expression blank, to not start searching the room for Eagle or my uncle. Because if Mac was here, he wouldn't be here alone. The club had come. Somehow, they'd worked out what Antonio was playing at.

By the time we stood at the unclaimed baggage counter, my nerves were getting the best of me. Not knowing what the club's plan was, but knowing they had to have one was messing with my head.

"Ma'am? Are you alright?"

The young man behind the counter eyed Antonio and his goons like he could do something about it if I said they were holding me hostage.

"I'm just a little overwhelmed, that's all. A reporter spoke to me the other day and told me you had a bag here that belonged to my father. He was on the United Airlines Flight 175 on 9/11. Apparently his checked bag didn't make the flight?"

That got the man's full attention.

"I'll need to check to see if that's correct. We did find a few bags that missed that flight when we did a cleanup a few weeks back. What was your father's name?"

"John Bennett. My name is Claudine Bennett, his daughter."

He gave me a small smile. "If I can see some ID, I'll go check the bags for his name."

After showing him my driver's license, he nodded, then headed off. As he walked away, I gripped the edge of the counter until my fingers turned white, my previous numbness completely gone now. I wasn't sure what was going to happen next. I wanted to turn and scan the area around me for a familiar face, but I couldn't. I knew I couldn't risk giving away that I knew they were here. *Fuck.*

The TSA guy returned and my eyes caught on what he was carrying. It was my dad's favorite bag. The one he always took with him when he traveled. The sight of the scuffed up faded black material had my mind reeling with memories.

And my stomach churned.

"Oh, God. I'm gonna be sick."

I turned on my heel and bolted for the bathroom, making it into a stall just in time to throw up the water I'd drunk. It was like liquid acid in my mouth as I continued to gag over the bowl. Would this day never fucking end?

Chapter 7

Silk

Knowing I couldn't hide in the airport bathroom forever, I pulled myself up and flushed the toilet before I unlocked the door and made my way to the sink. Grabbing a couple of paper towels on my way, I splashed some water on my face, the icy coolness a relief I felt all the way to my toes.

"Miss? Are you okay?"

I squealed and jumped about a foot in the air. Clutching my chest, I looked in the mirror at a middle-aged woman in a TSA uniform.

"Yeah, I just, ah, needed a moment."

She smiled gently and came closer, handing me a sealed bottle of water. "I helped Greg locate the bag. I know who you are, and fully understand your reaction. If you like, I can take you into one of the interview rooms where you can go through the bag in private?"

I frowned at her. Why did she assume I'd want to look through it here? Wouldn't any normal person take the thing home to do that?

"I also know who the man waiting out there for you is. Don't know why he's with you, but I'm guessing it has something to do with that bag of your father's. So, if you want a few minutes alone with it before he gets to paw through the thing, I can help with that."

I tentatively smiled. This woman was a complete stranger. Sure, she sounded like she was trying to help me, but I couldn't be certain she wasn't up to something. Regardless of what she might be pulling, I did want to go through that bag alone first and was grateful of her offer.

"That would be nice. I'm sure I'll end up crying, and no one needs to see that."

I followed her back to the counter and before following her through the door beside it, I turned to Antonio.

"I'm not trying anything here, I just want a few minutes to myself with his things first, okay?"

His gaze was hard, but he knew he didn't really have a choice in the matter. And I knew if I did try anything, he'd rain hell down on me for it. It was all there in his eyes. With a sigh I followed the lady, whose name I didn't even know, through the door into a white corridor then into a small room with a metal table bolted to the wall and a seat on either side of it. My father's old bag sat innocently in the center of the table.

"Fuck. I still can't believe it."

"Normally when bags are unclaimed for any length of time, they go to the auction house. I'm not sure why the stuff from flight 175 didn't get put through the normal channels. Guess things got crazy after the towers went down, and they got shoved aside."

"How did they get found now?"

"Most of the unclaimed bags we have come in now, only stay on site for a few hours, then it gets sent to our off site office down the road. We've been slowly going through all the storage rooms here at LAX and sorting out all the old stuff that's lying around. Last month, we found an old storage crate with five bags in it. When we saw the date, then the flight number we couldn't believe it. Guess someone called the media about it and they wanted to run this big story about finding the owners of the bags. If you haven't already heard from a reporter, I'm sure it won't be long before you do."

I forced my stare away from the table and back to the TSA woman, delaying having to open that damn thing. "That's how I found out it was here—from a reporter. Did they find next of kin for the other bags?"

She shook her head sadly. "You're the only one so far to turn up to claim anything. Maybe once the papers run their articles on the anniversary, others will come forward."

She moved over to the bag before she reached into her pocket. "I assume you don't have a key for the lock?"

I shook my head, I hadn't even considered the fact the bag would be locked. She pulled out what looked like a pair of modified pliers and made quick work of snipping off the small padlock.

She patted my shoulder. "We'll worry about the

paperwork after you've had a few minutes to go through it."

Then she strolled out and closed the door, leaving me alone with my father's belongings. I paced the room, shaking out my hands as I glared over at that fucking bag. It'd caused so much shit already. The continuous ticking of the clock above the door had me eventually reaching for it. I wouldn't have long before Antonio would find some way to get back here with me. Or have me dragged out.

Taking a deep breath I pulled the case closer to me and frowned at the weight. What the hell was in it? Bricks? No wonder he hadn't been allowed to take it as carry on. Tugging the broken lock off, I took hold of the zip and slid it over. My breath caught when the sides fell open to reveal a pair of jeans and a t-shirt. With unsteady hands I lifted the clothes free, my father's scent filling my lungs with my next breath before I placed them neatly on the table. What I discovered lying beneath had my chest tightening. Books. At least a dozen of them. All bound with string, tied like a present.

Lifting the first one out I glanced at the cover where my father's messy scrawl had written in thick black text the word "Charons". Without opening it, I grabbed the next one "Iron Hammers".

"Oh, Dad, what did you do?"

I kept going until I found one with "L.A. Mob" on it. Before I opened it, I shoved the others back in the bag, and covered them with the clothes once more. Then I sat and tugged on the string. The little bow came undone and the string dropped to my lap. I opened the first page to find an envelope taped to it. When I ran my finger over the paper, I could feel a key was inside. Curious, I lifted the lower part of the envelope up and found the name of a bank and a number had been hand written there. I assumed it was the details for the safe deposit box Antonio had mentioned. Knowing I didn't have much time before someone would come barging in, I quickly flicked through the pages. Numbers, dates, amounts. And notes. Of course, my dad was too lazy to come up with some kind of code. Nope, the crazy fool just wrote shit out in plain English. Deaths, drug deals, stolen money—the details were all there staring me in the face. A shudder worked through me, landing in my churning stomach. Closing my eyes, I took a couple of deep breaths. I knew my stomach was empty and there was nothing left to throw up, so I focused on pushing the feeling down, continuing with my deep breathing until the nausea passed.

What do I do now?

If Antonio found out I'd seen this shit, he'll kill me for sure, regardless of what he'd said earlier. Suddenly overcome with a sense of urgency, I grabbed for the string and retied the book so it looked like it had when I'd found it. Then I stood and re-zipped the bag, I didn't want Antonio to even see the other notebooks, let alone get his hands on them. That would be dangerous to everyone that had anything to do with any of the organizations those books related to.

Including myself, because one of those books was about the Charons, no doubt listing all their dirty deeds. That made me pause. *The club.* Of course! Mac was here, that meant there would be others here too. A plan was forming in my mind, when the door opened and the TSA lady came in, paperwork in hand.

"You ready to head off?"

"Not just yet. Can I ask a favor?"

She tilted her head. "You can ask, but I can't promise I'll do it."

I held in the urge to roll my eyes at her. I mean really, what did she think I was going to ask her to do? Shoot Antonio? "It's nothing illegal or anything, I promise. I just need a new lock for this bag, and for you to hold it for a few minutes for someone."

She frowned at me. "Is that wise? The mob may not have the power they once did here in L.A., but they're still powerful enough you don't want to defy them. Not if you want to live, at any rate."

"All he wants is this one thing. The rest are my father's personal belongings that Antonio has no need for. He'll probably make me throw them out before we leave the airport."

It wasn't a complete lie, I'm sure after he rummaged through, found and grabbed the books, he would, indeed, toss the rest in the nearest trash can. I let tears well in my eyes as I gave her a pleading look. She sighed and looked up to the ceiling for a moment. "Fine. Who am I releasing it to?"

"If I can make a phone call, they'll come to you as soon as I've left the airport. You won't need to hold it long."

I waited while she thought over my request. "Fine. Make your call while I go find a lock for you. You also need to sign these forms."

She placed the papers and a pen on the table, before she pulled her phone out with another sigh. Unlocking the screen, she held it out to me. I took her offering with a smile. "Thank you."

I didn't waste a moment to dial, and held the phone to my ear to wait, hoping he'd answer a call from an unknown number.

"Who is this?"

"Hey, Uncle Clint. It's me."

The TSA lady's face softened a little when she heard me say uncle, and she left the room.

"Fuck, sweetheart. Are you hurt? Did you get away? We're here in L.A., tell me where you are and I'll come get you."

"I'm fine. And I'm not really free of him. Not yet. I have to finish this, then I'll leave. Listen, I know you have men here at the airport and once I leave with Antonio, I need you to send one of them to come get Dad's bag. I've got what Antonio is looking for, but I don't want him to have Dad's things."

He growled over the phone. "I don't like this. We were going to snatch you as you leave the airport."

Panic flared inside me.

"You can't! You'll never get away with it here. There's too many people, Antonio has too many guards. And if you did manage it, he'd come after me again. I need to finish this, so he's done with me. Listen, he hasn't hurt me, and has promised all he wants is my help to retrieve something Dad took from him. We'll head downtown, to the East West Bank, I'll unlock the box and then walk away."

"Okay." He groaned. "Okay. We'll play it your way for now. Stay safe, sweetheart. And we'll see you at the bank."

"Love you too, Uncle Clint."

The TSA lady came in as I spoke that last bit and she gave me a sad smile when I hung up the phone.

"Here's a combination lock, you know how to set it?"

I slipped a few dollars into her hand along with her phone. It wasn't much, but it was all the cash I had on me. I didn't want her to be out of pocket for helping me. I took the small black lock with three gold dials from her. "Yeah, I got it. Thanks."

It didn't take long to get it set and locked on the bag. I then quickly signed the release forms saying I'd taken the bag.

"My uncle or one of his friends will come soon to grab the bag. Thank you so much for all your help."

Picking up Antonio's book, I followed her out of the room and headed back toward where I knew Antonio was, no doubt impatiently, waiting for me. Once she entered a code, the door let out a soft beep and I walked out alone. Antonio and his goons were standing where I'd left them, all staring at the door, as though they'd been waiting for me since I'd left.

"Sorry I took so long. It was harder than I thought it would be to go through his things." I walked straight up to Antonio and held out the book. "Found this with your name on it, figured it was what you were after. The rest of the bag was just clothes and toiletries. Personal stuff I'll come back to get later."

He gripped my wrist as he took the book from my hand, his grip tight enough to have a jolt of pain shoot up my arm. "Did you look inside this?"

I gasped. "You think I'm that stupid? The last thing I'll do is give you a reason to hurt me. Your name scrawled on the cover was enough to tell me it was what you wanted."

He narrowed his eyes at me for a moment, and he tightened his grip. My knees buckled a little, but I caught myself as he suddenly released me.

"If I discover you have hidden something from me by not bringing the bag, I will recount my promise."

Rubbing my wrist I stepped away from him, staying silent as I worried my actress skills weren't as good as I'd hoped. Then he nodded once and turned to head out of the airport, his goons making sure I followed him.

Eagle

I couldn't fucking wait to patch in and be a full member of the club. Being a prospect could suck at times. Like now. Mac and Taz were inside the airport strolling around, without their cuts on, pretending to be everyday travelers. Nitro, Scout and Bulldog were huddled together discussing whatever Bulldog's phone call had been about. Me? I was stuck here guarding the damn bikes. I was a fucking Marine, and my girl was in trouble but I couldn't be sent in because whoever took Silk knew what I looked like. I hadn't seen her since she was snatched and it had me on edge. I was also pissed off that I was being left out of the loop on whatever was currently being planned.

When they finished their chat, Nitro pulled his phone out while Scout and Bulldog headed straight for me. *About damn time.* I stood taller and focused on loosening my tense muscles. Looking like I was going to tackle someone probably wasn't going to get me far with the Club President and VP.

"New plan. Silk's going to a bank with Sabella and we're going to grab her from there."

I pulled my sunglasses off to glare at Scout. "What the fuck? We're doing what now? I thought we were grabbing her here."

And ending this shit. I wanted Silk where I could see her. Close to me where I could keep her safe, not in the back of some fucking limo with a mob boss and his goons!

"It's too risky, too many people. Silk's asked us to wait until after she goes to the bank. There's a deposit box he needs her to open for him, then she's free. At least, that's what he's told her. She wants to get him his shit so he has no reason to come after her ever again. Although, I highly doubt he really intends on simply letting her walk away after he gets whatever is in that fucking box. Assuming what he wants is even in the damn thing. So, we're going to be waiting at the bank to make sure she leaves with us, not him."

Nitro came over to join us, and as Sergeant in Arms, he took over explaining the new plan. The big bastard had been a Navy SEAL for years before he retired and joined the club. I had no problem following the man's lead.

"Right. Mac is collecting the bag Silk left for us. Taz is going to stay with him, watch his back. Us four are heading over to the East West Bank. I want you," he pointed to my chest, "waiting out the front with the bikes, ready to roll. Bulldog, I want you inside, near the entrance. Scout and I will be further inside the bank to delay anyone we need to. The second Taz and Mac arrive, I want Taz to stay with the bikes while Mac and Eagle come inside. Bulldog will tell you which way to go. Keep your cuts packed away, we don't need to be advertising we're in town. And no fucking guns. I know you boys are used to just shooting shit that's in your way, but we need to keep this quiet."

We'd stopped and removed our cuts outside of L.A.

None of us wanted to get in a fight with a local MC for not getting permission to enter their stomping grounds. We also didn't want anyone connected with Sabella to recognize the club insignia and report back to their boss that the club was in town. As far as anyone who saw us was concerned, we were just a group of guys on bikes. No MC affiliation at all.

"Hand-to-hand is fine with me. I'll enjoy pounding out some of my frustration on a few of these bastards. What's the plan once we have Silk?"

"If we get her before Mac and Taz arrive, we'll send her out to Eagle and you'll ride with her out of town. Once you're out a ways, contact your boys and meet up, then head home together. But hopefully Mac and Taz will be there by the time we get her. In which case, I still want her on the back of your bike as soon as you can swing it. Take Mac and Taz with you and ride home. We're going to hang back for a while, make sure you're not followed."

I fought the smirk that was trying to spread over my face. I'd put money on the 'what' they were staying in L.A. for, and it wasn't to make sure we weren't followed. It was to deliver a message. No one messed with those protected by the Charon MC and got away with it. No one. It stung that I couldn't be a part of that particular beat down, but with these three busy taking care of that, it meant I had at least a couple of days on the road with Silk with no overbearing relatives stopping us from taking things further. Taz and Mac knew full well how I felt about Silk, and I knew without a doubt that neither would stop us, or report back on anything that happened.

We all went silent as Sabella and his crew walked out of the airport. I could barely see Silk in the middle of all the suits. Efficiently, they all got in the limo and it drove off toward the inner city.

"Right. Let's move out."

With a nod, I followed Nitro's order, knowing Mac and Taz would only be minutes behind us. No way would they waste time getting to that bank when they knew what was at stake.

I couldn't wait for all this shit to be over, and I had Silk safely on the back of my bike, where she belonged.

Chapter 8

Silk

Once the door of the limo was closed, Antonio tore at the string holding the book closed. I shrunk back into my seat, and did my best to keep my gaze focused on his face, rather than his hands. I knew that if he knew I'd so much as peeked at the contents of that bloody book, I'd find myself in a whole heap of, no doubt painful, trouble.

When he opened the cover and saw the envelope, a frown creased his brow a moment as he examined it, then lifted his eyes to run over me briefly before he focused on the driver.

"Head downtown, to the East West Bank."

I relaxed a little when he tilted the book toward himself, so I couldn't see the pages, even if I was looking. He flipped through them quickly, muttering in Italian with what I guessed were curses.

"You are certain you didn't look in this book?"

I held his gaze steadily. "I delivered it to you in the condition I found it. Bound with string."

Technically, it wasn't a lie. And he didn't further

question me on it. Ripping the envelope from the front, he closed the cover and handed the book to one of his goons.

"Do not open that. Keep it safe until I request it from you."

With a nod, the big man slid the book inside his jacket, flashing the butt of a gun resting in a holster under his arm as he did. I took a deep breath to try to calm my nerves. I hoped I was doing the right thing, going with him so he had no reason to come after me again.

Antonio tore the top from the envelope and tipped it against his palm. A key and small card fell out. The quick flash of the card I saw had me thinking it was some kind of password. Random letters and numbers just like those were written on the page underneath the envelope. Antonio pocketed the card before smiling over at me.

"Here, take the key. You will need it to access the box, as the next of kin."

"Then I'll be free to go?"

He cocked his head at me. "You don't want to see what's inside that had me chasing you down?"

I shook my head. "Hell, no. Like I said before, I'd like to still be breathing tomorrow and I have no need for whatever is in that box." I gave him a small smile. "Hopefully, you'll be so busy looking at whatever it is, you'll let me go on my merry way."

With a frown he glared at me. "I'm finding it hard to believe you have no curiosity about what you've been kidnapped over."

"Let's just say, my self-preservation instincts are stronger than my curiosity."

He made a gruff sound that I think was his attempt at a chuckle, then the car came to a stop and once more we exited the vehicle and made our way into the bank. I gripped the small key tightly in my fist, praying that Antonio would keep his word and let me go once he had his stupid box.

With Antonio by my side, I walked up to the customer service counter.

"I've recently found out my late father, John Bennett, had a safe deposit box here. I have his key, and here is my driver's license."

I handed both over, figuring I'd give the woman everything at once to save her having to ask.

"Sorry for your loss, ma'am."

She held the key up close to her face and tilted it to read the number stamped into the metal. Then she turned to her computer and tapped away for a bit.

"Will you be taking the contents with you today, ma'am?"

"Please, call me Claudine. And yes, I'll be taking whatever is in the box with me."

She squinted at the computer and frowned. "It looks like there's two boxes assigned to that key. Strange."

I didn't know much about how these box things worked but that didn't sound right. "Aren't the boxes all keyed differently? How can one key open two boxes?"

"Oh, the actual key will only open one box. The other

box is a keyless one. We don't have many customers ask for them. It's easier to use a key to access them. This one has your name listed as its owner, actually. Now, let me print off these forms, and I'll get you to sign them. Then I'll take you back to the boxes."

As she fluffed around with the forms I thought over why there'd be two boxes. What would my father have left for me at the same place he was hiding mob stuff at?

"Right, here you go. Just sign here, and here."

She continued on and I followed her instructions, signing whenever she told me to. Finally, the forms were all done and with a smile the woman handed the key back to me.

"Follow me, please."

We entered a large room with walls lined with metal boxes. There was a large table in the center, where I guessed people normally went through their boxes.

"Excuse me, miss. Do you have private rooms for viewing the contents of the boxes?"

Antonio's question startled me. He'd been silent for so long.

"Ah, yes we do. Let me get the boxes, then I'll take you through."

Confidently, she walked through the room and stopped to scan the numbers about two-thirds of the way down.

"Here you go. This one here is the keyed one. I'll just be a moment while I get the other box for you. Please wait here."

She slipped through a narrow door at the end of the room and vanished from sight. I held the key out to Antonio.

"I'll give you the key, if you give me my phone back. This is the end for us. You can take your box to a private room and do whatever you need to, I'll take my box and leave. I've done everything you've asked of me. Now it's time for you to keep your word."

My voice came out strong, even though I was a mass of nerves inside. He frowned at me but clicked his fingers toward the goon who'd followed us in. The other two had waited back in the hallway. His man handed over my phone and battery to Antonio, who held them out toward me.

"We took the battery out to disable the GPS, nothing else has been done to it."

I took the items and he took the key. I'd just slipped the battery back in and turned my phone on when the bank lady returned with a smaller box. I heard a metallic sliding noise and assumed Antonio had slid the box from the table, but I didn't care. My whole focus was on the box in her hands.

"Ah, did you both want to open the boxes in the private viewing room?"

"No. I'll go through that one here. My friend here, will use the private room for his box."

The woman frowned a little but seemed to get over whatever her issue was quickly.

"Okay, well, sir, if you'd please follow me I'll take

you to the private room. Claudine, I'll come back and escort you out after I settle your friend in."

I grinned as she placed the box on the table. "Great. Thank you for all your help."

I waited until I was alone before I quickly pulled the box closer to me and opened the lid. *Shit.* Maybe I should have asked if they had a second private room. I set my handbag up on the table next to the box and quickly moved the several rolls of cash into my, thankfully, large bag. I carefully picked up the handgun, made sure the safety was on, and put that in my bag too. I had no idea if the thing would even work after sitting in a box for over fifteen years, but I sure as fuck wasn't going to test it out in a bank's strong room.

I moved to pick up the thick, heavy A4 yellow envelope and my eyes stung at seeing my dad's handwriting on it. A smaller piece of paper was folded and stuck below where he'd written my name. I carefully peeled the tape off so I could unfold and read the note.

"Fuck, Dad. What the hell did you do?"

My whispered words echoed in the empty room and I didn't hang around. The note clearly stated that if anyone related to the mob was with me, that I couldn't trust them and I needed to run, far and fast. After placing the envelope in my bag, I made one last check of the box to make sure I had everything, before I spun toward the exit. I rushed out of the room before I'd realized that the bank lady hadn't returned to get me. When I slammed straight into the solid body of one of Antonio's guards, I knew why she hadn't.

"Give me that envelope, and whatever else was in the box. Was it cash? More papers?"

He'd been watching me at least for the last minute or so. Dammit, I hadn't even thought to check the hall was clear, just barreled straight into danger.

I tried to break free of the tight grip he had on my shoulders but couldn't get his hold to even loosen a little. Letting my fury fuel me, I lifted my leg in preparation to knee him, and the bastard twisted so my knee landed against his thigh, not his groin like I'd planned. With a growl he spun me and slammed me against the wall.

"Always the hard way."

He took a fist full of my hair and pulled my head back. A scream tore from my throat when I realized he was going to slam my head against the wall. I pushed my hands against the cold marble with all the strength I could muster, trying to get my face as far away from the hard surface as I could. I would be knocked out from the blow at the least. Hell, with this bastard's strength, I'd be lucky to still be alive afterwards!

Next thing I knew, I was shoved from the side hard enough I went sprawling toward the floor. I managed to catch myself with my hands, rather than my face, and my wrists screamed in protest at the jarring. I didn't look back, but tried to get to my feet as I scrambled down the hallway. Hands under my arms lifted me to my feet and I tensed, gripping my bag with one hand and clenching the other, ready to swing around and punch.

"Shh, Silk. It's just me. Can you walk? I need you to walk with me, as fast as you can to the front doors."

Eagle. He'd come for me. I leaned back against him for a moment. "Yeah, I can do that."

He loosened his hold and I turned to look over his shoulder. Antonio's man was lying on the floor out cold with half his face beginning to swell up. I glanced down at Eagle's hands and saw the knuckles on his right were roughed up.

"That make you feel better, babe?" He growled as he led me across the main foyer of the bank. "Because let me tell you, it's gonna take more than one fucking punch to make *me* feel better."

I nearly tripped over my feet. Eagle had knocked that huge man out with one single blow? Wow.

Uncle Clint stood by the door, until he saw me. Then he strode toward me, helmet in hand.

"Here, put this on. I want you to get on the back of Eagle's bike and let him take you away. You understand?"

"Where's the bag? From the airport?"

I jumped a little when Mac appeared at my side. "It's safely stored on my bike, Silk."

Uncle Clint drew my attention back to him. "Mac and Taz will be riding with you. Scout, Nitro and I are gonna hang around, make sure no one follows you."

I winced. I knew full well what he meant by that. "Please, be careful."

He kissed my forehead before taking the helmet from

my hands and placing it on my head, quickly doing up the strap.

"Go on, before it's too late."

I rushed toward the door, with Eagle and Mac tight on my heels, and as I pushed against the glass, I heard Antonio call my name. Fear had me bolting out the door and onto the street, allowing Eagle to guide me. We jogged down half a block where Taz sat on his bike, next to Eagle's and Mac's. It sounded like all three were idling, ready to go in an instant.

Eagle didn't give me a chance to get on. He simply lifted me up and put me on the back before he slipped on in front of me.

"Hold on, baby."

Tucking my handbag safely between us, I wrapped my arms around his waist. The moment I did, he took off down the street, Mac and Taz thundering along behind us.

Relief at being free and clear of Antonio and his goons had tears pricking my eyes and I did nothing to stop them. The wind against my face dried them within seconds and there was no way I could contain my elation at riding away from all the shit Antonio had brought down on me.

Being pressed up against Eagle wasn't too bad either. His hard abs beneath my palms felt wonderful, and briefly, I wondered if he'd mind if I slipped my hands under his shirt. I soon decided not to try it, at least not today. I didn't want him to crash because he was distracted.

Eagle

When we stopped at a set of lights, I lowered my hand to her thigh, giving it a squeeze. I told myself I was doing it to reassure Silk, but I was mainly doing it because I could scarcely believe she was safely on the back of my bike. Her legs tightened against me and she rested her cheek against the back of my shoulder. Without my cut between us, I could feel the warmth from her skin through my shirt. It felt so fucking right to have her wrapped around me like this.

I hadn't really believed it would be so easy to get Silk away from that mob goon back at the bank. He'd been a huge bastard, but I knew I had power in my strikes, and in the end, it had only taken one well-placed punch to the side of his head to drop him. I winced as I remembered how it had sent Silk skidding across the floor. That had been unfortunate, but it was better than allowing the bastard to slam her head against the wall like he was about to do. My heart skipped more than one fucking beat as I thought about what would have happened if I'd been even a few seconds later than I had been. A shudder ran through me and she nuzzled her face against my back, soothing me with the caress. Part of me wanted to pull over and check her from head to toe for injuries now, but I resisted. When we next stopped, I'd make sure it was at a hotel where I could have some privacy to make one hundred percent sure she was unharmed.

About two hours later, Silk started squirming around behind me. Figuring she needed a break, I pulled into a motel on the outskirts of a small town, with complete confidence my brothers would follow me. The place looked a little worse for wear, but I didn't give a damn. We could all use a couple hours of sleep before we rode the rest of the way home. I didn't want to stop too often, but right now, I needed to check Silk was truly okay. And I couldn't do that the way I wanted to in public.

As soon as I pulled up, Silk slid off and stretched her legs, then her arms and back. Damn, she was sexy as fuck. The way she moved had my cock throbbing for some attention. Wincing, I swung my leg over my bike and, leaving Silk in Taz and Mac's care for a moment, I headed into the motel office.

I flashed enough cash at the clerk, he was happy to give me two room keys for the afternoon without needing any paperwork filled out. I went out and tossed one key to Mac. "You and Taz can crash in there for a couple hours. I made sure it had two doubles, so don't start bitching."

To the sound of them snickering like a pair of school girls, I snatched up Silk's hand and dragged her to our room. It was next to where Taz and Mac would be, and I figured they'd move my bike for me. If not, it could just stay by the front office for the afternoon. At this point, I didn't give a fuck. I was about to have Silk all to myself, in private.

In no time I had the door unlocked, us inside, and it slammed shut. I hung the old-school key on the hook on the back of the door, then prowled toward Silk. She was setting her bag on the table when she noticed me coming at her. With wide eyes, she backed away from me until the wall prevented her from going any further. She didn't say a word as I laid a palm against the wall on either side of her, boxing her in. I dropped my face into her neck to inhale against her skin and smiled when a slight tremor ran through her body. Her sweet scent filled my lungs and the tight bands around my chest loosened a little. I wasn't dreaming, Silk was really here, and unharmed. Or was she? I had a sudden urgent instinct, one I couldn't shut down, that demanded I check her thoroughly for injury.

She gasped when I grabbed the bottom of her shirt and ripped it over her head. Moving onto her pants, I was solely focused on getting her stripped naked. That is, until Silk took my face between her palms. The moment she did that, my entire body stilled and I looked up into her pale blue irises. I could guess she wouldn't find the wild look I had in my eyes comforting. I'd been going crazy the whole time she'd been gone. Now that I had her back, I wasn't going to fucking let her go.

"What are you doing?"

"Checking you for injuries. I'm sorry, but I can't stop. I need to do this, to make sure you're really okay."

She smiled gently, like one would to a crazy person.

Maybe I was crazy. "I don't need to be naked for you to do that." Dropping her right hand from my face, she rolled her shoulder forward to reveal the burn marks from a Taser. "This is the only wound I have, from when they grabbed me at Silky Ink."

There were bruises too, from when she'd been grabbed in the bank. Each bicep had a darkening patch right where the bastard's thumbs would have been. I gently wrapped my palm around her skin, below the bruise.

"You've got bruises too. Fuck, sweetheart. I'm sorry I didn't stop them from taking you. I should have risked it and taken a head shot."

There hadn't been much time to do it. Only seconds, but I should have at least tried. Staring at her injuries, my vision turned red for a moment as fury coursed through me. I knew she could have been hurt a whole lot worse than this, but the fact that she'd been hurt at all burned my soul.

Silk's fingers drove into my hair and twisted so I was forced to turn to look at her face again. Fuck, she was so beautiful.

"Eagle, I'm fine. It will all heal in no time. Yeah, I'm a little shaken up after it all, but honestly, I'm okay. I'd be a hell of a lot worse off if you'd killed the one that first grabbed me. You would have ended up in jail, then they would have come after me again. Doubt they would have taken such care to not hurt me if I'd cost them one of their own."

I shifted my hand to stroke over her smooth belly before I gripped her hip. She looked sexy as sin wearing just her black lacy bra, and her jeans' fly ripped open, revealing the matching panties.

"I swear you took ten years off my life when I heard you scream. I came running, but it was already too late."

She smirked. "You shot my kidnapper twice in the leg. Antonio put him on driver duty because he has to use a crutch to walk while it heals. He wasn't a happy man."

A growl rippled up my throat. "He'll be a whole lot less happy if I ever see him again."

I tightened my grip on her before I moved in to press my body against hers. The sexual energy crackled between us and I gave in and took her mouth with mine. That one taste I'd had two days ago hadn't been nearly enough. I had a feeling I'd never get enough of this woman. Somehow, over the past ten months, she'd become vital to my existence.

She thrust both of her hands in my hair, wrapping her fingers in it when I nipped her lower lip. She opened on a moan and I slipped my tongue inside to dance with hers. She was the best thing I'd ever tasted. My cock throbbed as I wondered what her cream would taste like. Not leaving her mouth, I slipped a hand up her spine, pulling her slightly away from the wall so I could get to the catch on her bra. The moment I had the thing unhooked, I broke the kiss and took the material from her body. As I'd guessed, her tits were fucking perfect. Smooth, white skin tipped with pierced rosy nipples that were already hard and waiting for me.

With another growl I took her mouth again. It was rough and hot, and when I wrapped my palm over her breast, kneading it before tweaking the metal bar through her nipple, she arched against me with a loud moan. I kissed a trail down her throat and kept going until I had my mouth on her tits. I kept working her over with my lips and teeth as I ran my hands down further and pushed her jeans and panties over her hips.

The way she writhed under my hands and mouth was so fucking sexy it nearly had me coming in my pants like a fucking teenager. When her boots stopped me from getting her completely naked, my frustration rose up.

"Dammit."

I scooped her up and tossed her on to the bed. She giggled as I attacked her boots until I had them off and could rip her jeans free. Once she was naked I stood up and took in the sight. Her parted lips were dark red from my kisses, the small love bites dotting her chest had me grinning. She'd wear my marks for a few days at least. After tearing my shirt over my head, I tugged on my belt, loosening the buckle before I undid my jeans. Her eyes zeroed in on what I was doing as she continued to squirm on the bed.

Toeing off my own boots, I shoved my jeans and boxer-briefs down in one movement. The way her eyes widened and her palms went to her breasts had me gripping my cock and giving it a few strokes.

"You gonna let me have you, Silk? Even though I

don't have my top rocker yet."

She licked her lips and her stare remained glued to my hand sliding over my hard length.

"Would I be lying here naked if I didn't want you to fuck me, Eagle? I don't give a shit if you have your patch or not. But you're not doing it without a condom."

I smirked as I reached for my discarded jeans, searching for my wallet.

"I'll wrap it up for you, baby. Don't you worry about that."

I pulled the condom out before I chucked the wallet back down on top of my jeans. I tossed the condom on the bed beside Silk before resting a knee between her feet.

"I've been waiting a long time to have you like this, baby. All soft and naked...waiting for me to ease that ache you have."

Silk

I struggled to tear my gaze away from his dick. He had it fisted in his hand and was stroking it slow and hard. Fuck. I wanted him. When he gripped my ankle with his other hand, my gaze followed the movement. His skin looked so dark compared to my incredibly pale leg. His Native American heritage meant his skin was a deep tan color all over and I wanted nothing more than to taste every inch. I ran my tongue over my lower lip at the thought.

"Don't tease, baby. That's not nice."

I blinked up at him. "How was I teasing? You're the one sitting there out of my reach, looking sexy as fuck."

Feeling cheeky, I ran my palms over my breasts, tweaking my nipples before running one hand down my torso.

"Guess, I'll just have to play with what I can reach."

As my fingertip grazed my clit a low growl filled the room.

"That's mine."

A moment later he was on me, shoving my legs apart and diving face first between them in one smooth movement. A brush of hot air against my flesh was my only warning before he set his mouth on me.

"Fuuuuck."

Unable to stay still, I bucked up against him as he thrust his tongue deep within me. Well, at least I did until he gripped each of my hips in his hands and held me still. I fisted one hand in his silky hair, and the other in the bed cover. The coil of desire in my lower belly building faster than it ever had before. Eagle alternated between swiping the flat of his tongue over me, nipping my clit, and thrusting his tongue deep in my pussy. Every move he made had me panting and shivering under the onslaught. My climax grew closer and I thrashed my head back and forth as I moaned his name. I groaned when he lifted his head to stare up into my eyes. It was more than a mere ache, my pussy *pulsed* with need. I licked my lips, ready to demand he put his mouth back on me, but stopped short when he released a hip and pressed two fingers deep within me, curling them forward until he found my secret spot. Before I could take a full breath I blew apart. With a scream, I arched up from the mattress, pressing myself firmly against his mouth once more as he began to lap at me again.

Panting, I lay in a contented heap, watching Eagle through half closed eyes. He reached for the condom and covered himself with it before he crawled up over me. As soon as he was close enough, I reached for him, wrapping my arms around his neck to bring him down to me. I licked at his lips, moaning as I caught a taste of myself mixed with his unique flavor. He took possession of my mouth in the same instant that he gripped my thigh, lifted it and thrust deep. My internal muscles were still recovering from my climax and rippled against his hard length. My body undulated beneath him, loving how he trapped me with his larger frame.

"So fucking tight. You feel so good, Silk."

He kissed me again, before he lifted up to get more leverage to pound into me. Every glide of his cock into me sent me higher. I ran my palms over his shoulders, down his pecs and pinched at his nipples.

"Fuck me, woman."

He leaned back to kneel as he lifted my ass in his hands. The next thrust in had him going deeper than ever and I threw out my hands to grab the covers, desperately searching for something to keep me grounded as he struck my g-spot with Every. Single. Stroke.

"Eagle!"

Stars and black spots swam across my vision as I struggled to drag breath in as my second orgasm hit me like a freight train. I heard my name a few moments before Eagle's weight was over me, pressing me into the mattress. As my mind came back online, I groaned. Damn man weighed a ton... and it was all hard muscle.

"Sorry, didn't mean to squish you."

He gave me another quick peck on the lips, before rolling off both me and the bed and took the few steps over to the bathroom. I couldn't resist watching his very fine ass as he strode away. Damn, but that man was certainly built to please. When he disappeared from view, I shifted around until I was under the covers. I was tired and could use an hour or two nap before I had to sit on a bike for who knows how long. The boys may want to do the rest of the trip without any more long stops. At a guess, we still had at least ten hours of ride time ahead of us. With only short stops, that was a long time to sit on the back of a bike. I'd been riding bikes forever, but even for me that was a long haul.

I was already drifting off when Eagle came back and pulled the covers off. My heart did a flip when, with care, he lifted my leg and wiped a warm washcloth over my inner thighs and pussy. He pulled the cover back over me before he turned and tossed the cloth back into the bathroom. Next thing I knew, I had over six feet of delicious male spooned up against me, his stiff dick pressed against my ass. I couldn't resist wriggling a little against him.

"Quit teasing me, woman. I only had the one condom, and we do need to catch some shut-eye before we head off again."

Chuckling, I snuggled back against him and let myself go, knowing with certainty, Eagle would keep me safe while I slept.

The next thing I knew, soft lips were pressing kisses over my bare shoulder.

"Hmmm."

"Sorry, baby. I wish I could let you sleep longer, but we gotta get up and get moving."

I rolled onto my back and stretched out, getting the kinks out of my spine as I always did when I woke. And was rewarded with a low tortured groan.

"You are a cruel woman, Silk. I'll leave you to grab a quick shower while I discuss with the boys where we're going."

That got my attention.

"I don't need a shower, and where are we going? I thought we were going home?"

I stood from the bed and moved around, gathering my clothes to put on.

"We're going back to Bridgewater, but I don't think going to your place or the clubhouse is a smart idea right now. I have no idea what kind of trouble Bulldog is going to kick up back in L.A. before they leave."

I winced. Yeah, Uncle Clint was no doubt delivering a

beat down that was going to come back and bite the club in the ass. Especially her, if they could get their hands on her.

"I know where we can go. Let's go find the others."

As soon as we were both dressed, I ran my fingers through my hair, hoping it didn't look like I'd just been fucked. I slung my bag over my head and grabbed my helmet before I followed Eagle out the door.

"That bag of yours looks damn heavy. Want to put it in my saddle bag?"

Anyone else, I wouldn't trust to keep it safe, but this was Eagle and deep down I knew he would never intentionally hurt me.

"Um, yeah. It kinda is now. That'd be great."

He gave me a funny look, but I wasn't ready to discuss what my father had left me in that box. I strode off toward where the bikes sat, Mac and Taz leaning against a wall next to them, both with smirks on their faces. I winced at them knowing what Eagle and I had done earlier.

"You two better keep your mouths shut about Eagle and me, or he'll get a beat down like you read about."

Both their expressions turned to stone on a dime.

"Neither of us would ever betray our brother, Silk. You don't even have to say it. You should know that."

"Yeah well, I didn't want to risk it. The cost is too high. Right, now Eagle said y'all don't think it's a great idea for me to be staying in town when we get back. I have a place. I normally take off for the week or so around the ninth of September, so I've got a cabin all booked and ready to go. I'm also not scheduled at the shop for a couple of weeks, so disappearing won't be an issue for me work-wise."

She wasn't sure what the three men were scheduled to do for the club, but she was certain Scout and Bulldog would handle it so they were all free and clear for the time they were gone.

"Where is this place of yours? And who knows where it is?"

"It's on the coast, about an hour's ride from my home. And no one knows, not even Gabs or my uncle. I go off grid every year. Uncle Clint doesn't like it, but he can respect my reasons for it and has left it alone so far. So, you three better keep it to yourselves. I do not want to have to find a new hiding spot because everyone in the club suddenly knows where to find me."

Although I pretty much suspected I would need to do just that, regardless. No way would these three be able to deny telling Scout or my uncle its location. As prospects, they didn't really have a say in the matter.

Losing the cabin was going to hurt like a bitch. I loved that house. If I could afford it, I'd have bought the place. But it was buy the cabin or start up Silky Ink. Naturally, I'd chosen my shop, especially considering the owner of the cabin was a lovely older man who had told me I could buy it from him whenever I could afford it—that he wouldn't sell it out from under me.

Chapter 9

Silk

Two hours after we arrived at my cabin, I still couldn't get rid of my final guard. The place I rented each year wasn't really a cabin. It was huge, with two bathrooms and four bedrooms. *Plenty of room for us all to have our own space.* Which was what I wanted desperately to have. I hadn't read my father's letter, or gone through his bag properly. I didn't want help to do either of those things. I wanted to be alone. But Eagle was refusing to be reasonable. At least Mac and Taz had finally gone to bed. The two of them had scouted the landscape surrounding the place for nearly an hour before they returned, announced it was safe enough for now, and headed to their rooms.

We'd been on the road until well into the night and were all tired, but I couldn't sleep. Not until I at least read my father's letter. The bag could wait, but his letter could not.

"It's late, Silk. Just come to bed already, and we'll continue arguing in the morning."

"You go to bed. I need a little alone time before I call it a night."

His gaze darkened. "I'm not leaving you alone. Until we're certain the threat from Sabella has passed, you're not to ever be left alone. You getting taken while I stood by your shop's entrance proved that point."

I threw my hands up in the air in frustration. "You'll be right next door!"

He shook his head. "No, I'll be right beside you."

I glared at him as my temper rose. This was such bullshit! With a growl, I shoved past him into the master bedroom. If he wouldn't leave me alone, then I'd just pretend he wasn't here. I dumped my handbag on the bed, the weight of it sinking deep into the fluffy comforter. Unzipping it, I pulled it open and began rummaging around for the letter.

"What the fuck is in your damn bag?"

I froze at the steel laced through his voice.

"What do you mean?"

He snatched the bag from me and up ended it on the bed, the contents spreading out. I snatched the envelope and held it against my chest as he pushed the rolls of cash into a pile, then carefully picked up the gun and checked it out.

"You had a gun on you the entire time and didn't try to use it?" He shook his head again. "Why didn't Sabella search you and take it away? Or the money. Isn't that what he was chasing? Money? I don't understand, Silk."

"I don't know what my father had that belonged to

Antonio, but I assumed it would be money. It's not my gun or cash. This is all the stuff that my father left me in a box at the bank. There were two boxes. When I went in with the key, they checked the system and there was a second box under my name attached to the key. I gave Antonio the key and his box, then once he'd taken them into a private viewing room. I opened my box, emptied it all into my bag and ran out of there."

Silently he reached over and tore off the note that I'd stuck back on the envelope. I tried to grab it but stopped when Eagle gave me a glare.

"That's not yours to read."

"If it affects your safety, then it sure as hell is mine to read."

I could feel my face heat with my fury. Who the fuck did he think he was?

"Personal messages from my father. *My dead father.* Are mine alone."

My temper was close to breaking. He was already scanning the damn note so there was no point in arguing really. But he was infuriating me. First, with not giving me time by myself, and now, with not respecting my privacy one little bit. When he held the note out, I snatched it from him and tightened my grip on the envelope. No way in hell was he getting to look in there first.

"So, I'm guessing your pops knew he'd screwed up with Sabella and that his days were numbered. I'm also guessing he knew the bastard would come after you.

Want to tell me what's in the envelope you've got a death grip on?"

"I don't know. I haven't looked yet. It's why I wanted you to go away for a while."

His expression softened and he reached out to stroke his knuckles down my cheek.

"You know I'm here for you. The fact Bulldog put me in charge of keeping you safe, is nothing more than a really good excuse for me to be here. Trust me, even if I wasn't anything to do with the club, I'd be chasing you down."

Frowning, I looked him up and down. He was as beautiful as ever, but his eyes looked tired and his shoulders were slumped. Was he telling the truth?

"I don't believe you."

Any hint of his weariness disappeared, and in the blink of an eye he was standing right in front of me. He tore the envelope from my grip and tossed it on the pile of stuff from my bag.

"You think I lose my mind over every female that gets kidnapped? You think I don't sleep with worry every time I hear a woman's been taken? Or do you think I devour every woman I can get my hands on, like I did you? I have *never* felt like this in my life. *You* are the only one who's ever had me so fucking twisted up in knots, I don't know which way is up."

As he'd spoken I'd backed away, his voice a whip that left me reeling. I couldn't think of what to say. I didn't even know what I truly wanted him to do. Did I really want him to go and leave me alone? The things I felt when he was near were both amazing and scary as fuck. I blinked as I licked my lips, his gaze tracking the movement. When he growled, I turned to run. I couldn't handle this right now. Not with my mind still spinning from all I'd learned about who my father had been.

The breath rushed out of me when Eagle caught me around the waist and easily lifted me until my feet were off the ground.

"Put me down! Don't touch me!"

He had my arms pinned, but my legs were free and I tried to kick him, but he managed to avoid each blow. My temper rose each moment he stayed silent while I thrashed against his tight hold. I needed to blow off some steam before I could think straight again and he wasn't helping by keeping me captive.

Suddenly I was flying through the air. At the same time I landed on the mattress, all my stuff noisily shifting as I landed. A scream tore from my throat for a moment before Eagle clapped his hand over my mouth.

"Stop it. Or do you want Mac and Taz in here for this?"

He released my mouth and I got one breath in before Eagle's hard body had me pinned down. I couldn't move an inch. Especially when he shifted his hands to hold my face still between his palms. I was panting hard, my attempts to fight him off, had me worked up. Each inhale pushed my breasts harder against his chest. My gaze focused in on his lips of their own accord. They were soft and I kind of wanted to nip at the lower one, suck on it a little, but I wouldn't. I couldn't give in to him tonight. I'd stupidly fallen into bed with him earlier, but that didn't mean I handed over my life to the man. I would never allow any man to control me, regardless of how good they were in the sack.

"I don't want *any* of you here. Why won't you let me have this? All I want is a little time alone."

He lowered his face down to mine and my eyes slid shut when he gently pressed a kiss to my forehead. Something deep inside me settled and calmed at the strangely comforting gesture.

Eagle
Her body relaxed beneath me as I pressed my lips to her forehead. How could I make her understand that I wanted her, not because I'd been told to keep her safe, but because I adored her? I wasn't sure if I loved her—I hadn't known her long enough for that level of emotion yet. But I did know her well enough to know that if I left her alone like she wanted, to read that letter, she'd fall apart and be forced to attempt to put herself back together again. I didn't want her to suffer through that alone, she didn't need to. I would always be here for her, but I wasn't sure how to make her believe it.

"Because, sweetheart, I don't believe you really want to be alone. You're going to want someone to vent to about whatever you read. Whether it's crying or yelling, you're going to need to let that shit out. You can unload on me."

She shook her head. "Just because we're good together in bed—"

With a finger pressed over her lips, I stopped her from talking. "Yeah, I love your body and want to have you in my bed each and every night—but I want more than that. I want to be your rock, Silk. I don't know how else to tell you, how to make you believe. So how about you give me a fucking chance here, and let me show you."

She blinked up at me, looking impossibly vulnerable. It made my heart bleed for her. I rolled off her and in a flash, had her settled between my thighs, with her back against my chest, as I leaned against the headboard of the bed.

"Grab the envelope and let's rip this band aid off. I'm dog tired, and I know you must be too. So, just hurry the fuck up and read the thing so we can get some shut-eye."

I bit back a groan when she leaned forward and ground her ass against my rock-hard cock. Dammit. I was trying to be a gentleman here, and she was teasing the shit out of me. With a huff, she sat with her back straight once she had the parcel. *Stubborn woman.* I shifted to sit forward, so my front was pressed against her back and I could wrap my arms around her waist as I rested my chin lightly on her shoulder. Naturally, she stiffened and stopped moving.

"What are you doing?"

"Offering you support."

She twisted to stare at me a moment before turning back with a shake of her head and a huff. "Whatever."

Carefully, she peeled the envelope open before she tilted it, so the contents slipped out on the bed. A crisp page of lined paper filled with messy handwriting was on top of a thick, bound stack of photocopied pages. From what I could see, they were ledger pages of some kind, but without a closer look, I couldn't tell for certain. Silk dropped the now-empty envelope and lifted the bundle of papers. After pulling on the string that bound the pages, she took one hand from it to lift the note. I snapped my hands up and grabbed the bundle before we ended up with pages all over the damn place.

She gasped at my quick movement, but didn't object when I held the bundle closer so I could read the first page. Definitely a ledger, of criminal activities by the looks.

"What is this shit?"

"It looks like a copy of the book I gave Antonio."

I flicked through the pages, reading random entries.

"Fuck me. This is a detailed report of years of the mob's dealings. No fucking wonder Sabella came after you to get it. Even with the time lapse, this shit would cause them one hell of a lot of trouble."

She shook her head. "It wasn't just the book that Sabella wanted. Inside the book was the key to the deposit box. I can only assume the box had either cash or bank account details. From what Antonio said, I think my dad stole a lot of money from them. And the L.A. mob wasn't the only one he had dirt on. There were a number of books in his bag, but only one of them was relevant to Antonio."

I set the pages down on the mattress before I used a finger against her chin to turn her face towards me.

"Books? He left more of these reports for you?"

She gave me a small nod. "There were six in the bag. It's the real reason I left it behind when I was there with Antonio. I didn't want him to get his hands on the others."

My instincts flared that I wasn't going to like what those books contained. "Who are the other books on, baby?"

She stiffened and her gaze hardened. "They're nothing you need to worry about."

"Like hell they are."

As much as I wanted to stay wrapped around Silk here in bed. I knew I needed to see those other books. Detangling myself from her warm, soft body, I strode out the room and into the lounge area, where we'd tossed the contents of all the saddle bags from our bikes when we arrived. It had been late and we were all tired, so we'd dropped it all here. The boys had done a quick search of the grounds, then headed straight to bed. I was jealous as fuck of Mac and Taz, sleeping peacefully, while I was here about to open what I suspected was going to be a fucked-up Pandora's Box.

"What are you doing?"

Mac's deep voice startled me. I hadn't been paying attention to my surroundings. Such a stupid thing to do. We still potentially had enemies after us. Without responding to him, I pulled her father's bag free of the pile and dropped it on the table.

"Investigating. Fuck, it's still locked."

Mac was by my side in a heartbeat. "These things are a piece of cake to get off."

My lips quirked as Mac pulled out a pocket knife. "Not that I have any doubt of your skills, brother. But we can't destroy the lock. Not without Silk knowing what we've done."

Mac returned his trusty Leatherman, the one that had earned him his moniker of MacGyver, to his pocket before leaning against the wall casually.

"You have any idea what's in there?"

I rubbed a palm over the back of my neck. "Books. Ledgers Silk's dad kept on various organizations."

Taz stepped out of shadows where he'd concealed himself. "Her old man was an accountant?"

I shook my head. "I don't think so. These ledgers are more about dirty deeds rather than tax returns. I have no idea who he's got dirt on. Other than the L.A. mob, that is. She handed over a book to Sabella this morning, and just now when she opened the package her father left her, she found a copy of that particular ledger." I sucked in a sharp breath. "Oh, fuck."

Mac was instantly on alert. "What?"

I shook my head. "Nothing you two need to worry

about. There was a letter from him in the package. I wanted to be with her when she read it. What's the bet the reason she didn't follow me out here to stop me getting the bag, is because she's in there reading the damn thing."

Taz tilted his head. "I don't get why it's a big deal for you to be there. It's just a letter, what could he have put in it that would affect you?"

I rolled my eyes. "Fuck, Taz, are you really that clueless? No wonder you're single. Silk's my woman, that letter is going to tear her fucking heart out no matter what it says. She's going to need a shoulder to cry on, someone to lean on. I intend to be that for her." I snatched the bag off the table. "We'll discuss all this in more detail tomorrow."

"See if you can get a look in that bag before then." After giving Mac a nod, I headed toward the master bedroom and Silk, hoping like hell she hadn't locked herself in the bathroom, or something crazy like that, trying to hide from me.

Chapter 10

Silk

A creaking sound alerted me to Eagle's return. I wiped away the tears on my face and took a couple of deep breaths, trying to rein in my emotions. Not that it helped. From the moment I read the first line of the damn letter I was crying. Anyone knows that something starting with the clichéd "If you're reading this, then I'm no longer with you..." is going to be heart-wrenching to read.

"Fuck, baby, I knew you shouldn't have read that on your own."

Through blurry eyes I watched as Eagle dumped my father's bag next to my handbag on the end of the bed, then pulled his shirt over his head. Even blurry-eyed, my gaze followed each ripple of movement his muscular abs and pecs made. Kneeling on the mattress, he easily scooped me up and sat with me cradled in his lap.

Needing comfort, I didn't fight him, just put my arms around him, buried my face against his throat and cried. I let out the pain of my grief, and my anger that the only reason I'd lost my parents was because my father was a damn fool.

Eagle's embrace was perfect. Firm, but gentle strokes of his palms over my hair and back soothed me until I ran out of tears. Hiccupping in the aftermath, he pushed my hair behind my ear, then ran his knuckles down my cheek, which had to be red and puffy. I'd never been a pretty crier. I must look like a total hot mess, but when I looked up at his face, I only saw compassion and sympathy. No revulsion at all. Was the man going for sainthood or something?

"Why are you doing this? For real. Do you want your top rocker that much?"

He flinched at my words before he leaned in and pressed another of those kisses to my forehead that made my soul sigh.

"Looking after you has nothing to do with the club, sweetheart. Sure, Scout told me to keep you safe, but I'm pretty sure he only did that because he knew full well I'd have done it regardless."

I lifted my hand to wipe away the last few tears from my eyes and face. I wasn't sure what the fuck to say to him, so I didn't say a thing. I rested my head back on his shoulder and toyed with the dog tags hanging over his pecs.

"Now I've had you, baby, it's going to be fucking hell to go back to acting like I haven't when we go back to the clubhouse. I want you, Silk. Not just to scratch some itch, but for the long haul. From the first time I saw you ride in that poker run last year, you've had my full attention."

My lips twitched with the start of a smile. "You saying you want me for your old lady, Eagle?"

"Fuck yeah, that's what I'm saying."

My heart swelled and a wave of warmth passed through me. I continued to fiddle with the metal dog tags as he stroked his fingers through my hair.

"Once we leave here, we really are going to have to be hands off until you patch in. You know that, right? Even if Scout knows how you feel about me, until you have your top rocker, we can't be together."

"You're underestimating my resourcefulness, Silk. It'll be hands-off in public, but I'll be sneaking into your personal space every chance I get. Don't you worry about that."

That made me smile, even though my heart still felt bruised from reading my father's letter. This wonderful man managed to make me smile. Wanting to stay in the moment, I decided to tease him a bit more.

"Is that right, big guy? And how are you planning on that?"

He held out his arm and rolled it in so I could see the outside of his bicep. He had his Marine Corps tattoo dead center but aside from that, his skin was ink free.

"Plenty of blank canvas for you to work your magic on, baby."

Instantly ideas started running through my mind. I ran my fingers over his collarbone and up to his shoulder.

"An eagle across here and over your shoulder would look fucking awesome."

He chuckled, his body shaking beneath me. "Bet you'll have the thing all planned out before morning, won't you? I have no idea how you do it."

I shrugged a shoulder, and kept tracing my fingers over his smooth skin, unable to stop now I'd started. "It's how I'm wired. I love designing tatts, especially big pieces." Wanting to see how far I could push him, I lowered my hand and gave his nipple a quick sharp pinch. He hissed and stiffened at the flash of pain. "Getting your nipples pierced would give you another reason to see me."

"Fuck, Silk. You're playing with fire."

Smiling I moved to straddle his lap. Leaning in, I pressed my lips to his as I tweaked both his nipples. Hard. He bucked beneath me, his thick, denim-covered erection pressing against my pussy and causing streaks of desire to shoot through me.

With a growl he pulled away from my mouth, gripped the bottom of my shirt and tore it over my head. He attacked my bra until I sat topless, my breasts swaying with my heavy breathing. With a smirk he flicked both my nipples, aiming at the small bars that ran through each one. My body stilled as arousal rolled through me. A groan escaped when he palmed both breasts and began kneading them.

"The piercing room has a lockable door right?"

"Uh huh."

I had no idea what he was thinking, all I could concentrate on was how fucking good his hands felt on me.

"I'll let you pierce one nipple, on one condition."

Fighting past the fog of arousal in my head, I stopped grinding against his lap and placed my hands on his shoulders to steady myself.

"And that would be?"

"You do it naked, and afterward I get to fuck you."

Heat flashed across my cheeks and spread down my neck. The thought of sliding my needle through his dark skin, then having him fill me was fucking hot as hell.

"The door might lock, but there's no sound proofing. We'd have to be quiet. And piercings don't take long, we'd have to be fast."

A wide grin split his face. "Oh, I can fuck you hard and fast, baby. If you can't stay quiet, I'll just have to find something to gag you with."

I rocked against his erection again as my pussy flashed hot. I was so fucking horny I was about to explode—and we both still had our pants on!

The next thing I knew, I was on my back and Eagle was looming over me. He took my mouth with his. Passionate, drugging kisses that left my mind spinning. Then he moved down, nibbling his way over my breasts, then teasing each nipple with tugs mixed in with his swirling tongue and hard sucks. I was writhing against his hard body by the time he got to my waist. He unbuttoned my jeans and I lifted my ass to help him slide them, and my panties, off. He slid down the mattress until he stood at the end. I was now completely naked and he stood there in his jeans, with his hot gaze running over me from head to toe.

"You are so fucking sexy, babe."

With that he attacked his jeans like he couldn't wait to have me. As he lowered the denim, taking his boxers with them, I sighed in appreciation. His thighs were as hard and muscular as the rest of him. And his cock was beautiful. Thick, and not too long, it stood proud. Ready for action. My mouth watered at the sight he made buck-ass naked. Every inch of him was taut muscle and strength. Then something he'd said earlier finally registered.

"You know, you gave me two conditions, not one. Does that mean I get to pierce your flesh twice?"

He stilled with one knee on the mattress to frown down at me.

"You ain't poking a needle through my cock, baby. No fucking way."

I pouted. "I thought marines were all tough and not afraid of pain?"

With a shake of his head, he prowled up the bed, each move mesmerizing me with the way his muscles flexed and shifted. "It ain't the fucking pain that's stopping me, sweetheart. It's the months of no sex while the bitch heals that has me saying no."

I lifted up so I was propped up on my elbows as he came to a stop over my lower half. "And just how did you know about the recovery time? You considered getting one, Eagle?"

"Nope, not me. Someone I know got one a few years back."

Did Taz or Mac have one? The way he winced had me thinking it had to be one of them. But before I could ask anything else he pushed my thighs apart and put his oh, so talented mouth to good use. Within seconds his skilled tongue and fingers had me squirming on the bed and my mind had cleared of anything that had worried me earlier. All I felt now was pleasure, and it made my heart swell even more for this hunk of a man. I knew at least part of the reason for this seduction was to distract me, and I gladly let him. Because, well, fuck. I wanted him too damn bad to resist.

Eagle

Even before joining the Marines, I always woke at sunup. It didn't matter if I'd been up till the early hours of the morning, didn't matter that I was worn the fuck out after spending more time fucking my woman than sleeping, once I did finally hit the sheets.

The sun was up, so I was awake. Of course, this morning it came with the benefit that I got to really look at Silk. Fuck, she was a stunning woman. She was fast asleep, half on her side, half on her front. Her face looked peaceful, no lines of worry marring the perfection of her soft skin. Her arm was up enough to show me the full expanse of skin over her ribs. A large tattoo covered the flesh. It was an epic piece of artwork. The New York skyline, complete with the twin towers, was behind a cross. An American flag was wrapped around the cross with the words 'RIP' and '9/11/2001' artfully written within it.

Unable to resist, I gently ran a fingertip over the design, and chuckled when she scrunched her face up and rolled all the way over onto her front. I pushed the comforter down past her toned ass. Silk worked out and kept herself in really good shape. She was still all woman though, with sweet curves that made my mouth water. I leaned down and nipped her butt. With a squeal she pulled away from me. Well, she tried. I hauled her back, rolling her over in the process.

"Morning, beautiful."

She opened one eye and glared at me as I moved to cage her body beneath mine.

"No way is it morning yet. Get off me!"

"Sun's been up for a while now. Definitely morning."

I lowered and pressed a kiss to the corner of her mouth and nipped her chin, then when she gasped, I took her lips, thrusting my tongue in to dance with hers. My cock had already been hard, and now it throbbed. I rocked my hips, rubbing the length of it against her bare mound as I continued to possess her mouth. When I couldn't stand not being inside her another moment, I pulled back to reach for a condom. I was really fucking glad I remembered to grab a box yesterday in our travels. As I leaned over, she started running her hands over me—lazy, gentle strokes that had a shudder running through me from head to foot.

"Fuck, that feels good, Silk."

With a moan she lifted her head and ran her tongue over my nipple.

Growling, I gloved up faster than ever before. I slipped a hand down between her thighs and circled her clit as I took her nipple in my mouth, flicking her piercing with my tongue. She tasted so fucking sweet everywhere. Keeping my thumb on her clit, I twisted my hand so I could get two fingers inside her. I groaned as I easily slid into her pussy—she was wet and slick already. Fucking perfect. I only teased her for a short while. I was too fucking desperate to be inside her to drag this out. Lifting her thigh, I lined up my cock at her entrance as she curled her leg around my waist.

Tilting my face up, I watched her expression as I slowly slid inside her. Her eyelids were three quarters closed and she looked as sweet as a sleepy kitten. The moment I was fully embedded inside her heat, her mouth parted and she arched up off the bed. Her tits were too much of a temptation to resist. They're the perfect size. Not huge, but big enough to fill my palm when I wrapped a hand around one to hold it up so I could torture her nipple while I started thrusting into her. I kept my movements steady, wanting this time to be different. So far, every time I'd taken her we'd been wild, fast and hard. This morning, I didn't want that. What I want was to wake her up from the inside gently, not fuck her unconscious.

Releasing her breast from my mouth, I moved to bury my face in her neck. The sensation of her slick walls squeezing my cock had me moaning and biting her shoulder. I made sure I left my mark between her neck and shoulder, where her shirt would hide it from public viewing. After giving my mark a kiss, I rose up, pressing a fist into the bed on either side of her shoulders to keep my weight off her as I continued to slowly fuck my woman.

Her palms smoothed up my chest and around to the back of my neck where she tangled her fingers in my hair to drag my face toward hers. I went willingly, pressing my lips to hers and eating at her mouth as I continued to flex my hips, thrusting deep into her.

When a tingle ran down my spine and my balls drew up, I leaned back, kneeling between her spread thighs and teasing her clit as I focused on the sight of my thick cock sinking in and out of her slick heat.

"Fuck, baby, look at us."

She whimpered and her legs tightened around my ass, holding me deep inside her for a moment before she relaxed enough for me to make small thrusts into her. A quick glance up had me grinning. She'd propped herself up on her elbows, her gaze locked on where we were joined. I gave her clit a pinch and she fell back on the bed yelling out my name. Her back arched and she clenched so damn hard on me I had no choice but to follow her over, coming hard inside her heat.

I rested my face between her breasts as I waited for my brain to begin firing again. Every time I touched Silk it was magic. I'd never had such explosive sex. Fast or slow, this woman left me devastated in the wake. Pulling my now-sensitive cock from her body had us both wincing a little. It had been a long fucking time since I'd gone this many rounds in one night.

"C'mon, baby. Let's get cleaned up."

"Hmm."

She stretched like a sleepy kitten, arching up off the mattress and making my blood heat. I growled at her.

"You keep tempting me like that, I'll fuck you again."

After that last round, I'd thought my cock would be sated for hours. But at the sight of her spread out before me, thrusting her tits up toward me, I could feel it stirring to life again.

"Oh, no you don't. I think I have gravel rash on the inside after that marathon."

Barking out a laugh at her words, I gathered her up and carried her to the adjoining bathroom to get cleaned up.

"Gravel rash, huh?"

She wrapped her arms around my neck and threaded her fingers into my hair as she nuzzled her face against my chest.

"What can I say? I'm not used to having so much sex in such a short amount of time, Eagle."

My breath caught. What did she mean by that?

"Want to clarify that one, babe. Do you mean you

haven't had sex in a long time or that you haven't had a marathon sex session for a long time?"

She pulled her face away from my skin to frown up at me. "Are you jealous?"

Of course I was fucking jealous! Another growl rippled up my throat. "Just answer the damn question."

A wide grin broke over her expression. "Oh, you are so fucking jealous! This is classic."

She was laughing when I set her on the bench next to the sink. Standing between her thighs I caged her in.

"It's not funny, and you still haven't answered me."

"Oh, it's completely adorable. I kind of want to drag this out so I can enjoy big, bad Eagle being all sulky that his new toy might have been played with recently by another."

Wrapping a hand in her hair, I firmly pulled until her face tilted up. Then I nipped her jawline, hard.

"Answer me."

My voice was a rough growl and it echoed around the small tiled room.

"There's no one but you, babe. I haven't had sex since before you joined the club. It's actually quite difficult for me to get away from the club long enough to have a lover, so I haven't had many—"

"How many?"

"Two. Both of them ran for the hills when they found out who my uncle was."

I released her hair and began kissing along her jaw, soothing where I'd nipped her earlier.

"See? That wasn't so hard, was it? You know I won't run for the hills. I already know all about your family. You don't need to worry about that with me."

I was inexplicably pleased that she'd had so few lovers, and that she hadn't taken one since meeting me. I hadn't taken a woman since before I first saw her. Simply hadn't had the interest. The club had plenty of whores around, and prospects were welcome to use them so long as they didn't have a job that they should be doing at the time.

I grinned as I considered that Taz had certainly made up for my lack of interest in them. I was fairly certain he'd taken every whore the club had at least once since we'd arrived.

Chapter 11

Silk

I'd pulled on some yoga pants and a loose t-shirt and was toweling my hair dry when I finally left the bathroom. Eagle had joined me in the shower, but had left me to wash my hair by myself, saying if he didn't stop touching me he really would fuck me again. I chuckled. The man was insatiable. But I hadn't been kidding about the gravel rash. Eagle was not a small man and I hadn't had sex for about two years before he took me the first time yesterday. My pussy needed a fucking break to recover.

A smile curved my lips and warmth spread through my chest when I entered the bedroom. Eagle stood by the bed. He'd made it, neat as a pin. I was pretty sure it would pass a military inspection. He was now putting all the stuff back in my bag that we'd obviously knocked onto the floor during the night. Each time he leaned down to get something from the ground, I got an epic view of the incredibly sexy way his ass filled out his jeans. He had no shirt on and I was thoroughly enjoying the sight he made. I must have made a sound as he stilled, then turned toward me. Heat spread over my cheeks when he smirked and raised an eye brow.

"Guess we made a bit of a mess of things, huh?"

"Nah, we didn't even break anything."

I rolled my eyes before turning back to the bathroom to dump my towel and quickly drag a brush through my hair. When I returned, Eagle was lifting my father's bag onto the mattress. My breath hitched and I reached out to run my palm over the rough material of it.

"You ready to open it? I really think we should work out what those other books contain. I need to know who else will be potentially coming after my girl."

Through the ache in my chest a spark of humor flared. "Your girl, huh?"

"I think I've well and truly claimed you now, Silk. The moment I get my fucking top rocker, the whole world will know it too."

Taking a deep breath, I pulled my hand away. "Maybe after some food. I need breakfast. Then I'll open it and you can help me work out exactly how much my father fucked up before he died to leave me in the middle of all his shit."

My voice sounded bitter but I couldn't help it. Until earlier this week, my life had been good. I worked hard, had a job I loved. I owned my own business, sort of. I was happy and content with where I was. Then, in one move, my dead father had swiped it all out from under me. I truly doubted Antonio was going to leave me completely alone after what went down. Especially considering the club no doubt delivered a beat down on the man after I left.

With a sigh, I spun and strode out of the room, for the moment not caring if Eagle followed or not. The kitchen was empty when I entered and I frowned as I stopped still to listen. The house was silent.

Eagle came up behind me, resting his hands on my hips. "What's wrong?"

"Where are your boys? The house is too quiet."

He rubbed his cheek on my head. "They're probably both checking out the surrounding area more thoroughly. Setting up some alarms to warn us if we get uninvited visitors."

I shook my head but didn't ask anything else. I was fairly certain I didn't want to know what kind of 'alarms' they were making. I opened a cupboard and snatched out the box of cereal.

"Who stocked this place?"

"I pay extra to have the cupboards and fridge stocked. That way I can come up on my bike. Lucky for us, I'd been planning on leaving yesterday to come up here so it's all here, ready to go."

Pulling out a bowl, I glanced at Eagle. "You fine with cereal for breakfast? Or you want to cook something? I'm big on simplicity, personally."

"I'll eat anything, babe."

With a smirk, I took down a second bowl and set things up on the table for us.

Naturally, the bastard waited until I'd taken a mouth

full before he spoke again.

"So, what did your dad have to say in that letter?"

I glared at him as I slowly chewed my mouthful. He had this innocent expression on his face that I didn't buy for a moment. I didn't want to discuss that letter. *Didn't want to think about my father's plea for forgiveness.*

"It didn't say anything relevant to what's happening with the mob."

His eyes narrowed. "That's not the only thing I care about, Silk. It clearly upset you. I didn't force the issue last night because I thought you could use some time to wrap your head around whatever that shit was. I want to know about anything that is important to you, and the reason why your father did all the shit he did is obviously going to be important to you."

His tone was so deep and serious it had me wincing in guilt for trying to hold back from him.

"I don't want to talk about it."

My voice cracked and I stared down into my bowl as I ate the rest of my breakfast as fast as I could, hoping he'd hurry up and forget all about the stupid fucking letter. Deep down I knew he wouldn't, though. At some point, I was going to have to tell him about all my father's lame excuses that didn't make one bit of difference to anything.

Eagle

I remembered why I'd never bothered with a relationship before. Women were a pain in the ass. Maybe I should just take the damn letter while she wasn't looking and read it. But that wouldn't help get her to talk about it with me.

There was a small part of me that wanted to know what was in the letter and books since I was pretty sure the FBI was going to be very interested in them. But the main reason I wanted to know was so I could help Silk deal with it. No matter what her father had written, it would feel like a betrayal. Whatever his reasons were to keep secret files on various organizations, they were why Silk was orphaned and now hunted.

I rubbed the back of my neck as I followed her into our bedroom. She'd not said one word to me since telling me she didn't want to talk about it and I was worried. Silk was a strong woman. Seeing her so closed off, stiffly walking around, was simply unnatural for her. At a guess, I had maybe another half an hour before Mac and Taz would return to the house, so I needed to make the time count. She wouldn't want them seeing her like this, and I didn't want them to witness me being all soft and gentle. I had a hard-ass reputation to maintain.

Once in the room, Silk went directly to the bag on the bed and palmed the lock. By the time she had it unlocked, I was by her side. The zipper sliding open was loud as a siren in the silent room, and her body stiffened when the bag gapped open to reveal men's clothing. Needing to touch her, I pressed my palm to her lower back and made slow circles. A little of the tension left her body at my touch and I smiled, relieved she found at least a little comfort in our connection.

She knew what was in the bag, had seen it all back at the airport. I guessed with the pressure of Sabella standing over her, she'd done a quick job of finding what he'd wanted and not focused on the other stuff. With both hands, she carefully lifted the shirt to her face where she inhaled.

"It still smells like him."

A faint trace of a citrusy scent reached my nose as she placed the shirt on the bed, and stacked the jeans and other items of clothing from the bag with it. When she lifted out and opened a smaller bag, a shudder ran through her. I moved to stand close behind her, drawing her body back against mine as I wrapped my arms around her waist. I pressed a kiss to the top of her head as she fingered her father's toiletries. A simple comb, a throwaway razor, a small can of shaving cream and a bottle of Tommy cologne. She removed the lid and a strong alcoholic smell filled the air. With a groan she recapped the bottle.

"That's not how I remember it smelling."

"It's gone bad. All perfume loses its scent after a few years. Can't remember how long exactly, but I'm guessing it's less than fifteen years."

She twisted her head to look at me with a frown.

"How in the hell do you know that?"

Heat crept up my neck. I never got embarrassed! I

certainly never shared the fact that I knew some finer points about perfume with anyone. The boys would have had a field day with that, if they knew. I shuddered to think what kind of nickname I'd have ended up with if the Marines had known when I entered boot camp.

"Ah, one of my foster mothers worked at a perfumery. It was all she'd talk about, so I picked up a few things."

Her expression softened and she reached a palm up to cup my face. Closing my eyes, I leaned into her warm touch. This woman was so far under my skin, I should probably be terrified—running as fast and far away from her as I could—but I couldn't do it. I'd never wanted to be tied down with a woman or child, but with Silk, the thought of marrying her and having her belly swollen with my child often filled my dreams. This woman was my home.

"I didn't know you grew up in the system. How old were you when you lost your parents?"

I took a deep breath. I didn't talk about my past. Not with anyone. Mac and Taz knew the basics, but no details. Normally, I'd refuse to answer. I could easily side-step it with a question of my own, focusing back on Silk's father. But for some fucked-up reason, I wanted her to know. Wanted her to see all of me.

"I have no clue who my parents are. My mother dumped me at a hospital in Charlotte, North Carolina when I was only a few days old. I assume one, or both, of my parents were part of the Waccamaw Siousan tribe, but I've never tried to join them there. I don't know what

I'd do if I ever came face to face with either of them. I mean, what kind of person abandons her newborn baby like that?"

Emotions rose up in me that I hadn't felt since I was a teenager. I shook my head to try to get rid of them, but stopped when Silk turned and caught my face between both her palms. She then pulled me down toward her. Opening my eyes slightly, I watched her as she pressed a soft kiss to my mouth.

"I'd never be able to abandon any child, especially my own. She may have had an excellent reason for doing it, but you'll never know. And no matter how great that reason is, it'll never take the hurt away. You're allowed to feel pain over it. I know I do."

Tears ran down her cheeks and I brushed them away with my thumbs. "What did that letter say, sweetheart? What reason did he give you?"

"He said things got out of hand. That he'd never meant for it to go as far as it did. Initially, it was him trying to better his brother. The Charons weren't a *real* MC. Not like the Iron Hammers, so he joined them. Well, he prospected with them. Before he got patched in, he'd discovered that selling information was a great way to make money. He didn't say who asked him to go, just that he was asked to go north to gather secrets. Turned out he was good at finding out information he shouldn't know. I guess he got greedy when he figured out it was easier to steal money from those he was investigating, rather than simply sell the information he found.

"He stole from the L.A. mob. That was what Antonio was after—missing millions my dad had taken from his family." She paused to scoff. "Crazy bastard put it all in an offshore account and siphoned off the interest to live on. He didn't even live large on the stolen money. In the letter he said he was fairly sure Antonio's family would catch up to him at some point, and that he hoped I wouldn't be hurt when they did. He said he was sorry and that if I hadn't already, I should go find my Uncle Clint for protection."

Her voice cracked and I pressed her face against my chest as I wrapped her tightly against me, trying to take away the pain that was wracking her body. My poor girl. Her father's jealousy, then his greed, had cost her so much.

"I'm so fucking sorry, baby."

She didn't respond, just tightened her arms around my waist. I could feel the dampness of her tears against my bare chest and it had my heart aching for her. I stood there, simply holding her, stroking her hair and back as she cried and shuddered against me. I couldn't remember a time when I'd willingly held a crying woman. I'd tried to comfort a couple of foster sisters over the years when they'd been upset, but I hadn't wanted to have their tears on me. With Silk, I wanted her to lean on me. I needed her to give me her tears and her pain so I could help bare the load for her.

Fuck, I was in so deep with this woman and I had no idea how she truly felt about me. Did she feel the same connection? Or was I simply convenient because I was around and was willing to stand up to the club for her?

Chapter 12

Silk

I hated all this crying shit. I rarely cried, and I certainly never cried in front of others. But I'd bawled all over Eagle twice in the last day! When I finally got my tears under control I pulled back from Eagle and my face flamed with heat. His chest and abs were wet from my tears. I wiped my palms over him, trying to wipe the liquid away. The muscles tightened beneath my touch and a tortured groan emanated from him.

"Baby, you have got to stop doing that. Fucking playing with fire, woman."

"But I've got you all wet."

He groaned again. "Just stop talking before I throw you up against the wall."

My lips twitched as I shook my head. Trust Eagle to find a way to distract me with sex.

"Let me go splash some water on my face, then we can go through the rest of the bag."

I slipped from his arms, and instantly a chill ran over my skin. Rubbing my arms I quickly went and washed my face and dried off. I took a washcloth back to Eagle with a smirk.

"Thought you might appreciate a wipe over. Want me to do it?"

His gaze darkened as he snatched the cloth.

"We'll never get to those books at this rate. Quit teasing me, woman!"

I watched as he made fast work of wiping down his chest before he turned to throw the cloth into the bathroom. The ripple of the muscles in his arm and chest as he did it made me sigh. And him growl. Again.

"Okay, okay! We're looking at books."

I nearly told him if he put a damn shirt on, I wouldn't be so distracted all the time. But I stayed quiet. I liked how he looked with his bare chest on display. All those perfectly sculptured muscles begging to be licked. And inked. Fuck, but that man needed more ink on his sexy body. He'd been right last night when he'd said I'd have the eagle tatt all planned out in no time. I had a good idea what I wanted to do already. As soon as I finished with this shit, I'd find my sketch book and get to work on it. I could use the distraction. When I drew, I entered another world. All my worries vanished and it was just me and the image.

I pulled the five remaining books free and stacked them in my arms, then reached over to snatch up the envelope that had the copy of the sixth ledger in it.

"Probably easier to look at these out on the table." I paused to catch Eagle's gaze. "Can I trust you, Mac and

Taz with this? Trust that they won't rat me out to the club or the cops?"

"Fucking hell, Silk. You know you can trust me. And you can trust Taz and Mac with your life, baby. They have loyalty to the club. We all promised that when we prospected in. But our first loyalty will always be to each other, and you're mine, so you come before the club. Unless it's going to put you in immediate danger, they won't say a word to anyone about what those books contain."

I held his gaze a moment longer before nodding and heading out toward the kitchen. Like everyone, I'd heard stories about how tight men who went to war together were, and from watching how Mac, Taz and Eagle were with each other, I believed it. The three men were like blood brothers. Actually, I suspected the bond they shared was even stronger than that between biological siblings.

When I got to the kitchen, Taz and Mac were getting themselves coffee.

"I guess you've both finished playing MacGyver and rigging up the yard?"

Taz smirked and Mac roared with laughter. "Guess Eagle told you about me then?"

Tilting my head, I frowned over at him "No, he hasn't said anything about you. Why?"

Mac shoved a hand into his pocket and came out with a well-used Leatherman multi tool. "Mac is short for MacGyver, darlin'. I never leave home without this baby, even before I was a Marine."

Taz interrupted. "And he can do just about any damn thing with that thing, too."

"Or without it." Mac shrugged a shoulder. "I'll use whatever I can get my hands on to do what I need to get done."

I shook my head with a chuckle. "That must have come in handy on missions. So, can I walk around outside safely? Or, is there, like, a map of where to avoid so I don't get blown up?"

There was a sparkle in his eyes as I spoke that lightened the tight bands on my chest. These three men were genuinely good guys. Eagle was the only one that made my body come alive with a glance, but Mac and Taz were easy to talk with and I certainly felt well-protected with them surrounding me.

"Nothing will blow you up. I only rigged up some alarms to let me know if we have company coming. Nothing too dramatic—yet. If we get someone sniffing around, or we get word someone is going to be—then I'll step up my toys."

I shook my head at him again.

"Well, until that time arrives, if it arrives. I've got something to pass the time. I'm not ready to pass this onto the club, or the cops, yet. Not before I go over it all to see what it is. My father left me all these books. Ledgers on various organizations, including a copy of the one I handed over to Antonio in L.A. yesterday."

I hadn't taken my eyes off the men as I'd spoken, and

other than Mac briefly flicking his gaze to Eagle, they'd stood before me stony faced and deadly serious.

"You got an idea what they're about, right?"

"I had a quick flick through the mob one before I handed it over. Looked like a list of details on various criminal activities. I only had a few minutes alone with the bag, I didn't want to risk getting caught looking. When Antonio asked me if I'd looked, I'd told him I hadn't."

Mac folded his arms across his broad chest. "That would be the real reason you had us collect the bag. You didn't want the mob to get these other books. Sabella didn't figure out that you'd taken a peek in his ledger?"

I placed the stack down on the table as heat flashed over my cheeks. "Um, no he didn't. I was very careful to tie it back up how it was when I found it, and when he asked me if I'd looked I told him I hadn't. I'm pretty sure he believed me."

"Well, the very fact he didn't kill you on the spot would indicate you had him fooled."

I couldn't prevent the shudder that ran through me.

"Yeah, he was nothing but polite to me, but I could sense the violence in him. That it wouldn't take much to push him over that particular edge. I did everything I could to stay on his good side."

Fury suddenly radiated off Eagle and I turned to look at him before he spoke. "Guess you gave up on that theory at the bank. You do realize, if I'd been even a minute later than I was, you'd currently be in hospital with your skull crushed?"

Or I'd be dead. He didn't need to say it. My skull tingled as I remembered how that guard had pulled my head back ready to slam against the marble wall.

"There were two boxes at the bank. One that opened with the key that had been in the front of his book, and another one that was under my name and didn't have a key. Antonio wanted to see what was in my box. I managed to use the bank staff in a way that gave me a few moments alone with my box. But when I left the room to leave the building, Antonio's thug was waiting for me."

Mac glared at Eagle when he opened his mouth and he closed it before uttering a word. Mac then turned his gaze back to me.

"What was in your box? What would Antonio have wanted from it?"

"There were several rolls of cash. I haven't counted it to know how much is there. A handgun, that I only checked to see if the safety was on before stashing it in my bag. I've no idea if it's loaded or if it will work. And finally, a large envelope. There was a note stuck on the front of it saying if anyone from the L.A. mob was with me, that I needed to get away from them as fast as I could. To find a safe place before opening the envelope."

Mac was nodding in an absent way that made me think he was deep in thought.

"I think it's all about the money. Antonio said things to me that were fairly vague, but when I put them all together with what I now know about what my father did, I think Dad stole enough money from the mob that it crippled them. They want it all back."

"How about you go grab those rolls? I think we need to know how much he left you to figure out how much of a hard-on Sabella is going to have to get it back."

My heart rate picked up at the thought of Antonio or his goons coming after me again. I'd hoped it was all over. Sure, I knew the three men were here with me to protect me against him if he did come back. But I'd thought it was a hypothetical. My uncle and the club playing it safe, not a real threat.

Eagle briefly gripped my shoulder. "I'll go grab your bag."

His voice was barely more than a whisper and I nodded as I continued to struggle with the fact that I wasn't as safe as I'd thought I was.

Suddenly a glass of water appeared in front of me.

"Here, luv. Take a drink and don't worry so much. You've got yourself three marines to make sure nothing ever happens to you. They got you that first time because we didn't know all the facts. Now we do, we'll make sure you're covered twenty-four/seven."

"Thanks, Taz."

Taz was a total charmer, always had women trailing him around the clubhouse when he was in. I lifted the glass to take a sip while he continued talking in that Australian accent of his.

"And you know, if you ever get sick of Eagle there,

I'll totally take over the night-time undercover duties."

I choked on the water and started coughing, my eyes watering. I coughed and wheezed for a bit before I could finally get a full breath in. Before I could get a smartass comment out, Eagle came back. He carefully placed my bag on the table in front of me before he slowly turned toward his friend. Taz's eyes peeled wide and he stepped away.

"C'mon, mate. I was just mucking around. I know she's your girl, I wouldn't really make a move on her."

A loud crack tore through the room when Eagle landed his fist against Taz's jaw. The other man didn't try to avoid the hit. I was pretty sure he could have, if he'd wanted to.

He rubbed his jaw testing the joint. "Fuck, Eagle. Did you have to hit so hard?"

"Just making sure you remember to not hit on my girl, whether it's pretend or real."

Not sure what to say to either of them, I took another drink, cleared my throat and began to empty out my bag on the table.

Eagle
Deep down I knew Taz had simply been trying to cheer up Silk. She'd been having a mini panic attack after Mac told her Sabella would most likely chase the money she'd received. I still wasn't sure about that. Scout, Bulldog

and Nitro had stayed behind to, no doubt, deliver a beat down on at least Sabella and whatever guards he had with him at the time. Depending on what was in the box he got from the bank, Sabella may decide it simply wasn't worth chasing down Silk for the bit of cash of his she potentially had. Then again, what did I know about the mob and their methods? Fuck all.

Silk had carefully emptied out her bag on the table. There were eight rolls of hundred dollar bills and an older style Glock. Mac grabbed the gun off the table and quickly had it pulled apart.

"Serial number's been ground off, but it looks good. With a good clean and oil, it should work perfectly." Mac left the gun in pieces and moved to the cash. "Looks like we've got some counting to do."

"The rolls look the same size." Silk lined them up, and they did look like they were all the same. "Maybe just counting one will be enough?"

Mac shrugged. "Up to you, darlin'. Counting all of them will be more accurate. But counting one will give us a good idea of how much you've got."

"And really, it's not like we're currently pressed for time. Might as well get it done right the first time, yeah?"

Taz was still rubbing his jaw, but he didn't look like he was gunning for me over the punch.

"Yeah, okay. Let's get it done."

Silk tossed a roll to each of us, then took one for herself. Before she took the rubber band off, she reached into her bag and came out with a notepad and pen, which she set in the center of the table.

I took the band off my roll and started counting the notes. They'd been curled in a roll for so long they were a bitch to try to flatten out. In the end I stopped trying. I'd just roll the fuckers back up when I was done.

The room was silent except for the sound of paper shifting against paper as we all counted. As we each finished, we wrote the total on the pad. Silk took the pad when we'd all finished.

"Well, looks like he was consistent. Each roll has a hundred notes." She paused for a moment and I figured she was doing the same math equations I was. "Fucking hell. I have eighty thousand dollars sitting here in front of me."

My heart dropped. That was a lot of cash. "He'll come for it if he knows this much is missing."

Mac nodded in agreement. "We have to assume with this amount, he'll realize your dad didn't give him all of what he stole. Especially if that ledger you gave him details what he took."

Silk grabbed the envelope and took the contents out. "Guess we go over this and work out exactly what he's written in here. We might get lucky and he didn't mention the details of his own dirty deeds."

Yeah, I doubted we were going to be that lucky.

"All three of us don't need to help you do that. How about we go over these other books? Who are they each for?"

Mac's questions had Silk reaching for the pile of

bound books.

"There's one on the Charons. Not sure any of us should even glance at that one's contents." She put that one aside and grabbed the next one. "Iron Hammers. This one needs to be read carefully, to see if we can find something to use against them. Scout might just be able to get them to stop trying to take over our town."

"I'll take that one and go through it. I can help Scout use anything we find in there."

Silk gladly handed the book over to Mac and I couldn't help but smile at the easy way my girl had fallen into sync with my boys. She clearly trusted them—not enough to give us access to the club's secrets, but enough for now. Willingly letting us help with the other books was a good start.

"Who do you want Taz? I've got the N.Y. mob, Ice Riders or Satan's Cowboys. Any of you ever heard of either of those MC names? I don't think I have."

"Satan's Cowboys are up north of Texas. They're a huge club and not one you want to get mixed up with. The other one I haven't heard of. Let me look it up." I pulled out my phone and pulled up an internet search. "Right. Ice Riders are a club up in Boston. No idea how big they are, it's not like they're going to advertise the kinda information we want on their public website. I'm sure Scout would know if they're a club we need to be careful with."

"I'm not ready to call in Scout yet. Not until I've gone over this book of Antonio's. The moment the club gets wind of these ledgers, I'll be cut out from knowing anything about them and this shit is affecting *my* life. I want to know the details."

"Give me the Cowboys' ledger. I'll sort that one."

She handed Taz the requested book before turning to me. "Which one do you want?"

"I'll take the Ice Riders. We need to work out if that club will be coming to look for blood. Whoever finishes first can take on the N.Y. mob one."

We all sat down with our ledgers and I rolled my shoulders and neck before I pulled the string to release the book I held. Opening the cover, I cursed.

"What?"

I tore open the envelope taped onto the first page. "Another key. Do you all have keys in the front?"

As the others opened their books, I reached for the N.Y. mob one and sprung the string free to check that one.

"Yep."

Mac and Taz spoke at the same moment I revealed the same envelope in the mob one.

"What the fuck was my father thinking?"

I wrapped my arm around her shoulder and pulled her against me, kissing her head when she rested her face against my chest.

"I have no idea, baby. But we'll work it out, I promise you that much." I looked at the page under the envelope. "My key is for a bank up in Boston. What about you boys?"

Mac spoke first. "Mine is down in Galveston."

Then Taz. "Mine's up in Dallas."

Silk flicked up the N.Y. mob envelope. "New York."

With a finger under her chin, I tilted her face toward mine. "Got seven days till the anniversary. You alright to do some traveling over the next couple days? Go round up all these boxes and see what we end up with?"

"We can't do that without the club, Eagle. Not when there's other MCs involved. And I will *not* go to New York. No way, no how."

I leaned in and pressed my lips to hers, for a brief kiss.

"I'll ring Scout after you finish with that book and sort something out."

With a nod, she turned back to the ledger in front of her and I looked up to Mac and Taz. The FBI would want to know about all of this. But I wasn't sure I could turn in the ledgers on the MCs, especially not the one on the Charons. Since prospecting in nearly a year ago, I'd grown to really like the club. Enjoyed being a part of it. The MC family was similar to the one we had with our Marine family. I wasn't sure I wanted to risk ruining that by handing over information to the FBI. Information that was at least fifteen years old and may well be useless to them anyhow.

Once Silk was engrossed, I nodded to Mac and Taz and we slipped into the kitchen, out of earshot, but where we could still see Silk.

"You know they'll want all of those."

Trust Mac to say exactly what I'd been thinking.

"I'm not willing to risk our place with the club for this shit. Either of you know exactly how long the statutes of limitations are on these types of crimes? I don't, but fifteen years is a long fucking time. They probably can't do shit with them anyway."

Mac got in my face, going toe to toe with me. "Brother, even if they can't go after them for the crimes in the ledgers, they can follow the trails and find current crimes. We should hand them over."

"And then what? We walk away from the club?"

"Away from Silk you mean. You really hooked on this girl, aren't you?"

I shook my head. "It's not just her. I mean, yeah, I don't want to leave her. But it's the club too. Don't you guys like being a part of it all? Being surrounded by men that understand us, how we operate. Not only do they accept who and what we are, they welcome us with open fucking arms."

Taz finally spoke up. "I don't want to leave either. I like the Charons, and once we patch in, we can start actually participating."

The man had a sly grin on his face and I rolled my eyes as I stepped back from Mac.

"You participate with any more of the club whores and they're going to move your bed into the whore room and call it yours."

"The free pussy sure is nice, but that's not what I was referring to. You heard about what went down last month? With that fucking senator's aide from Dallas?

That is what I want to be involved with. Would have loved to have been on the crew that beat that fucker into the ground. Fucking asshole."

They were silent for a few moments. Of course I'd heard about it. A big shot senator and his aide had passed through town last month, and on their way the aide picked up a young girl and brutally raped her. He did enough damage that the poor girl would probably never be able to have kids. Then the bastard pulled some strings and walked away with nothing more than a slap on the wrist. Yeah, the Charons had a reputation for doing bad things for good reasons. The fact the aide wouldn't be able to ever get hard again meant he couldn't ever rape another female. Of course, with the level of brain damage he was left with, he probably wouldn't remember what sex even was.

It was what the fucker deserved.

"Yeah, as much as I know vigilante justice ain't how it should be done, when the system fails, it's good to know the club will step up to make sure it's served."

Mac sighed. "Guess we're not going to do our job on this one then?"

"Nope. Maybe we can give them the N.Y. mob one? They don't need to know about the club ledgers. We'll just tell them about the two mob ones. Give them a copy of each, they can deal with that shit?"

Mac nodded. "That'll work. And I don't want to walk away from the club either. I wasn't sure I'd like it, but I honestly do. Like you said, it's a family that truly understands what kind of men we are."

"Guess now all we need to do is somehow get a copy of those two books without Silk knowing about it."

Taz stepped forward. "I'll do it. Tonight while you're sleeping, I'll grab them and photograph them with my phone. That should be enough, then I can email it through to our guy. If you could get Silk to leave them out on the table that would be handy.

I chuckled. "Yeah, that won't happen. She'll lock them in her father's bag. I watched her unlock it earlier. The code is three-six-eight. And make sure we're fucking sleeping before you come into the room. You do not need to be seeing my woman naked."

Taz smirked. "So you want me to make sure you're fucking before I come in? Or sleeping? Pick one bro!"

With a growl I lunged toward him and with a howl of laughter he ran back to the table out of my reach.

"Fuckin' Aussie jarhead."

Mac chuckled as he followed me back to Silk. "Yeah, he is. But at least he keeps things interesting."

Having been his spotter for twelve years. I knew better than anyone how that man could inject humor into just about any situation.

Chapter 13

Eagle

Turned out those books weren't anything I was comfortable discussing over the phone. I'd rung Scout and requested we meet up. So an hour later, I sat at a cafe near Silk's hideout. Damn woman was adamant that the club not know the exact location of her cabin.

I had to agree with her that they wouldn't leave her be if they knew where she went, so I was trying to help her keep it secret. Although I hated not having her in my sight, I was confident Mac and Taz would keep her safe. I was also pretty fucking certain Scout wouldn't want Silk in on this conversation.

The deep rumble of a couple of Harleys had me looking further up the street to see Scout had brought Bulldog with him. By the time I took a mouthful of my coffee and set the mug back down, the two men had parked in front of the cafe and were striding toward me. I stood to shake both their hands.

"Silk not here?"

"Mac and Taz have her covered. I didn't think you'd

want her involved in this particular conversation."

Scout pulled out a chair and Bulldog went inside, presumably to order them each a coffee. Scout kept the conversation light until he returned. The moment Bulldog sat down, Scout leaned in and held my gaze.

"What's this about?"

"It's about the incredibly deep shit Silk's dad managed to bury himself in."

Bulldog hissed out a breath and his body tensed.

"Sorry, I know he was your brother, but the man was a fucking idiot to think he could get away with this shit. Honestly, he was lucky that plane took him out. It would have been a helluva lot less painful than what any of the organizations he'd gotten involved with would have pulled if they'd known what he'd done."

Bulldog rubbed a palm over the back of his neck. "I know John had his issues. I'm not going to bust your balls over being pissed at him. Just spit it out."

"Silk told you about the book Sabella wanted?"

Scout's voice was rough. "Pretend like we know nothing and lay it all out."

"There were six ledgers in that bag at the airport. The names on those books? Charons, Iron Hammers, Ice Riders, Satan's Cowboys, L.A. Mob and N.Y. Mob. Silk had a quick look at the one Sabella wanted and it looked to be a detailed record of a lot of the mob's dealings, from murders to drug deals. It also had a key taped into the front of it. That was what opened the safety deposit box." I glanced at both the men's knuckles. The flesh was scabbed over and beaten to shit. "I don't suppose either of you got a look inside that box when you were making sure we weren't followed out of there?"

"Brief glance. Looked like a few rolls of cash along with bank statements."

I nodded. "There was a second box at the bank, in Silk's name. It contained rolls of cash, a gun and a thick envelope. A note taped to the front of that told Silk that if she was with anyone from the L.A. mob, she should run as soon as she could."

"I gather she's had time to open it by now. What was in there?"

"A copy of the L.A. mob ledger, along with a letter. I haven't read it but from what Silk told me, he explained why he did what he did. It would seem he was approached to gather information when he was still a prospect in the Iron Hammers, then before he patched in he was sent up north to gather information on someone else. At some point he figured out it was easier to steal from organizations, rather than spy on them. Obviously, he worked out at some point it would came back to bite him on the ass, so left these boxes around the country."

Scout leaned in closer. "Boxes? You've looked in the other ledgers then?"

"All but the Charons. We completely agreed with Silk when she demanded that book remain untouched by all four of us. We don't need to know club secrets that will, no doubt, just make things awkward." I paused to pull the book from where I'd stored it inside my jacket. "Here.

No one's opened it since John last shut it. If it's like all the others, there'll be an envelope on that front page that contains a key to a deposit box. On the page under the envelope will be a bank address and box number."

Scout pulled the string off and sure enough, there was a key in the front. He quickly flicked through the pages.

"Fucking asshole. How'd he even get half of this shit?"

Bulldog tensed. "Don't look at me. I never once told anyone anything about what we do at the club."

Scout shook his head. "I know it's not you, brother. This shit starts before you were patched in. We need to get down to Galveston to see what he has stored there on us."

"The Iron Hammers' box is down there too. I was wondering if we might be able to use whatever it contains to get them out of our town for good?"

"That'd be fucking brilliant if we can pull it off. But without seeing what's in there, I can't say. Silk up for a road trip? It's still a week till 9/11."

"She'll do what she has to. You know that. But she's refusing to go to New York. The Cowboys' box is in Dallas and the Ice Riders' is up in Boston. The only one she's flat out refusing to go get is the N.Y. mob one, which I can understand. Maybe we should just toss that one to the cops or something?"

Bulldog shook his head. "Nah, we'll keep it close for now. If the L.A. guys come gunning for us, we might be able to use it to buy them off our backs. We'll get Silk to sign a release to allow them to get the fucking box."

I nodded. It might work. Although, if any of those bastards came near Silk again, I wasn't planning on letting any of them walk away, so they wouldn't need to be bought off.

"Right. Well, when do you want to head down there? Silk's pretty determined that neither of you know where her little hideout is located so I can head back to get her and the boys, then meet you back here in town."

Scout was silent for a moment, clearly in deep thought.

"Yeah, we'll go down there with just the six of us. I'll put the club on alert, and if we get in trouble, they'll be ready to ride. But I'd prefer if we could slip in and out of there without the Hammers knowing we were ever in Galveston. It's getting too late to do it today, so we'll head down first thing in the morning. Meet us here at eight. That'll get us to the bank just as it opens. We'll worry about the other boxes after 9/11. They've already been sitting there for over fifteen fucking years—another couple weeks or months isn't gonna to make a difference."

With a nod I rose to my feet. He was right to have the club on alert. Galveston was firmly Iron Hammer territory. If we got caught down there, things could get bloody.

Bulldog stood too. "Before you go, I've got something for you." The man strode back to his bike and returned with a couple of bags he'd pulled from his saddle bags.

"Silk had these packed ready to bring with her. Figured she'd appreciate having some fresh clothes and her other shit."

I fought down a smile. Silk had begun to bitch about her lack of clean underwear already. "Thanks for that. I'm sure she'll appreciate it."

Bulldog narrowed his gaze a moment before Scout came and slapped the man on the back and broke the moment.

"Settle down. You know he's going to take good care of her. Once 9/11 is done passed we'll sort out you, Taz and Mac patching in. All three of you have more than earned it."

No way could I hold my grin in at that. That top rocker was worth its weight in gold. Not only getting me deeper in with the club, but also making it so I wouldn't have to sneak around to see Silk.

"Thanks, man. I can't wait."

The man smirked at me. "I can't imagine why."

Yeah, the President knew how I felt about Silk. Hell, I was pretty sure the entire fucking club knew by this point. It wasn't like I tried to hide it, and the moment that top rocker was on my back, I'd be claiming her for my old lady in front of them all.

Silk

Once I finished looking over that damn book, I went and made myself a hot chocolate. The things I'd read would forever be in my mind. So many people killed or injured. I truly had been lucky to escape them with only a few bruises. It also made it clear to me that there was no way in hell they'd simply let me walk away, especially if they'd read that whole ledger and worked out how much money Dad had stolen from them. He hadn't detailed the transactions he'd interfered with, but if I could figure out which ones he tampered with, it wouldn't take Antonio or one of his men long to figure it out. Then they'd come for me.

I took my cup out to the front porch and sat on the porch swing, watching the driveway for when Eagle returned from his meeting. I hoped Scout didn't demand I go to New York. I could handle collecting all the others for them, but not that one. So far I'd managed to avoid going to New York since 9/11. I had no desire to see the site where the twin towers used to stand. It was all part of my history that I wanted to forget existed.

A deep rumble had my thoughts clearing and a smile spreading over my face when Eagle rode up to the front of the cabin on his own. I hadn't been entirely sure he would manage to convince Scout and my uncle to not come see that I was fine with their own eyes.

The sun caught his thick, shiny, black hair as he pulled his helmet free and hooked it over a handlebar. He was a beautiful male, that's for sure. I sighed as he swung his lean leg over the bike, giving me an excellent view of him from the back. His jeans clung to his butt like a second skin and I couldn't tear my gaze away from the sight.

When he turned, I felt my cheeks heat as I quickly glanced away. Dammit. I'd been busted checking out his ass. Again.

"Hey, baby. Like what you see?"

I lifted my mug to take a mouthful of rich, chocolaty goodness before I responded.

"How did it go?"

"Coward."

Yeah, I totally was. But, whatever. I risked a glance up at him and he stood there holding two very familiar looking bags. After setting my mug down, I was on my feet in a moment and rushing toward where he stood at the top of the stairs.

"You got my bags? How did you know?"

He carefully dropped them both to the ground and caught me when I tried to reach for them.

"Your uncle brought them for you. Where's my welcome home kiss?"

Heat raced over my cheeks again. "Sorry."

I leaned into him, lifting my face and he lowered his, Eagle's soft lips on mine causing a shiver to run through me. His hands roamed over me, until one was on my lower back, pressing my hips against his while the other gripped the back of my neck, holding me still as he devoured me. My hands weren't idle either. I ran them up his arms and into his thick hair. I loved how the silky strands felt against my skin.

He slowed the kiss and nibbled on my lower lip, kissed the corner of my mouth, then nipped at my jawline before he pulled back. My brain was barely working with all the arousal coursing through my body, and I went lax as I rested my head on his chest. The scent of leather and Eagle filled my lungs and my knees went even weaker.

Damn man chuckled at me a moment before he scooped me up in his arms and headed inside.

"I rather like that my kisses have this effect on you. Now I know how to win any arguments we might have in the future. I just need to get my mouth on you."

I lightly slapped at his chest. "I don't think so. I let you affect me this time. If we're arguing, I won't let you distract me so easily."

"That sounded like a challenge, baby. Of course, I'm not sure how to test it because you're going to always do what I tell you, so we won't ever argue."

That had me laughing hard enough my eyes watered.

"You are deluded if you think I'll do what I'm told!"

He grinned down at me. "There's one place I know you do exactly what you're told."

The heat in his gaze had goosebumps rising on my skin and my breaths turning into shallow pants, but I couldn't look away. I'd never had such an intense man. Maybe it was a Marine thing. Everything they did, they did thoroughly.

He dropped me on the bed, then delivered a hard, fast kiss to my mouth.

"Stay right there."

He strode from the room and I rolled off the bed. Yeah, right. Like I was going to stay in bed in the middle of the freaking afternoon while he went off to do whatever it was he was doing. I headed to the bathroom to use the toilet, and after washing my hands I splashed some cold water on my face to try to cool off a little. Eagle was tying me in knots. And I worried he was right—he'd bind me to him so tightly, I would do whatever he told me to do. Would I lose myself in him? Lose my independence?

"Why are you not where I left you, sweetheart?"

I squealed as I jumped about a foot in the air. "Fuck, Eagle! Scare the shit out of me next time. Make some noise when you walk, would you?"

He wrapped his arms around my middle and nuzzled his face into my neck. "Sorry, babe. After so long in the Marines, I'll probably always walk silently. Want to tell me why you're not on our bed, waiting for me?"

I pressed back against him, rolling my body against his.

"I needed to pee, Eagle. And I didn't think you were serious about me not moving at all. I'm still in the room. Sort of."

"Hmm. Well, I had plans for you on the bed. Guess I'll have to mix things up a little now with some punishment. Ever been spanked, Silk?"

I stilled and met his gaze in the mirror over the sink. "Not since I was a young girl. I'm not a child, Eagle. You can't spank me because I didn't do what you told me to."

His eyes darkened. "That's exactly what I'll do. But don't worry, I'll save that for next time. This time I'll go with something a little more creative. Something that'll have you burning for me. Oh, and trust me, I'm fully aware of how much you are not a child."

Before I could say another word, he had my shirt up over my head and my bra on the floor. He palmed both my breasts and I forgot all about being mad at him. A shiver ran through me as he kneaded, then tweaked the bars through my nipples.

"Fuck, Silk. You're so responsive. Put your hand on either side of the sink, and hang on."

Lust swirled through my mind and I didn't even think to deny his request—not if it meant he was going to keep touching me. The moment my fingers were wrapped around the cool porcelain of the sink, he tore at the zipper of my jeans and tugged them down. With quick, jerky movements, he had them wrapped around my ankles, restraining my movements.

"Eagle."

His name came out a moan and he rose up behind me, pressing his clothed body against my naked back and ass.

"Ah, Silky. Look how fucking sexy you look."

He held my chin so I had to look in the mirror, to see my pinkened cheeks, parted lips, and hooded eyes. He'd barely touched me and I looked like I'd been fucked hard.

"Keep watching, babe."

My gaze followed his hands as he stroked my torso and hips, loving the contrast between his dark skin and my pale flesh, then his hand slipped between my thighs and cupped my pussy. I spread my legs as far as I could with my ankles restricted like they were, as he slipped a long finger deep inside me.

"Soaked already."

In lazy strokes, he teased my folds and clit. I tried to move into his touch, to get more friction but he stilled me by gripping my hip with his other hand.

"Oh, no. You don't take what you're not given, Silk. Now, for the punishment part—you're not allowed to come. Not till I tell you to. You do? I'll stop and walk away, and I won't touch you again until tomorrow night."

I whimpered as I tried to writhe against him. A whole day without him touching me? Now that would be punishment. But I wasn't sure I could hold back. I'd never tried to withhold an orgasm before.

"I don't know I can do that. I've never tried to hold it off, and you've got me so close already."

He moved his hands back to my breasts, leaving my core empty and aching.

"That's what makes it a punishment, babe. I get to tease and back off until you're burning so hot for me, you'll be begging for me to fuck you. You'll hate it and love it at the same time. And when I finally drive my cock deep inside you, you'll come so fucking hard we'll both see stars."

His words had me rubbing my thighs together, wanting what he was selling. I swallowed past the lump in my throat and locked my gaze on his.

"Promise?"

Chapter 14

Eagle

True to my word, I kept Silk on the edge for as long as I could stand the burn. She was sexy as fuck, standing before me with a white knuckle grip on the basin as I worked her body up, then let her cool off just a touch before I drove her up again. She whimpered and writhed, and her skin had flushed all over. I knew I'd never forget how she looked in this moment. Her eyes were a little wild as she held my gaze in the mirror.

"Please, Eagle. I can't take any more of this."

Ah, there was the begging I'd been waiting for.

"Hmm, you beg so sweetly, baby. But I need to you to hang on just a little longer. I want us to come together. Can you do that for me, Silk? Hang on just a little longer?"

She moaned and rolled her lower body against mine. "I'll try."

Her voice was throaty and had my cock jerking. I tore my shirt over my head and ripped open the fly of my jeans, freeing my rock-hard erection. Slipping a condom from my pocket, I suited up quickly and leaned over her back. Her skin had a light sheen of sweat over it and she slid against me in a way that had a groan rising up from my throat and echoing around the small room.

I nipped her ear and kissed down her neck before I pressed my palm between her shoulder blades to lower her over further. The jeans around her ankles meant she couldn't spread her legs far, but she was doing her best to spread herself wide.

"You are the sexiest woman I've ever seen, Silk."

Her response was to whimper and tilt her ass up toward me. With a growl, I pressed my cock between her thighs and thrust in deep.

"Fuck!"

With her legs together she was even tighter. I wasn't going to last long. I let myself go for several thrusts before I slid a palm up between her breasts and lifted her torso so she stood before me, her back to my chest. Instantly, she wrapped her hands into my hair and I took a firm hold of her hips as I continued to fuck her hard.

"Watch us, Silk. See where I'm going in and out of you. How fucking good that looks? I'm never going to get enough of you, baby."

My gaze was riveted on the sight of my dark, thick, latex-covered cock entering her pale body on each stroke. My darker skin tone against her lighter one was fucking perfect. A tingle ran down my spine and my balls tightened in preparation. Silk was whimpering, her body strung so tightly I worried she might literally shatter.

"Come, baby. Let it go and take me with you."

Our eyes met in the mirror and the fear in her gaze had me wincing, but before I could say a thing her body clenched down on me and I couldn't think anymore. I heard her scream my name, heard my roar echo around us, as stars filled my vision.

When I could breathe again, I blinked my eyes clear and found myself leaning over her, pressing her body down over the sink.

"Fuck! Sorry, baby. I didn't hurt you did I?"

Her head was on her arm and tears tracked down her cheeks from her closed eyes, but there was a serene smile on her lips that had me hopeful I hadn't injured her. She didn't respond to my voice so I carefully pulled free of her body and disposed of the condom. Then I gently lifted her in my arms and strode over to the bed. Keeping her against me with one arm, I used my other hand to tug the covers back before I wrestled her limp body onto the sheets.

I pressed a kiss to her forehead before I removed her shoes and jeans. She still hadn't woken up. Going back into the bathroom, I wet a cloth with warm water and returned to her. With more care than I'd realized I was capable of, I cleaned her up, then tucked her in.

She looked so sweet, all sex-rumpled, and I wanted nothing more than to curl up next to her, but I needed to go check in with Mac and Taz and let them know about tomorrow. Then I'd come back and wrap myself around my woman.

Back in the bathroom, I gave myself a quick wipe-down before I straightened my jeans. I didn't worry about adding a shirt. There was no way in hell the whole town hadn't heard what we'd just done in here.

When I walked into the lounge room it was to low catcalls.

"Oh, shut the fuck up, both of you."

"Damn, so touchy. Did you not do it right? Sex is meant to chill you out, mate."

There was a part of me that was scared shitless at how much Silk already meant to me. That sex we'd just had was easily the most powerful I'd ever experienced. And I was no fucking virgin. But I didn't want to think about that—I was simply going to enjoy the moment and push all that emotional shit right down.

"We're riding out in the morning. Meeting Scout and Bulldog in town at oh-eight-hundred, then riding down to Galveston. We're going to collect two of the boxes. One for the Iron Hammers and one for the Charons. Scout wants to hold off on the others until after 9/11."

Mac leaned back with his arms folded over his chest. "They're the logical ones to deal with first. Not sure I like the idea of waiting on the others, though. Word will spread that her father had ledgers on organizations he worked for and we'll end up in a ton of shit if we're not careful."

I'd had the same thought as I'd ridden back. "Gotta start somewhere. Once we see what's in these two boxes, I'll suggest we don't waste time getting the others. Even if we don't do shit with them, at least if we'll have them here and if the clubs come for them, we can deal with it quickly—"

"And without involving Silk. Once she collects the boxes, she can be out and clear of it all."

I looked to Taz after he interrupted me. "Damn straight. The other thing Scout said he'll sort out once 9/11 passes is our top rockers. Looks like we've earned our way all the way into the fold, boys."

Both men grinned broadly before Mac grew serious.

"Speaking of which, I don't think we should hand over all the ledgers. Taz has copied them all but I vote we only hand over the L.A. mob one for now. I've got a bad feeling of what will happen if we just give them everything."

I nodded. "I was going to suggest the same thing. My instincts are screaming for us to be careful with what we hand over. I know they're supposed to be the good guys, but we know all too well that nothing is ever that black and white."

We were all silent for a while. I didn't doubt they were remembering the same thing I was. One of our final missions was something we never spoke of. I tried to never even think about that place. Our unit had been sent in to capture a few men that had gone rogue, and not for the first time. They'd left their base early one night without leave.

When we tracked the fuckers down to an orphanage, we couldn't believe what we found—several naked girls and a couple of naked women, all dead and all clearly sexually assaulted. It was a fucked-up mess. We found the missing men in a room at the rear of the building. One man with his pants open and his cock hanging out was lying dead with his throat cut. A sobbing woman huddled in the corner near him. The other three men were engaged in hand-to-hand combat that was vicious and intense enough none of them heard me and my men enter the room. We quickly detained the three of them. The two shirtless ones smelled of sex, and the way their eyes flicked around, I'd been certain they were high on something. The other man was in full combat gear, everything where it should be. He stilled the moment he saw us, dropped to his knees and put his hands on his head. He'd claimed he heard the other three men talk of their plan the night before, and when he noticed them gone earlier, he'd headed off to try to stop them. Tears filled the man's eyes. He'd been too late.

We'd been ordered to bring the men in to be dealt with. While the two who decided raping and murdering innocent women and children was a good idea deserved everything they got and more, it fucking flat-out sucked that the one that was trying to save the innocents most likely ended up with a dishonorable discharge and had maybe even been charged with murder. None of us had heard what had happened to any of the men once we handed them over to their commanding officer.

"I won't bring down someone for doing the right thing again. No fucking way."

"Amen, brother. Fucking amen to that."

Taz and Mac responded at the same time. Yeah, none of them had liked what they'd had to do that day. The Charons fit the three of us perfectly, for reasons the club would hopefully never know.

Silk

I woke to the sensation of fingers trailing over my skin.

"Hmmm."

I arched up to get more contact and Eagle pressed his palm against my tummy with a laugh.

"Such a greedy girl. Unfortunately we don't have time for me to take advantage. We have forty minutes before we need to be in town."

My breath hitched as my eyes flew open.

"What?"

Eagle was lying next to me, freshly showered and fully dressed already.

"You distracted me when I got back yesterday, I didn't get a chance to tell you what our new plans were. Scout and your uncle are joining the four of us for a ride down to Galveston to get the Iron Hammers' and Charons' boxes from the bank down there. We need to meet them in town at oh-eight-hundred."

My heart ached. "I can't believe my dad collected shit on his brother's club. What kind of person does that?"

"A desperate, jealous one. C'mon, go grab a shower

and I'll make you some breakfast. I brought in your bags last night." He nodded toward the dresser and I glanced to see my two bags sitting there neatly. "We don't have that long, so quit tempting me with this sexy as fuck body of yours, and go shower."

With a chuckle, I rolled out of bed and stretched. Then laughed when he growled at me.

"I'm going, I'm going."

I went over to dig through my bag for an outfit before heading to the still-steamy bathroom. I inhaled deeply when I entered. It smelled like Eagle, my new favorite scent. It was leather and pine, and all male goodness.

Twenty minutes later I walked into the kitchen dressed in my bike gear with my hair in a braid down my back. I slung my jacket over the back of the chair and sat down as Eagle brought over a bowl, along with a mug of coffee.

"Here you go, baby. Make it quick, we need to get moving."

He pressed a kiss to my temple before he moved away to grab a mug from the counter for himself as my heart did a stupid fluttering thing. I dove into eating my cereal and kept my gaze down. I wasn't sure how the fuck we were going to go hands-off when we went back to Bridgewater. Nor was I sure how the fuck I'd become so addicted to him in such a short amount of time. Did he feel the same way?

I hoped Scout would give the three of them their patches soon. Then I'd know for sure how Eagle felt. No way would he try anything in front of the club if he didn't want me for his old lady once he had his top rocker. Daughters of the Club were protected, and even patched in members couldn't go sniffing around us if they weren't fucking serious about making us theirs for the long haul.

When I took my dishes to the sink, Eagle snagged my arm.

"You okay? You look worried."

I shrugged. "Just thinking about everything. I'm fine, really."

He frowned at me a moment before nodding. "Right. Well, let's get moving. I don't want to keep the Prez and VP waiting."

That made me smile a little. "Yeah, patience has never been a virtue either Scout or my uncle have ever been known for."

I followed Eagle out and down to the bikes.

"Shit. I don't have mine."

Eagle smirked as he handed me a helmet. "Guess you'll have to sit behind me again. *Such a pity*."

Feeling cheeky, I returned his smirk. "I don't know. Taz's bike sure does look comfy."

Taz barked out a laugh when Eagle growled. "Sure is, Silky-girl. You just slip on over here and I'll show you just how smooth it is."

"Like fucking hell you will. Get on my bike, Silk."

I laughed loudly before wrapping my arms around his waist. "You're too easy to rile up, Eagle. Of course I'm riding with you."

He leaned down and kissed me hard and fast before he slapped me on the butt.

"Get moving, before I decide to do something that will make us all extremely fucking late."

Heat burst through my face at the thought of him bending me over his bike to spank and fuck me. I cleared my throat as I put my helmet on and climbed on the back of Eagle's ride. Normally, I preferred to ride by myself on my own bike, but the only way I was going to be able to touch Eagle while Scout and my uncle were around was going to be like this. And I had a feeling I'd need the calming effect his presence had on me today.

Once he was in front of me, I shifted so I was pressed against his back. I wrapped my arms around his waist as he took off, with Taz behind and Mac in front of us. All three of these men were so damn protective. I knew without a doubt Scout would give them their top rockers soon. They were a perfect fit for the club.

It was only a short ten-minute ride from the cabin to get to the local town and I appreciated being able to enjoy the scenery, and the wind in my face, rather than having to focus on the road and riding. It was a nice change. Although, I did miss not being in control of the beast I was sitting on and couldn't wait to ride my own baby again. I guessed it would be after 9/11 now before I got the chance for that. No way was I returning to Bridgewater before then. Especially now that everyone knew about my connection with the attacks. They'd all look at me with pity or try to talk to me about it, when all I wanted to do was forget the fucking day ever happened.

Chapter 15

Silk

Aside from my uncle glaring at Eagle the whole time, the meet-up in town was quick and uneventful. I wasn't sure how Uncle Clint was going to react once Eagle was patched in and we became official. *If that's what happened.* I was still holding back from telling myself it was a sure thing, just in case he didn't have the balls to claim me as his in front of the club. Deep down I was fairly certain he would, but there was this niggling little doubt that wouldn't allow me to truly believe it until it happened.

Now we were approaching the center of Galveston and I could feel the tension coming off the men. This was Iron Hammers territory and if they caught us in town, there would be trouble. Eagle pulled up between Mac and Taz, and I got the impression the three of them did it automatically, without thought. Keeping a woman protected was like second nature to them. I pulled my leg over the seat and handed my helmet to Eagle to store away. He rose from the seat, and once off the bike, I saw his hand begin to reach for mine, before he caught himself. I winced as I turned from him to walk into the bank. This hands-off in public thing was going to suck, and be fucking hard after having full access to each other at the cabin.

The five men all surrounded me as we walked, and had me feeling like some sort of pop star with bodyguards everywhere. The thought had me chuckling a little as we made our way into the building.

Just like in L.A., it didn't take long to hand over the keys and my identification to get access to the boxes. Once again, there was another box for me, just one this time, but a note had been left connecting it to both the club boxes. Guess whichever box I found first would have given me the information I needed for both of them. The teller gave me the keys back after I signed the paperwork to release the contents.

"Would you like to open them in a private viewing room?"

"Yes, please. That would be great."

The bank teller eyed my guards warily and I smiled at her. "Don't mind them. They're my family and a little over-protective."

With a slight nod, she led us all back to a private room with two chairs and a large table, before leaving to get the boxes.

"Mac and Taz, I want you boys in the hallway keeping watch. Silk, we need to just empty those boxes into your bag and get the fuck out of here. Every minute we're in town is another minute the Iron Hammers have time to find out we're here. Until I get to examine what's in their box, I don't want them knowing about the damn thing."

I smiled at Scout. "I understand. I had just about all the excitement I can handle back in L.A. I'm not looking for any more."

He squeezed my shoulder briefly as his face tightened with a flash of pain before he moved away. The club really was my family, and like any over-protective uncle, Scout hated that I'd been taken and hurt.

It was only a few minutes before the teller returned with the boxes.

"When you've finished, just leave the boxes and keys here on the table and go. I'll come back later and sort them out."

Scout handed me the un-keyed one and tossed my uncle the key to the Iron Hammer's box. Both men had brought a bag in with them, and they made quick work of unlocking the boxes. I shook myself back to attention and opened my box. No gun this time, but there was a wicked looking hunting knife. Thankfully, it was in a sheath so I wouldn't cut myself on the thing by accident. I put it in my bag, along with another thick envelope. This one just had a note on the front, saying to be careful and to read it when I was alone. My eyes stung as I thought about what bullshit excuses he'd have written in this letter. I wasn't sure I wanted to read the damn thing at all, but I knew I would. Ultimately, I missed my dad and wouldn't be able to resist.

The rest of the box contained more rolls of money. Only three this time. Assuming they were the same as the last ones, and they looked the same size, that was another thirty thousand dollars. Fuck, that was more than a hundred grand total from just two boxes. How much more would we find in the others?

Eagle snatched the cash and tossed it in my bag as I stood there in a trance. I snapped to attention with a muttered apology and the look in Eagle's eyes nearly had me going to him for comfort. Until my uncle cleared his throat.

"Right, let's get moving."

I glanced over at Scout and my uncle, and they were both zipping their bags closed. I had no idea what they'd found, but both their faces looked strained.

"Where are we going after here?"

"If we can get clear of town without catching the attention of any of the Iron Hammers, we have three choices. One is we go back to the clubhouse, second is we go to Silk's secret hideout, and the third option is the old quarry about half an hour out of Bridgewater. What's it going to be Silk? Make it fast."

My whole body tightened. "Fuck me. I don't like any of those options! I guess the clubhouse, but I don't want to be seen. I don't want, or need, any fucking pity from the club."

"Right. Done. Let's go. And Silk, in the middle of the day on a Tuesday, there aren't going to be many at the clubhouse, so you've got nothing to worry about. You can go back to your hideout as soon as we've gone over the boxes and we know they don't contain anything that will bring you harm in the immediate future."

With a nod and stinging eyes, I marched from the room. I hated being emotional and was grateful I managed to hold the tears back from spilling over. I rarely cried, and since those mob assholes had grabbed me, I'd found myself on the verge of tears way too many times for my liking. I was not that wussy, girly-girl that cried over every fucking thing. I was a tough chick who rarely shed a tear for anything.

It just appeared my tear ducts had forgotten that fact recently. Stupid, fucking things.

Eagle

By the time we pulled into the Charon's clubhouse I was more than ready to be done with this mission. Tension radiated from Silk as she clung to me while we rode. I wanted to wrap her in my arms and take all her worries away. If I could get even half an hour alone with her, I could give her what she needed to clear her mind. But that wouldn't be happening until much later.

I knew it would only be a matter of weeks before I got patched in—but it was going to feel like a fucking year now that I'd had her, and would have to stand clear until I got my top rocker.

I stayed a step behind Silk as we followed the others

inside the clubhouse. The place was the quietest I'd heard it in a long while. There were two of the new prospects cleaning the bar area, but there appeared to be no one else around. I was so fucking glad I didn't have to do cleaning duties anymore. Thankfully, there were enough newer prospects to do the truly shitty jobs. I guess Scout could see early on that Taz, Mac and I had skills better used elsewhere. From almost day one, we'd been put on security and watch jobs. Boring as hell, but at least I hadn't been cleaning up blood and cum from the fights and orgies that seemed to take place nightly at the clubhouse. That shit made one hell of a fucking mess.

Before entering, we all put our phones in the small open lockers that lined the wall outside the doorway to the meeting room. Scout closed and locked the door after we were all inside. Silk's steps faltered as she entered and I wondered if she'd ever been in here before. Women weren't typically allowed in church, so she probably hadn't. Scout marched straight up to the table at the head of the room and dropped his bag. Bulldog followed suit, then Silk placed hers next to them both.

"Right. Let's see what John left us all, shall we?"

With that, Scout unzipped, then unloaded his bag on the table. I locked my jaw to stop it from dropping. Silk's father was either extremely clever, or a complete fucking moron who'd gotten lucky too many times. Scout had emptied the Charon's box. It had contained a stack of old VHS tapes labeled with locations around Bridgewater and the surrounding area together with dates. Fuck. I could imagine what they would have on them. There was a large envelope, that when Scout opened, revealed a stack of grainy photos. I'd need a closer look, but like the videos, it didn't take much to imagine what they were. He also pulled out one single roll of hundred dollar bills that looked the same size as the ones we'd counted out back at the cabin.

"Silk had rolls like that in her box from L.A. They counted out to ten grand each."

Scout looked up to me frowning. "How many? And don't glare at me like that. I have no fucking intention of taking it off her, I just want to know how much John fucking stole so I can work out if the mob is going to keep coming for her."

My shoulders relaxed. I hadn't realized I'd tensed up at his words.

"You know, I am right here? In the room with you? There was eighty thousand in the box from L.A., then three rolls in the one I just got. So a hundred and ten grand to me so far. Assuming all the rolls are the same."

She reached into her bag and took out the cash, along with the knife and envelope.

"He left you a weapon?"

Silk shrugged. "There was a handgun in the L.A. box."

"Motherfucker." Bulldog's voice was rough with anger. "What? He thought if you got caught in his mess, you could fucking shoot your way out? Or take on an entire MC with a fucking hunting knife? You know, if the bastard wasn't already dead, I'd be tempted to kill him myself for the shit he's dragged you into, Silk. This whole thing is fucked up."

Silk's body went ramrod straight and my fingers itched with the need to take her into my arms. She was hurting and I wanted to comfort her. I kind of wanted to fucking throw a punch at Bulldog too. Sure, if John was still alive I'd have some choice words to say to the bastard too—but I wasn't going to say that in front of his still grieving daughter. The man was still her father.

"Fuck, Silk. I'm sorry, sweetheart. You know I loved your father. Hell, even with all the shit he pulled, he was my brother and I would never have truly hurt him. It just guts me that he's left so much shit for you to deal with."

She nodded, and her shoulders lowered a little. That seemed to be enough for her uncle, who then started unloading his bag. This was the Iron Hammer's box. Considering John had been a prospect, I had no idea what kind of dirt he could have collected on them. Turned out to be only two VHS videos, but three envelopes.

Bulldog ripped them open and photos spilled out onto the table. Women. Fuck that, they weren't women, they were girls. Teenagers, too young to be doing the shit they were. I couldn't help myself, I whipped out my hand and snagged Silk's wrist, yanking her to me where I buried her face against my chest to block her eyes.

"Don't look at that shit, sweetheart. It's nothing you need to see."

Her body shuddered against me and I knew I hadn't

been quick enough, that she'd seen at least some of those depraved photos.

Scout cursed and gathered up the photos. "I'll have to find someone with a machine that can play these tapes, but I can take a guess that the Iron Hammer ones are going to be more of shit that's in these photos. Charons have never done that shit, so the tapes on us won't be anything like that. At a guess they're beat downs, shit like that. This is fucked up. Especially, if he's got copies stashed anywhere else. Fuck!"

Silk nuzzled me a moment before she took a deep breath and moved away. I forced myself to stay still, to not keep her against me. Thankfully, neither Bulldog or Scout looked like they were going to make a deal out of me grabbing her, but I didn't want to risk bringing their wrath down on me. Especially when they were riled up from those photos.

Chapter 16

Silk

For as long as I lived, I was never going to forget the images of those teenagers being stuck with needles and cocks. Another shudder ran through me as I paced away from Eagle. I wish I could have stayed wrapped in his arms, pressed against his hard body, breathing in his scent. But that wasn't going to do anything other than get him beaten up if Scout or Bulldog saw the display. In an attempt to distract myself and the men, I reached for the thick envelope my father left for me in my box.

"Let me read the letter he left me. At a guess the envelope will have copies of the ledgers for both clubs. But I have no idea what the letter will say."

Ripping it open, I pulled the contents free and sure enough, the two bound bundles looked to be copies of the ledgers.

"Here are the copies of the clubs' books."

I tossed them onto the table and took the letter with me to go sit in a chair a little way away from everyone.

My dearest Claudine,

I have no idea if this is the first of the boxes you've found. If so, there are more. I am so terribly sorry this has fallen on your shoulders. It was never my intention. Of all the boxes I've had to leave for you, this is the one I'd hoped you never have to see…

I skimmed over all the bullshit excuses he'd written about in the last letter. They didn't help any more now than they did when I'd read them. It was still all his fault for his selfishness, greed and jealousy. I got serious about reading again when he quit with his apology.

Please, do not look at what the other boxes here contain. It's nothing good. If neither club are chasing you, hand it all over to the police anonymously and run far away from Texas, Boston, Los Angeles and New York. If you have been in contact with your uncle, go to him. He'll know what to do with the boxes.

The thing that had my heart pounding and sweat breaking out over my face was a line he'd scribbled out after saying I wasn't to look in the boxes. Holding the paper just right, I could see his words underneath.

Your mother wouldn't want you to see her like that.

I shook my head. "No. Hell fucking no."

My eyes stung. It couldn't be. My mother had been one of those young girls the club had forced drugs and sex on? With my quick glance at the photos, I'd seen girls being pinned down to have needles shoved in their arms. I couldn't bring myself to read the rest. I rose and pushed past Eagle to get to the table. I dropped the letter and reached for the Iron Hammer's envelopes. My uncle tried to stop me.

"Sweetheart, you don't want to see them."

I spun on him and glared hard. "I *have* to see them. Trust me, I know I don't want to, but I need to."

I turned back, vaguely aware of Uncle Clint picking up the letter I'd tossed aside, as I tore at the envelopes, tipping all the depraved images out in front of me. I shifted them around on the table until I caught a familiar face. I froze and swallowed.

"Fuck."

My curse echoed around the now-silent room as I lifted the image to look more closely at the face of the young teen whose face was oh-so-familiar.

"Are you fucking kidding me?"

My uncle's enraged voice came from beside me.

"It's her, isn't it?"

My voice was barely more than a whisper. His strong arm came around my shoulders and pulled me in against his chest. I went to him, seeking comfort from the man who'd been a father to me since that day, fifteen years ago.

"Yeah, honey. That's your mother."

There was a moment of shocked silence in the room before the cursing started. I stayed with my face pressed against my uncle's cut, wishing I would wake up to find myself in Eagle's arms and discover this had all been some horrible nightmare. My mother had been a club whore, most likely forced into the role as a teen. Was John even my biological dad? I took after my mother in appearance. I had pale blue eyes like my dad, but plenty of people had them.

Steeling my courage, I pulled back and held my uncle's gaze. "Was he even my real dad?"

He cupped my face and wiped my tears with his thumbs. "Honestly, honey, I have no clue. But he loved you as though you were his own. Just like your Aunty Rose and I do. Do you want us to investigate it? Try to figure out what happened? Or do you want to leave it alone? The choice is yours."

I blinked up at him, my mind a hazy mess. "I can't think right now."

He leaned in and pressed a kiss to my temple. "You don't have to answer me right now, Silk. Why don't you go up to your room and lie down for a bit? We'll finish up here, then Eagle, Mac and Taz will take you back to your cabin. Let me know what you want to do when you get there. We'll lock all this down till then."

I nodded and numbly headed toward the door.

"Silk?"

I turned to face Scout. "Leave the photo, honey. You don't need to remember her like that."

I'd forgotten I still had it in my hand. I looked down at the image of a young teen being pinned down by her shoulders as another man had a needle in her arm. Her mouth was open in a scream. Bile rose up in my throat and I dropped the thing, feeling as though it had burned me, then spun to sprint from the room.

I didn't stop until I slammed into my room upstairs,

and made it to my little bathroom. Dropping to my knees, I threw up in the toilet. I wretched for what felt like hours, my energy leaving me with the contents of my stomach. I couldn't make my legs move, so I just rested my head on my arm and closed my eyes.

A warm palm rubbing my back snapped me to attention.

"What?"

"Shh, sweetheart. C'mon up off the floor."

I reached out without hesitation to take my aunt's hand. She helped me up and I let her lead me to the sink. Just like she'd done when I'd been sick as a teen, she washed my face with a cloth, before she led me back out to the bed. I felt like a zombie. My brain wasn't firing right so I just followed Aunty Rose's lead. I knew I could trust her, so I didn't need to think. My heart hurt from all the betrayal my father had inflicted. It made it worse that they were both gone. Who could I ask questions? How the fuck could I get to the truth if I wanted it? Did I want it? It could lead to all sorts of shit with the other club, and for what? My parents were dead. Nothing was going to change that.

I sat on the bed and Aunt Rose sat beside me, pulling me against her. I went willingly and didn't even try to stop the sobs that tore free from me.

"Oh, sweetheart. I'm so sorry this is all happening. You go ahead and let it all out. I've got you."

I didn't say a word, I couldn't. I simply wrapped my arms around her and let myself release all the pent-up emotion.

Eagle

I fucking hated this bullshit. I forced myself to stay still as Silk bolted from the room like the hounds of hell were chasing her. I knew the clubhouse was safe and she wouldn't have any problems between here and her room, but still. It stuck in my craw I couldn't go take care of her.

"Motherfucker! My brother was such a stupid bastard. I'm calling my old lady. She'll come and sit with Silk."

As Bulldog stormed out of the room, Scout came up to me.

"I know you're feeling her, and I know you want to go to her, but I need you to stay here. Just because we didn't see any Iron Hammers this morning, doesn't mean they don't know about our visit. Word is already spreading about what happened in L.A. Trouble will follow us sooner, rather than later, and I need the skills you three have to help keep the fall-out to a minimum."

I clenched my jaw a moment, breathing away my emotion, before I gave the President a nod.

"So, what's the plan going to be?"

I stopped speaking when Bulldog returned.

"Rose is on her way. The prospects on duty know not to let anyone else anywhere near the first floor until I say so."

Scout gave him a nod and I relaxed a little. Silk's aunt was probably the best person to handle this situation. Our relationship was so new and I was severely limited in what I could do for her while pretending we hadn't become lovers.

Scout adjusted his bandana before speaking again. "Easiest thing to do with this shit is to blackmail the bastards. Give them a couple of the photos, tell them we have more, plus videos. If they try so much as to step foot into our territory again, we'll release them to the cops and the media. They might be old, but that shit is sick and I'm sure the cops would find some way to press charges for it. Especially, if some of those girls are still being used by the club."

Mac stepped forward. "What about getting the women out? Those photos clearly showed they were forced. If they're still there, that's over fifteen years of rapes they've lived through. And it doesn't take a genius to work out they did this more than fucking once. They could have a fresh batch of teens being abused in there now."

I grabbed Mac's shoulder as Scout folded his arms over his chest watching us.

"I hear you, Mac. Trust me, this fucking shit doesn't sit well with any of us, but the Iron Hammers are a big club. We don't have the manpower, or the resources, to just go down there and break their fucking doors down. That'll end in a bloodbath none of us want. We will get them out, but it'll take time and careful planning. Right now, we need to be prepared to get them off our fucking backs about our trip this morning once they find out we visited. And if we can stop them from pushing into our territory while we're at it, all the better."

Bulldog was pacing the room and didn't seem to be paying much attention.

"Brother? You with us?"

He jerked to look at Scout. "Why the fuck did he not come to me with any of this? If he wanted to get his woman out of the club and leave, why didn't he fucking come to his brother, instead of running off to become some kind of fucked-up information broker. Motherfucker!"

I winced when he spun and put his fist through the wall. I was pretty tempted to do the same thing, but busting my knuckles up wasn't going to help Silk. I stepped back to stand with Mac and Taz, while Scout went to deal with Bulldog.

Mac nodded toward the door and I returned the gesture. The meeting was over and Bulldog needed a few minutes to process. I could understand that. In his position, I'd need more than a few minutes to adjust to the fact the world just started spinning in the opposite direction.

We grabbed our phones and headed to the bar. Taz slipped behind it as Mac and I sat on stools.

"This is some seriously fucked-up shit."

Taz slid a drink in front of me, then another to Mac. I didn't care what it was—didn't even look before I picked up the glass and threw back the liquid. The trail of fire down my throat made me think it was maybe whiskey, the expensive shit the club kept for special occasions. Or for when someone really wanted to forget shit they'd seen, and needed a hand with the task.

"Again."

Taz refilled my glass and it went the same way as the first. I went to ask for another one when the bastard shook his head.

"Not if you want to go back to that cabin with Silk tonight. We all need to stay sober enough to ride. I figure we've got time for what you just had to wear off before we'll be heading out, but I won't let you risk things by getting plastered. You can finish getting sloppy drunk later, once we're back at her cabin and Mac and I have you covered."

I cursed under my breath. I knew he was right, but that didn't mean I had to like it.

"You think she'll want to know?"

I glanced at Mac. "About whether her dad was her biological father? I have no idea. With her folks dead, I don't see the point. Clearly her mother was being passed around that fucking club, probably unwillingly. By digging around, she could find herself with a new daddy trying to bring her into their fucked-up club. A man who won't give a fuck about her, other than she's fresh meat for his club." I shook my head. "No fucking way will I allow that to happen."

Mac scrubbed his palm over his face, then over his

cleanly shaven head. "I can't sit back and do nothing about them raping women. For all we know, they're kidnapping teens and getting them hooked on drugs so they can use them however the fuck they want."

I wasn't sure exactly what had happened in Mac's past, but whatever it was, it made the man extremely protective of women. Especially those that had been mistreated. For all the times we'd gotten drunk in the past and started talking secrets, Mac had always remained tight lipped about his childhood. The fact he was with Taz and me, and not with his family was enough for me to know he either didn't have any family left, or if he did, they weren't on speaking terms anymore.

"The Charons' reputation is that they don't let shit like this slide. They'll come through, but like Scout said, we can't simply storm the place." I lowered my voice so only Mac and Taz could hear me. "And if we go the other way? What's the bet they have someone on the inside and they'll just kill any girls they currently have and dispose of them before anything can be done."

I had a hunch Mac was wanting to get the FBI involved, but there were too many leaks in government departments. We needed to give the club a little time to sort something out. And they would. The Charons were known for seeking justice when it was needed. Eventually, that would rain down on the Iron Hammers.

"And if they take a little time? We'll have our patches and be able to join in."

Mac tilted his glass toward me in agreement before he took a final gulp. I turned to glance up the stairs. Not being with Silk when I knew she had to be hurting like a motherfucker was ripping my insides up.

"Ain't the only thing a patch will change, huh, mate?" I grunted at Taz's quiet remark. They both knew how I felt. Hell, they'd both been listening to Silk and me going at it for the past what? Forty-eight hours, as though we were a pair of damn rabbits.

Chapter 17

Silk

It was getting dark when we finally got back to the cabin and I still felt empty inside. I'd cuddled up behind Eagle for the ride, not even trying to get them to let me ride my own bike. I knew as well as they did I wasn't up for riding. I wouldn't have been safe with the way my mind couldn't focus.

I went to swing off the bike but Eagle gripped his palm around my thigh, holding me to him.

"Just wait for Mac and Taz to check first."

"Oh, yeah. Of course."

With a sigh, I closed my eyes and rested my head against Eagle's back, rubbing my cheek against the soft leather of his cut. His palms caressed my knees as we waited for the men to give the all clear. Once Mac called out it was safe, Eagle released me and I got off. I stretched and walked up to the front door. On autopilot, I made my way to the bedroom and didn't even bother stripping, I just let myself fall on the bed where I curled up on my side and stared out the window into the darkness.

I vaguely heard Eagle come in and go through to the bathroom. I just couldn't seem to shake free of the thoughts in my head. Had Mom wanted me? Was I the result of her being raped? Did my father rape her? Was some other Iron Hammer my biological father? What would happen if that was the case and the club found out? Would they come for me, demanding I belonged to them, not the Charons? A shudder ran through me. I somehow doubted daughters of the Iron Hammers were taken care of in the same way as the Charons did theirs. And even if they did, the Charons were my family. I didn't want to leave.

"C'mon, baby. Let's get you cleaned up."

Eagle scooped me up from the bed and I snuggled into his bare chest as he strode across the room. His scent filled my head and the questions eased off a little. I nuzzled my face against his chest, and when he hissed, my lips twitched. A small burst of joy flared inside me.

He perched me on the counter next to the sink and I ran my gaze over his body. He'd already stripped, and I could see every one of his firm muscles, including his thick cock, that twitched under my gaze. With a growl, he made quick work of getting me naked, then I was back in his arms as he stepped into the bath that he'd already filled.

"I've never had a bath with someone else."

"Can't say I have either. Not a lot of bathtubs over in the Middle East, and even fewer people I've ever wanted to share one with."

I chuckled as he lowered us both into the warm water. He settled back against the end of the large tub and easily placed me where he wanted me. I ended up with my back to his front, his thick erection nestled between my butt cheeks, and my head on his upper chest, just below his shoulder.

"Hmmmm."

His hands began stroking my body, but stayed away from my breasts and pussy. His strokes were tender and gentle, especially with how the water made his skin glide against mine. I lifted one hand up to wrap around his neck, burying my damp fingers in his silky hair.

"I love how your hair feels. I could spend an entire day running my fingers through it and be happy."

With each pass through the strands I could feel the tension leave my body. He pressed a kiss to the top of my head.

"I wish I could give you that. An entire day where nothing happens, so you could spend the time with your hands in my hair, or on my body, and be happy."

My eyes stung with more stupid, fucking tears.

"It's like a fucking leaky tap. Once you turn the bastard on, it's nearly impossible to turn the damn thing off!"

"Um, babe. I'm sorry, but I have no clue what you're talking about."

Sitting up, I scooped up water in both my palms and splashed my face before I responded. "Fucking crying.

It's a waste of time. All it does is make your face red and splotchy. Then, the next morning you feel fucking hungover from being dehydrated. And does it help? No, it doesn't bring the dead back, it doesn't undo betrayal. Doesn't change that my parents lied to me my whole life and now they're gone so I can't get any fucking answers!"

Eagle leaned against my back, wrapping his arms around me.

"Let it all out, Silk. Crying might not feel like it's helping, but keeping it all bottled up is so much worse. It'll eat away at you until you can't take it anymore. And we're in a bath, surrounded by water. Your skin is soaking in water and I'll make sure you drink plenty so you don't wake up sore in the morning. I'm here for you, Silk. Whatever you need, all you have to do is ask."

I twisted around so I could look up into his face.

"Make it all better? Make it so my parents wanted and loved me?"

My voice came out a broken whisper, making me wince. I wasn't this freakin' weak fragile female! I shook my head and snuggled against him. "Ignore that. I'm just tired."

Eagle held me against him, stroking my shoulder and hair randomly.

"I wish I could make it all better for you, babe. I can tell you, your father loved you. If he didn't, he wouldn't have left those failsafe boxes for you. If he'd not loved you, he wouldn't have cared that you could be potentially caught up in his web of shit. He left weapons, money and material for blackmail for you to save yourself with. That's not something a person does for just anyone.

"As for your mother, I haven't heard much about her at all. But at a guess, when she found out she was pregnant with you, she did everything she could to escape that club. It would have been scary for her. Hell, she moved clear across the country. Again, not something a person does lightly. I think I can safely assure you that your parents loved you very much. And before you start questioning your father's DNA, it takes more than genetics to be a family."

Such pain filled his voice. Lifting a fingertip I began to trace random patterns over his chest as I remembered what he'd told me about not knowing his parents. "Did you have good foster parents?"

His body tensed and his hand gripped my upper arm tightly, before he blew out a breath and loosened his hold.

"There were some good and some bad. None that ever bothered to bond with me, if that's what you mean. No, the only family I ever had was in the Marines, and now the MC. Taz and Mac? They're my brothers. I don't have any blood relations, but I couldn't imagine having a closer bond than what the three of us have. It's that bond I see between the club brothers. It's why the three of us were drawn to the MC in the first place. We were sick of dodging bullets, so we retired, but we missed the comradery of being in the Marines. The Charons have a similar feel to it."

I frowned at that. "Why the Charons? I mean, there's probably thousands of MCs across the US, and Texas isn't your home state. Why Bridgewater?"

He shrugged, tensing slightly. If she hadn't been lying on him, she would have missed it. "Not real sure, baby. We were kind of aimlessly riding around the country when we heard about the poker run. Figured we'd go and see what it was all about."

Nodding against his shoulder, I kept trailing my fingers over his skin. He was hiding something, but I didn't have the energy to dig deeper into it. And really—what did it matter how he found his way to Bridgewater, Texas? The important thing was that he had made it here and planned to stay.

Eagle

When Silk started to fall asleep, I rose from the bath and stepped out with her still in my arms. I set her on the counter, and the poor girl was so out of it, she just sat there docilely, while I dried her off, then quickly wiped myself down. I lifted her in my arms again and smiled when she nuzzled against me like a sleepy kitten. I didn't like how quiet she was. It wasn't like her, but she'd had one hell of a bomb dropped on her earlier, so I wasn't surprised. Although, I did like how she sought me out for comfort. I tucked her into bed and climbed in behind to spoon up against her. I didn't make any moves to take her—she didn't need that tonight. She needed gentle caresses and a good night's sleep.

I stroked her hair and down her side, steering clear of her oh-so-tempting tits with her pierced nipples, until she went to sleep. I stayed there a few minutes more, watching my woman sleep as my mind spun. I wanted to protect her, to prevent any more shit from coming down on her head. But how?

With a sigh, I rose and chucked on a pair of jeans before I padded out to the kitchen. Mac and Taz were both there, nursing beers. I grabbed one from the fridge before I sat at the table with them.

"The area all clear?"

Mac nodded. "None of our alarms have been activated. We're solid."

"Great."

It might be all clear now, but we all knew how quickly things could turn to shit. It was for that reason I knew, like me, the other two wouldn't have more than one beer tonight. No matter how much we all wanted more.

"How's Silk handling it all?"

I shrugged at Mac's quiet question. "She's gone real quiet. She's gotta be hurting. Feeling betrayed and questioning her whole world. Finding out her mother was a club whore, having been forced into it by the looks of things, is rough enough on its own. But she's also now questioning if her dad was actually her biological father. It's a fucking messed up situation, and with both of them dead, there's not much we can do to prove anything."

Taz cleared his throat. "Is it wise to even try? What if he wasn't? What if some bastard Iron Hammer is her dad and he finds out when she starts digging? They could come for her. I'm not sure if they'd treat her any better than they did her mother. Is it worth the risk?"

I looked my brother in the eye. "No. It's fucking not. I told her straight up that family is more than genetics. Clearly, her dad adored her. From everything I've heard, that man doted on her and he left all these boxes for her just in case she got caught up his web of shit. I don't want her anywhere near that other fucking club."

I took a long draw on my beer.

"I sent the copy of the L.A. mob ledger tonight. Mr. Smith was rather excited over it. I think we're now his favorites."

I was glad Taz had taken on the role of liaison with our FBI contact. I couldn't stand the man. Nor did I get the need for bullshit fake names, but it seemed as though to be in the FBI you had to like bland, boring as shit, fake names.

"Hopefully they can do some serious damage with the information and Sabella won't have the time or manpower to come after Silk for the money she has."

"Or he could realize the only place the information used against them could come from was in that book, and he'll come gunning for her."

Mac's voice was low and quiet, but it hit me in the chest like a sledge hammer.

"Yeah, well. If he does, we'll be waiting for him this time. And we'll take care of that bastard permanently."

Taz sighed. "I thought we left the Marines because we were sick of killing? What the fuck, man?"

I shrugged again. "I don't want to ever take another life, but I won't let anyone hurt Silk. She's it for me. I know it in my soul. I won't allow a threat to her life to exist if I can help it. I don't expect anyone but me to pull the fucking trigger."

Mac wrapped his hand around my forearm. "We're brothers, Eagle. We always, *always,* have each other's backs. None of us wants to ever take another human life again, but that doesn't mean we won't, if we have to. All three of us have the skills and knowledge to do what needs to be done to make sure your girl stays protected."

Well, fuck. Emotion put a lump in my throat. I truly loved these men. My family. I wasn't sure if I'd ever feel about the men in the club like I did about Taz and Mac, but that was fine. So long as I had these two by my side and Silk in my arms, I'd be a happy man.

With a nod, I lifted my bottle to drain the last of the liquid.

"Well, I'm going to go crash. See you two in the morning." I paused a moment. "Thanks. For everything."

Before they could respond, I pushed the chair back and hightailed it out of there. That had been the first time I'd put into words exactly how much Silk meant to me and I wasn't entirely sure how I felt about it. On one hand, I'd never been happier. Silk was like a missing piece of me. We simply fit together.

But I wasn't sure how to handle the fact my world now revolved around one sexy blonde tattooist. I mean, how the fuck had that happened? In my entire life, I'd never needed anyone. Sure, my Marine brothers were fucking great and I didn't want to be without Taz and Mac. It would crush me to lose them. But if I lost Silk? The bottom would fall out of my world. Even the thought of it had me breaking out in a sweat.

This was heavy shit, and I wasn't even sure if Silk felt the same way about me. I stood in the doorway a moment and drank in the sight of her. She'd rolled onto her side, her hand thrown out to where I should have been. An ache started behind my sternum and I raised my fist to rub over it.

Silk was such a strong woman, both in body and spirit, yet while she slept, she looked fragile. With a quiet sigh, I entered, shut the door carefully and stripped. I eased into the bed, lifting her hand and placing it over my heart. With a soft moan, she wriggled in against me, throwing a leg over mine and grinding her pussy against my hip. I groaned when my cock sprung to life with its own demands, but I didn't move to take her.

I had to grit my teeth to stop from rolling her over and mounting her when she nuzzled her face against my chest with a moan. She was asleep and needed the rest desperately. I kept repeating that in my mind as I fought my impulse to take her. Dammit, was being a gentleman always so fucking hard and painful?

Chapter 18

Silk

The days passed in a blur as I tried to get my head straight. The men took turns checking the land around the cabin each morning and again at night. They even spent some time each day sitting up on the roof, binoculars in hand. Aside from thinking a lot, I spent my days sketching. I had several new tattoo ideas roughly outlined and I was nearly finished with Eagle's artwork. So far I'd even managed to keep it hidden from him. I wanted to surprise him with the finished thing, so when he was near me, I worked on other images. Immersing myself in my artwork, I'd managed to regain a level of peace I hadn't thought possible after the bomb I'd discovered back at the clubhouse however many days ago it had been.

I'd also spent a fair amount of time with all three men, getting to know them. Eagle never left my side for long, but that didn't stop Taz from flirting. It was pretty obvious he enjoyed stirring up his buddy. I didn't honestly think he wanted me to come climb into his bed after Eagle had finished *attempting* to satisfy me.

"What's that grin for?"

I turned to Eagle. "Just thinking about how funny you looked chasing Taz around the house with your hunting knife last night."

He frowned at me with a low growl, which just made me laugh. Taz walked in with a wide grin.

"The offer still stands, darlin'. You just come to me, baby, and I'll make sure you're well and truly satisfied."

I grabbed Eagle's arm when he went to stand. "Settle down, babe. You know he's joking."

"I'm sure a broken nose would drive home the point."

Mac strolled in with four beers. "Settle down, boys. You both know full well Silk ain't going anywhere with anyone other than Eagle."

I closed my sketch book and took a bottle when Mac offered it, then sat back to take the first sip.

"Hmm. Damn, that's good."

Eagle was still grumbling under his breath when he took a bottle from Mac, put it down on the coffee table, then took mine and set it there as well.

"Hey! Give that back!"

Then I was up against his chest before he sat down where I'd been, with me now in his lap. I slung my arms around his neck and nipped at his jaw.

"You know I'm yours and would never give in to Taz, no matter how charming he is with that Australian accent of his."

"Hear that? She thinks I'm charming."

Taz exaggerated his accent and had a gleam in his eye when Eagle tightened his grip on me.

"You have no reason to be noticing any man's charms other than mine. And I will always, always, make sure you're fully satisfied."

Mac shook his head with a chuckle, then he turned his icy blue gaze to me.

"So, Silk, how long do you normally stay up here? Much longer and we're going to need to go grab some more supplies."

I snuggled into Eagle's embrace as a chill ran up my spine. With the three of them here to keep me distracted, I'd managed to not think about 9/11 for days now.

"Ah, normally I go back two or three days after the anniversary. Sometimes I stay here for up to a week after. If I'm sketching, I often lose track of the days."

"I gathered that happened. You have no idea what the date is today, do you?"

Eagle stiffened and gave Mac a low growl. I frowned and thought back over how many days we'd been here. We went to Galveston on Tuesday. I pulled out my phone I hadn't even glanced at in days, and turned it on.

"The twelfth?"

Yesterday had been the anniversary and I hadn't even known. I'd spent most of the day playing Monopoly with the men. Apparently Marines are highly competitive, no matter what they did. It had made for a highly entertaining few games.

"You all kept track of the days, though? You all knew

yesterday was 9/11?"

Eagle pressed a kiss to the side of my head. "Yeah, babe. We all knew. But none of us wanted to bring you down. You'd been relaxed and having fun. That's why you come up here each year, isn't it? To escape the hype and to relax?"

Emotion had a lump forming in my throat and I swallowed to try to clear it.

"Yeah, but not to forget completely. Never to forget."

How could I have forgotten? Missed the day? Not thought of my parents at all!

Eagle tightened his grip when I tried to stand.

"Silk? Look at me." I flicked my gaze to meet his. "I'm sorry, baby. I thought you didn't want to dwell on it. If I'd known you wanted to do something on the day, I would have told you. We can do it today. Whatever you normally do, we can do it today."

The pain and regret in his eyes had me leaning forward to press a kiss to his lips.

"I just need some time on my own. Give me an hour or so before you come looking for me, okay?"

He cupped my face and kissed me again before he helped me stand. I walked away without looking back. I went for the back door and out into the wilderness. Mac had shown me the traps around the yard, so I avoided them all. Turning away from the cliff that dropped down into the ocean, I made my way into the national park that the cabin backed onto. Surrounded by trees, I stopped to take a deep breath. I loved how the air smelled out here.

I'd often thought about moving into this cabin permanently. It wasn't that far from Bridgewater and my shop.

I started walking again. Further up the mountain there was a large rock that was big enough to sit on comfortably. It was also above most of the trees, so it had an excellent view. I would often spend hours sitting up there but I hadn't gone up at all this trip. Maybe that's why I felt so overwhelmed still. I hadn't taken the time for my usual meditation sessions I normally took on these trips.

Once I arrived at the large boulder, I climbed up on the flat surface and settled in. Closing my eyes, I lifted my face to enjoy the warm sunshine. Continuing to take deep breaths, I started to process all the thoughts in my mind. One by one, I worked through them. First off was my parents. What had really happened all those years ago when they left Texas? I tried to work it all out. Mom had been a club whore, forced into the role as a teen, by the looks of those photos. Thinking back to my childhood, I couldn't see her using drugs by choice. She'd always been softly spoken, always did everything Dad told her to do. But I couldn't recall a single time where she'd had so much as a glass of wine. Mom had loved my father with all her heart. I remember seeing the look in her eyes when she'd look at him when she thought no one could see her. Total adoration. Same with Dad—he loved Mom. He always made sure she had what she needed, and pretty much anything she wanted, he made sure she got. Not that she ever asked for much. We'd lived simply up in Boston, but it hadn't stopped us from being happy.

Now that I was thinking through things with a clear mind, taking into account my parents' personalities, I knew no matter what had happened, both Mom and Dad wanted me and loved me. That would have to be enough. If I started digging into the Iron Hammers, they could easily decide to take me and claim I was one of them. The Charons would fight for me—even if I wasn't the niece of the VP, the club would go into battle for me. But it was a war that would have fatalities and injuries and I didn't want any of my club family hurt. Especially for something that would change nothing. John was the man who raised me and claimed me as his own. That was good enough for me. He was my dad, always would be.

I couldn't help but grin when I thought about those boxes he'd left. Both so far had a weapon. I'd put money on the others being the same. He'd loved me enough to leave me a way to defend myself, if his enemies ever caught up with me. And I had the knife on me. The sheath it came in fit snuggly inside both my hiking boots and my riding ones. I felt closer to my dad with it on me.

Like I had a little part of him with me all the time now.

Eagle

I felt like a fucking heel.

"Don't beat yourself up over it, mate. We all assumed

letting the day pass unnoticed was the best way to go."

Mac cut in on Taz. "If she didn't have the ledger shit hanging over her head, I wouldn't have said anything today. Trust me, I don't mind hanging out here. She's found a fucking great place. I'm actually wondering why she doesn't live here all year round. I would in a heartbeat in her shoes."

Taz wriggled his eyebrows at me. "Yep, even with the amorous soundtrack each night, I'd totally stay here indefinitely."

I threw a cushion at Taz as I chuckled. "Asshole. You're just jealous."

Now that I thought about it, by staying up here, Taz had put himself through one hell of a dry spell for me and Silk.

"I appreciate you both staying here with us. I know you'd both prefer to be doing other things this past week or so."

Taz's glare would have been enough to kill a lesser man. "What the fuck, mate? I know I've been living the man-whore life since joining the club, but pussy will never be more important than watching my brothers' backs. I can live without sex just fine, it's just nice to not have to."

Yep, that was Taz. Went from rip-shit pissed to cracking a joke in under a minute. I was about to make another crack about his need for pussy on a regular basis when a jolt ran down my spine. Something was about to go down. I jumped to my feet at the same moment the alarm sounded.

"Where?"

I barked out the word, knowing full fucking well Silk had gone outside for her alone time. We'd fucked up. Again.

"North west. Up the mountain around a hundred yards."

"Fuck. I can't believe I let her go alone! I should have known better."

I rushed to our weapons, and Mac handed me my Glock. I already had my knife strapped on to my belt. "Take a breath, brother. We have a mission to complete first, then you can beat yourself up for being fucking human. We all got slack. We'll debrief after we make sure your girl is safe. It could be a deer that's set it off, or Silk forgetting where one was."

I shook my head. "Not with how my senses are twitching. Shit is going down right now. Let's move out."

As we'd always done things, Mac took the lead, directly toward the triggered trap. I stayed with him until we got closer, then broke off into the shrubs. Taz hung back and covered us both. I'd never been so grateful for my time in the Marines that gave me the skills and the brothers I needed to save my woman. *Again.* Maybe I'd tether her to my side from now on. That way, I'd always know where she was.

"Heads up."

Right. I mentally shook my head. I had more

important things to do right now, other than kicking my own ass.

We didn't have coms, so the three of us made sure we could see each other as we arrived at the triggered trap. Mac crouched and examined the ground for a moment, then signaled us toward the north.

We continued being careful to stay silent until I heard Silk scream. Then I went as fast as I could without giving away my location. Someone was hurting Silk. Whoever it was, was about to die.

I slipped around a wide tree trunk, catching a glimpse of Silk, which left me silently cursing before I moved back into cover. Glancing around until I spotted Mac and Taz, I used hand signals to tell them three men had Silk. My heart rate was pounding, but my mind was calm. Just like in war, this was a battle. I needed to use my head to successfully complete it, then I could let my emotions rise up. The fact my woman was being beaten wasn't what I needed to focus on. No, it was the fact that two of the bastards had their backs to me, and the third was side on. Silk was being held between them, standing so I couldn't use a gun without risking her. Taz could take one out with his sniper rifle... if he had it. We hadn't brought it with us, unfortunately. I pulled my knife free and looked to Mac. He'd been our top for so many missions, it was natural to check in with him.

I watched his signals and nodded when he was done. It was difficult to block out the men demanding Silk tell them where the rest of the money was, to ignore the sounds of their hands landing against her. But she wouldn't suffer for much longer. They were all dead men—they just didn't know it yet.

Waiting for Taz and Mac to get in position seemed to take forever, but I knew it had only been moments. Less than a minute. Then we were on the move again. We each had a knife in our fist as we crept across the small clearing to where they were standing near a large rock. Sabella needed to train his men better. All three were so focused on Silk, they had no idea they weren't alone.

I stayed hunched down until I came up close to the back of one of the men who was hitting Silk. Keeping an eye on my brothers, I needed to rise at the same time as them. I took a firm grip in the bastard's hair before I swiped my blade across his throat. Taz had moved at the same time as me, and we each tossed the rapidly dying men aside to focus on the one holding Silk.

Seemingly oblivious to the fact Mac stood behind him with a knife to his throat, the fucker had his own blade pressed against her neck, and his other hand was behind her back, presumably holding her arm up to prevent her from moving—not like the knife at her throat didn't do that trick on its own. I didn't focus on her at all, I couldn't. I knew the moment I saw Silk bloody and beaten, I would lose focus and switch from being Eagle the soldier, to Eagle the lovesick idiot.

Taz stepped to the man's side and pressed the muzzle of his Glock against his ribs.

"Release her now."

As Mac spoke, Taz wrapped his free hand around the guy's wrist and jerked it away from Silk's skin. The moment his hold on Silk loosened, she tore free and threw herself at me. I wrapped my arms around her, holding her firmly against me, doing my best to ignore the sobs that were wracking her body. She was alive and I had her now. She would survive this.

"How many came with you?"

The man's eyes bugged but he remained silent, until Taz pulled the muzzle away from his ribs, aimed at his foot and fired. The sound of the gunshot and his scream had birds rising from the trees and Silk clutched me tighter with a squeal.

"You got plenty of non-vital places we can shoot, if you want to keep this up."

"Th-th-three. Just us three."

Mac looked me in the eye. "Take her away from here. Call the club and let them know. We'll let Scout take the lead on clean-up."

I gave him a nod and pulled my phone out to shoot off a text to Scout. It was going to take some time to get back down to the cabin holding an injured Silk, and I wanted these bodies cleaned up sooner, rather than later.

Seconds later a reply came saying the club was on its way. Silk was going to hit the roof that her secret cabin was about to become public club knowledge, but this was more important.

"Club's on its way."

I moved Silk so I could scoop her up in my arms. She

wrapped a fist tightly in my shirt and buried her face against my throat with a shudder.

"I got you, baby. Let's get back to the cabin and get you cleaned up before your uncle gets here."

For the first ten minutes or so that I walked down the mountain, I could hear the screams and pleadings of the bastard Mac and Taz were questioning. Hopefully they were getting some answers in between all the man's begging. Namely, getting firm confirmation that it was the mob who had come after her, so we could then go deal with them.

By the time I got back to the cabin, Silk was silent and still against me. I made my way into our bedroom and then to the bathroom. I wanted to clean up Silk and assess her injuries before the club arrived. She was mine, and therefor mine to take care of. Even if I couldn't make it official or public yet, it was the truth. And her being so still was scaring the fuck out of me.

Chapter 19

Silk

I hadn't seen Eagle in his warrior mode before today. Sure, he'd knocked out that goon back in the bank with a single punch, but I hadn't seen him do it, hadn't seen the icy look he got in his eyes. The cold way he moved and acted. Eagle had always been so warm with me, I'd been shocked to see the ice-man side of him when he'd killed that man, then carelessly tossed him aside.

Antonio's men had hit my face enough my eyes were swollen to the point I could barely see. But it was enough to witness my three guardian angels come to my rescue with blades slashing and bright, red blood flying. I didn't like the impersonal way Eagle had handled me, but I was certainly grateful they'd arrived in time to save me. Antonio had told them to get his money, then finish me. I was certain of it.

I was even more grateful Mac sent me away before they *questioned* that final man. Gah, everywhere on my body seemed to hurt. So much so, that even with Eagle being careful, I'd nearly passed out by the time we arrived back at the cabin.

When he placed me on the counter next to the sink in the bathroom, I groaned as pain shot through my torso. I wondered how many of my ribs those assholes had broken. Eagle's big, rough hands cupped my face and forced me to look into his eyes. I held my breath, not wanting to see more of the unfeeling stone-cold stare I had before. When our gazes met, I softened instantly, leaning into his palms with relief. His dark irises had warmed back to the Eagle I'd fallen for. Fuck, I loved him. I'd fallen completely in love with this beautiful man.

Sitting up on that rock, after I thrashed out the issue of my parents, I'd examined my feelings for Eagle. It hadn't taken long for me to realize the man owned me, heart and soul, already. Did he feel the same way?

I lifted my own hand, gritted my teeth against the jab of pain it caused in my side, and ran my fingertips over his face lightly.

"Thank you."

His face twisted into a frown.

"It's my fault you're hurt. I should have never let you go off alone like that. I got complacent and you were harmed. Fuck, Silk! You could have been killed!"

"I needed to be alone, Eagle. It was my choice to go out there without one of you watching my back. Antonio has been silent the entire time we've been here, and it's been weeks. None of us thought he was going to come for me." I frowned up at him. "Actually, you got there so fast, I'd assumed you had followed me. How did you know I needed help?"

"Instincts. I get this tingling up my spine whenever something is about to go to hell. I got that a split second before they tripped one of Mac's traps. We grabbed weapons and ran."

"That's one hell of an early warning system. Bet that came in handy when you were deployed."

His body stiffened at my comment, but he didn't speak.

"Sorry, didn't mean to bring up bad memories or anything. I'm just trying to say thanks for coming to save me. Again."

His lips twitched into a smile for the briefest of moments. "You really do need to stop getting into trouble. But I'll always come for you. You're my heart, woman. Do you understand what I'm saying?"

I tilted my head and blinked, trying to get my eyes to open further so I could take in his expression. His gaze had turned serious, but not in an icy way, like earlier.

"You saying you care about me?"

"It's more than that, Silk. I fucking love you. I've never loved anyone before. I didn't think I ever would. I was happy with just having my Marine brothers, until I saw you riding that bike of yours like you owned the fucking world. Now, I can't live without you. So you have to stop getting fucking kidnapped. My heart can't take it."

Tears leaked down my cheeks and emotion clogged

my throat, making it hard to talk.

"Love you, too."

He squeezed his eyes closed, then leaned in to kiss my forehead. The gesture had a wave of warmth flowing over me.

"Right, let's get you cleaned up."

He ripped the seams of my shirt so I didn't have to raise my arms. It had blood all over it anyway, so it was already ruined. The moment the material fell away from me, he started cursing.

"Not sure you're going to be able to have a shower, baby. It'll hurt too much."

I didn't say anything as he bent to the cupboard and rummaged around. I let my eyes close. My face hurt almost as much as my ribs. I jerked when a cool washcloth gently passed over my face. The cold wetness felt great, but the roughness of the cloth scraping over my raw wounds fucking hurt.

"I'm sorry, baby. I know this is stinging like a bitch but let me get the dirt off. I need to see if you need to go to the hospital."

I groaned and opened my eyes. I did not want to go to the fucking hospital.

"They punched my ribs and face, and my shoulder hurts from having my arm pinned behind me. My ribs feel like they might be broken, but my face is more of an ache. Help me take a shower. The sting from that will be less painful than that devil cloth."

The thunderous expression on his face had me leaning

away from him. He looked downright frightening. *I would not want to run into him in a dark alley looking like this.*

He shook himself before he spoke again. "Fine. Let me strip off, then I'll help get your clothes off. We need to be quick though. I do not want your uncle to catch us in the shower naked together."

I smiled, until I winced when my busted lip hurt.

"You might want to move your stuff out of our bedroom if you get time, then."

"Oh, fuck. Yeah. Good idea."

Keeping my eyes closed, I let Eagle guide me as we showered together. His hands were beyond gentle as he soaped up and rinsed off my body. I did my best to keep any wincing to myself but he knew. His cussing was a clear giveaway, so I stopped trying to hide it.

Before I knew what was happening, I was dried and lying on my bed.

"Back in a minute. Need to grab my kit."

I let my body relax against the sheets as I focused on trying to take deeper breaths. I hadn't had broken ribs before, but I'd been around enough men in the club who'd had. I'd heard them talk about how easy it was to end up with pneumonia if you didn't force yourself to breathe normally. I was completely naked but didn't have the energy to care that someone other than Eagle might come in on me. I'd hear the club arrive—the rumble of Harleys couldn't be hidden easily.

With my eyes closed I didn't hear Eagle return. I

jumped a little when he stroked my hair back.

"Can you sit up for me, baby? I've got some painkillers for you, and I want to help you put some clothes on." I tried to smile at him. Uncle Clint finding me buck-ass naked in bed wasn't going to end well. "You're breathing too well for you to have a punctured lung, so whether the ribs are cracked or broken, all we can do is ice them and give you some painkillers."

With Eagle's hand behind my back, I managed to sit on the side of the bed. I swallowed the two pills he handed me and drank the entire glass of water. Once more with Eagle's help, I stood so Eagle could help me dress in underwear, a pair of sweats and a baggy t-shirt, before he lifted me and laid me down once more.

"This is going to hurt, but I need to feel for broken bones on your cheek and jaw. I also need to tend to a couple of these cuts."

I nodded and held my breath as he poked and prodded me, then carefully put me back together with butterfly bandages.

"All done. I don't think anything's broken. Once the swelling goes down, you might want to get some x-rays, just to be sure. I'll go get some ice to put on your ribs and face."

Whatever medicine he'd given me was starting to work its magic, as my brain went fuzzy on me. I tried to nod, but had no idea if I'd managed to pull it off before I slipped into sleep.

Eagle

By the time I returned with a couple of ice packs, Silk was fast asleep. I gently placed one pack over her eyes and another over her right ribs, where the worst of the bruising had been. She didn't even flinch at the cold against her. I'd given her some fairly heavy pain meds that would make sure she slept for a good six hours, at least. Hopefully, some of the pain would have subsided by then. She'd certainly feel better if I could get the swelling on her face to go down some, so she could see properly when she woke.

Forcing myself to leave her be, I quickly shoved my stuff into my bag and headed down the hallway to Taz's room. It had two twin beds so I dumped my bag on the floor at the end before I rummaged through it to find some clean clothes. Being in nothing but a towel when Bulldog got here was not going to help my cause. I was fairly certain I was going to feel his wrath as it was. This was twice now that I'd been in charge of Silk's care when she'd been taken, or hurt. I was just hoping it would be Bulldog on his own, not the whole fucking club coming at me for a beat down. I did help save her both times. Surely that counted for something, right?

Before I could get myself too worked up, the loud rumble of Harleys filled the air. I went in to Silk to remove the ice packs and check she was still peacefully sleeping. A little of the swelling around her eyes had gone down, so hopefully by the time she woke, she'd be able to see clearly. I quickly set the timer on my watch to let me know when the packs needed to go back on. I had a feeling I was about to be distracted from watching the clock.

I opened the front door right as half the bloody club pulled up. Fuck, I was screwed. Especially since Taz and Mac weren't back yet. I kept my jaw clenched as Scout walked up the stairs. Bulldog was on his heels, along with Silk's aunt. Scout stopped and ushered the other two to go ahead of him.

Without a word, I turned and led them inside, directly to Silk's room.

"She's going to be fine. Her ribs and face are injured. I've strapped her ribs and I've had ice on them and her face. She's got another ten minutes before the ice needs to go back on. I've also given her some strong pain meds, so I doubt she'll wake up for at least another few hours."

Rose gripped my arm briefly as she passed by me into the room. At least she seemed to be on my side, although I doubted she knew I'd been part of the reason her niece had been injured in the first place. The woman let out a gasp as she dropped to her knees beside the bed. Bulldog ignored me completely as he passed me and went to his wife. I slipped into the kitchen and grabbed a chair, before returning to the bedroom.

Unsure what my welcome would be, I moved toward them and placed the chair behind Rose.

"Here's a seat for you, Rose. I need to take the others

up the mountain. Unless you need me here?"

Bulldog turned his furious gaze to me.

"Rose can take care of Silk. I'm going up that mountain with you."

I didn't bother questioning him, I knew Scout would leave at least a couple of men at the house to guard the women. I risked a glance over Silk's face and body before I turned and left. I made it out to the lounge room, which was now full of club members, all looking pissed off, before Bulldog was on me. He grabbed my shoulder and spun me around to face him.

"What the fuck were you doing when she got snatched this time? This is the second time you've let the club down. Let Silk down."

Before I could answer, his fist came at me. I could have blocked it, could have delivered a blow of my own, but I didn't. Bulldog's left hook hit me square in the jaw, but I didn't move an inch.

"I let you get that one in because I know I deserved it. You won't get another freebie, though. I don't care who you are. We've heard and seen nothing since we've been up here. None of our traps or alarms had been tripped. So, today, the day after the anniversary of her parents' death, when she wanted a little alone time, we gave it to her. The moment an alarm was triggered, we all ran for her. Thanks to our quick reactions, she'll be fine. We killed two of the three, and Taz and Mac are still up there with the third. You want to waste time here fighting me, or do you want to go see if he's dead yet?"

I had no clue how this was going to end. If the club really wanted to punish me, I'd get the beating of my life and be in worse shape than Silk. No way could I fight my way out of this many men. But I would try. For the right to be with Silk, I'd take the beating. It was how the club worked. I'd seen others receive similar treatment when they'd royally fucked up.

Scout stepped between us. "Enough. Dealing with these bastards comes first, then you can have a go at Eagle." He turned and pointed to two younger club members—no prospects had come with them. "You two stay here and guard the women. The rest of you follow us. Eagle, let's move out."

Resisting the urge to rub my aching jaw, I spun and headed out the door and up the path toward where I'd left Mac and Taz.

"We know who sent them?"

I glanced to Scout who was now beside me.

"I'm guessing they're Sabella's men. Not sure if you'll get a chance to question him. Although I guarantee you Mac will get any information he has before he kills him."

Considering Taz had already shot the bastard in the foot before I left, I was fairly certain all three men would now be dead. I knew Taz and Mac wouldn't leave the dead bodies lying out in the open to be found, so I'd guessed they were waiting for me to bring the club up to them.

Without needing to remain silent, or needing to be

careful of Silk's injuries, we arrived to the site a lot faster than I had returned from it earlier. I stood to the side to allow the others to pass me. Mac and Taz both stood on the now-bloody rock with a crumpled man between them. The bastard wasn't going to be moving on his own any time soon, but surprisingly, he was still breathing.

"Scout, if you have anything you want to know, I'd recommend making it quick. He's not got long left."

"What did he tell you?"

"Not a lot. Sabella sent them here to get the money John left Silk. Seems Sabella isn't happy with the amount he received. There also seems to be some confusion about a copy of the ledger Silk handed over. Looks to me like Sabella has a leak and the feds got a hold of at least some of its contents. Naturally, the bastard is laying the blame on Silk."

My head rung with what Mac was saying. Sabella didn't have a fucking leak. The club did. Us. We'd done this. By handing over the book to our fucking contact, we'd dumped Silk in deep shit. Of course, if Mr. Smith had done his fucking job, no one would have known they'd gotten the information from that ledger. I was done with this undercover shit. I'd never liked Mr. Smith, and this clusterfuck proved he didn't give a shit about his informants, or innocent people. I wouldn't be handing over any more of those fucking ledgers to him, that's for sure.

I was suddenly extremely grateful we'd decided to keep the existence of the other ledgers to ourselves. I held Taz's gaze for a few moments, then Mac's, and saw the same conclusion in their eyes. The FBI would be up for a fight to get anything out of any of us on anything, especially anything that affects this club or its families.

"Bulldog? You finish him. By the looks of it, you boys have worked him over, but good. He'd have told you anything he knew. Then I want them bagged and loaded. We'll put them on ice until we can deliver them back to their owner. We need to think of some way to get this fucker off Silk's back permanently."

I cleared my throat. "I've got a suggestion."

Scout came to stand in front of me as Bulldog went over and put a bullet through the downed man's skull. "Let's hear it."

"We give him the N.Y. mob's ledger. Silk doesn't want to ever go there, and you said yourself you don't want to bring their attention to us here. I'm sure Sabella could use that kind of information for his benefit, and easily make more money than whatever he thinks Silk has."

Scout crossed his arms and glared at me as he was clearly thinking it over.

"It could work. I want it copied first though, just in case the New York boys ever come looking for us."

With that, he turned back toward the mess of bodies and started giving orders to have them wrapped in the thick, black plastic some of the men had brought up with them.

"You three head down and get cleaned up and packed

up. We're heading back to Bridgewater. We've got a couple cages for these fuckers and for Silk and Rose."
I didn't like that she was being moved while injured, but I knew better than to argue. My heart sunk as I realized she'd be taken to either the clubhouse or Bulldog's place. I potentially wouldn't see her for weeks. For that reason alone, I wanted to take out Sabella.

Chapter 20

Silk

I floated out of my drug-induced haze to a world of pain.

"Eagle?"

I needed more of those painkillers, and more sleep. Maybe a week or so worth would do it.

"Shh, honey. Try not to move so much. What do you need?"

That was not Eagle's deep voice, but my aunt's.

"Water?"

My throat was dry, making it hard to speak. I wanted to know where Eagle was. If my uncle had injured him, I didn't care how much my ribs hurt, I would get up and go deal with him. A small, warm hand slid under my shoulders to help me sit up and a cold glass was pressed against my lips. I swallowed down a few mouthfuls before the glass was removed. I tried to lift my arm but Aunt Rose stopped the movement.

"I'll take it off, just lie back down first."

Once I was horizontal again, she peeled what turned out to be a wet cloth from my face. I blinked several times to clear my blurry vision and discovered I was in my room at the clubhouse. Of course, I'd been moved from my cabin back to the safety of the club. No matter how much I understood the logic of the move, I was still pissed off at having my freedom taken from me.

And my time with Eagle was also over now. Until he got patched in, I wouldn't be close to him again. And depending on what Scout believed about how I'd come to be hurt, he may not get patched in. The club could easily blame the three men for my being left alone to be hurt. That wouldn't end well for Eagle, Taz and Mac. Not at all.

I looked over to Aunt Rose. "Where is he?"

She winced. "I'm not entirely sure. Scout and your uncle are not happy with him for leaving you alone like he did. He's been in charge of your security twice now when you've been taken or attacked. The club isn't going to just let that go, no matter how you feel about it."

"It wasn't his fault. Maybe if I talk to Scout? Tell him how I ended up alone?"

My Aunt's gaze ran over me, seeing way too much.

"You really like this man?"

"I love him. If he had his top rocker, I'd already be his old lady."

She sighed heavily. "I thought as much. I'll go get Scout, but I'm not sure you can change what is going to happen. If it hasn't happened already."

"How long has it been since the attack?"

"Two days, honey. You've woken a few times, but

we've kept you on pain meds so you could sleep through the worst of the pain."

Two days later and it still hurt this much? I hated to think how much pain I'd have been in if I hadn't been drugged up. Aunt Rose left to get Scout and I stared up at the ceiling and tried to plan out what the fuck I was going to say to try to convince him Eagle didn't need to be beaten.

"Hey there, sugar. You feeling any better?"

I turned to face the club President, a man who'd always been there for me since the day I arrived, fifteen years ago.

"Hey Scout, I've been better. I wanted to ask you about Eagle."

He closed the door and moved to sit in the chair where Aunt Rose had sat earlier.

"Yeah, your aunt told me that. You know I can't discuss club business with you."

"You can if it affects me. And any punishment Eagle gets over this *will* affect me."

He sighed in much the same way as my aunt had. What was with that?

"He's failed as your guard twice now, Silk. We can't let that go. You know that."

"Are you going to refuse him a top rocker?"

Scout was silent as we stared at each other for a minute or two. "He takes his punishment without complaint, without passing out too quickly, he gets a clean slate."

"Passing out? What the fuck is the punishment?"

I tried to sit up but Scout held my shoulder down with his large palm.

"That, I won't tell you. Club business is not any concern of yours. We all know you two are feeling each other, but if he fails this? He's out and you'll not be allowed to see him. He needs to atone and prove he's serious about being part of the club and about being your old man."

A growl slipped out before I could call it back. I was in the clubhouse and speaking with the President. I needed to stay respectful. But I was struggling.

"Sorry, Scout, but I fail to understand why he needs to atone for anything. He saved me three days ago. If it wasn't for his instincts and Mac's alarms, they wouldn't have found me until it was too late. Those men weren't going to let me walk away."

Scout took my hand between his palms. "Don't growl at me again, girl. And pointing out how close you came to being killed is not going to help your boy. He should have followed you and kept watch the entire time you were out of the house."

I wanted to growl again, to rant and rave, but the serious, stubborn look on Scout's face told me all I needed to know. He wasn't going to change his mind.

"Can you tell me when you plan on delivering this mysterious punishment at least? And what about Taz and Mac?"

"Eagle has chosen to take the punishment for all three

of them. Taz and Mac were following his lead on this occasion, so the fault lies with Eagle. And I can't tell you when, but by the time you're back on your feet, he will be too. Assuming he passes."

At that I glared. He was pushing me to a point where I was about to not care I was in the clubhouse.

"I'm not happy with you right now. Really not happy."

The bastard had the gall to smirk at me. "I get that, sugar. I really do. But you're important to all of us here at the club and any man who wants you for his old lady better be strong enough, and brave enough, to stand up for you."

With that he stood, kissed the top of my head and turned to leave.

"I'll send your aunt back in with some food. You need to start eating now that you're awake."

I stayed silent as he left my room. What could I say? There was nothing I could do to prevent what was going to happen to Eagle, if it hadn't already gone down. Fuck! I wanted to throw things, vent some of this anger and frustration, but even raising my hand slowly had my ribs letting me know they didn't like the plan. No way did I have the ability to trash my room. And what good would it do anyway? Scout had condoned whatever the fuck was going to happen, and no one could over-ride that.

Minutes later, it wasn't my aunt that came in but my uncle.

"Hey darlin', good to see you really awake."

"Really awake? As opposed to what? Pretend awake?"

Yeah, I was being a bitch but just at the moment I really didn't care. Uncle Clint clearly didn't take my tone to heart as he chuckled and came to sit by me with a bowl of mac and cheese.

"You've been in and out of it for days. We've gotten a little soup into you, along with pain meds, but you weren't with it enough to have a conversation. Or to bitch anyone out."

"Don't suppose you could talk to Scout?"

His expression grew serious. "Eagle knows he deserves what he's going to get. There's nothing you can do to change that course."

"It's bullshit. You know it is. We were at the cabin for a full week with no sign of anyone. Want someone to blame? Blame me. What's the only way they could have known where I was?"

He winced and moved in the chair. "They put a tracker on your phone."

"So who's at fault? Me. I'm the stupid one who kept my phone without even thinking to check it over. I had it turned off until that morning. I'm sure if I asked one of the boys to look over it, they would have found the tracker. But I didn't even think about it. And before you say they should have, they didn't know that Antonio had taken my phone from me in the first place."

He filled a spoon with the gooey mac and cheese. "Well, I sure as shit ain't letting you go through what

He's about to go through

he's about to go through, so just accept the beating you already got as punishment and shut up and eat."

Shaking my head, I accepted defeat and opened my mouth to be fed like a fucking toddler. How long did it take for ribs to heal again? I think Eagle had said something about it being three to five weeks. Fuck. I probably wouldn't see him again until after I was healed.

It was going to be a long fucking month without seeing him every day. Especially knowing he was going to be hurt. At least he had Taz and Mac. I knew without a doubt both of those men would take care of him.

Eagle
"Are you fucking nuts?"

I glanced over to Taz after I threw back a shot of whiskey.

"Why should all three of us go down for this? I was in charge, and I fucked up. Club rules. I'll survive it, then we'll all patch in and it'll all be behind us. And I'll get the girl."

Mac shook his head at me. "You know we're more than capable of handling our own punishment? There is no need for you to take on three times what you should have to."

I laughed. "Read between the lines, brother. This shit has nothing to do with what happened up on that mountain and you know it. Sure, the club's pissed Silk got hurt. But they're more pissed that a prospect has come in and taken a Daughter of the Club for himself. Just because we haven't stepped over any public line, doesn't change the fact that everyone knows what's going on between us. Scout and Bulldog, along with everyone else, know full well the moment I get my top rocker, I'll be claiming that woman. This beat down? It's more about me proving I'm willing to step up for Silk. And I am. Fuck, I'm a Marine! These boys won't break me."

"Well, at least half these boys are ex-military so they may well fucking break at least some of you."

"Taz, you're not funny, man."

"Wasn't trying to be, mate."

He put another shot in front of me and I threw it back. Hopefully with my mind half-buzzed I'd not feel the blows so much.

"That's enough. Don't want you falling down drunk before they even land a punch. And whatever they manage to break, we'll take care of you, 'k?"

"Yeah, I know, Mac. Fuck, wish it was Silk but she's going to be flat out trying to get better herself for a good while yet. Last thing she needs is to know I'm fucked up too."

Mac gave me a nod. "She knows. That girl's spent too long around the club. No way she didn't work out you've got some pain coming your way."

Taz took over. "Knowing Silk, she's tried to convince them to leave you alone."

"I did see Rose come down and send Scout up there yesterday. I didn't even think of her trying to save my ass."

Fuck, she was one in a million. I had to survive this shit for her. A whisper of sound alerted me to someone coming up from the basement, and I froze, waiting for what I knew was coming.

"You ready, Eagle?"

I took a deep breath, held each of my brothers' gazes for a moment then turned to stand, facing Scout.

"Yeah, let's get this shit over with. Just to be clear, Mac and Taz are clear of punishment right?"

Scout shook his head a little. "Yeah, you crazy fucker. You're taking all the hits on this one." Scout looked over my shoulder. "You two stay up here. Either of you try to get downstairs, it's not going to end well for you. I'm leaving six men up here to keep guard on the clubhouse, and to make sure you don't try anything."

He rattled off the names, but I wasn't listening. I was too busy taking in each of the men who stood behind Scout. The ones who were going to be laying into me real soon. Looked to be about a dozen men. I should probably be grateful Scout hadn't called in the whole fucking club.

With a head tilt from Scout, we were off toward the basement. I hadn't been down there before, but could take a guess at what I'd find there. I rolled my shoulders as we marched down the stairs. It rather felt like I was heading to the gallows. I glanced at the men around me. They looked serious, but not 'I'm about to kill someone' serious. Thankfully.

I was led into a room with Scout, Bulldog, Keys, Arrow and Nitro. The hierarchy of the club were all here. Fuck. The others stayed out in the hallway and the door was closed. There was a single bulb hanging in the center of the space. I was surrounded by concrete, and the floor had a drain in the center. Yeah, only one reason they had this room. I winced. This shit was going to hurt like a motherfucker.

"You know why you're here?"

Scout's voice was deeper than usual, and a little more gravelly.

"Twice, I've been in charge of Silk's security when she's been taken or hurt. I also suspect this is more about the fact you all know that I want her for my old lady."

Because they knew full well it didn't matter how closely Silk was being watched, the mob would have gotten to her eventually. And that first time was on them, not me. If they'd told me sooner who was after her, I'd have been by her side, not standing out in front of the damn shop. The shit at the cabin was on me, though. I'd been kicking my own ass from the moment it happened. We'd all gotten complacent after a full week with no sign of anyone.

Bulldog stepped forward with a growl. "You ain't good enough for our girl."

"She's no girl, and I may not be good enough, but thankfully, she doesn't seem to care. Once I'm patched in, and have claimed her, you better stop withholding information from me that I need to make sure she's always protected. If I had known who was after her earlier, I would have had someone standing beside her twenty-four/seven, instead of just me at the door of the shop. And tell me, did you get word that they were coming after her again this last week?"

Bulldog's expression tightened and his fists clenched.

"Yeah, I thought so. If you'd given me a heads-up, she wouldn't have been allowed to leave the damn cabin at all, let alone by herself. You tied my hands behind my back, and now you're fucking pissed I didn't keep her safe. Don't you think that information would have been fucking helpful? You think I like that she's lying up there with fucked-up ribs and face because I wasn't there? And if my instincts hadn't kicked in, if me and my boys didn't have the skills we had, Silk wouldn't by lying upstairs at all, would she? She'd be fucking dead. All because you assholes didn't want to share club business with a fucking prospect. If anyone deserves a beat down over this shit, it's you five. Not me."

I paused to roll my shoulders and take a deep breath. I was angry and spouting off, but I wasn't about to be put through this shit for something I didn't fucking do.

"And you all know it. So, like I said before, I suspect this has more to do with me proving my worth to have Silk once you see fit to give me my top rocker. Tell me, am I allowed to fight back, or am I supposed to stand here and take the licks without raising so much as a finger?"

Scout spoke up again. "You can fight back. No killing anyone. I know you Marines are trained well, but I don't want anyone dying here today. Nor do I want half my club out with fucking broken bones. We still need to deal with Sabella, and we can't do that with a bunch of crippled men. After this is over, we'll discuss changing what we tell prospects in the future, especially when it comes to security issues."

With a nod, I fell back into a fighter's stance. Naturally, Bulldog was the first one to come at me with a fist flying toward my jaw. I jerked out of the way and delivered a blow to his stomach.

"Told you I'd only let you get that one free shot in."

Bulldog wheezed and stumbled back, but it only took him a moment to collect himself and come back at me. This time it wasn't just him. Obviously, the others had been waiting for Bulldog to start things. I caught sight of Scout moving to open the door as the other four all came at me at once. Every one of these bastards was big and they all knew how to pack a punch. I did what I could to avoid hits and throw out a few of my own, but it was useless, and before long I was pinned up against the wall, my arms being held against the rough concrete as the men all took their turns at me. I got a few good kicks in, taking down a couple of the lower-ranked members. Unfortunately, I couldn't keep it up. Not with my upper body taking blow after blow.

The third time I turned my head to spit out a mouthful of blood, my head swam and black spots invaded. Fuck. I was going to pass out. I tried every mental trick I knew to stay alert, to block out the pain. Then Bulldog filled my vision and this time, there was no avoiding his fist. My head jerked to the side and stars filled my vision before it went black.

Chapter 21

Silk

As soon as I could sit up comfortably, I started sketching.
I knew Eagle had gone through his punishment, but no
one would tell me anything. Like what condition he was
in, or even where the fuck he was. My mind was whirling
with the worst-case scenarios. Although, if he'd been
killed surely they'd tell me that? And no way would Mac
and Taz still be hanging around if that happened. I'd only
been downstairs a couple of times. It still hurt if I moved
too much and stairs were not my friend. But when I had
gone down yesterday, Taz had been behind the bar and
Mac on the front door.

Shaking my head, I focused back on my sketchbook.
I'd nearly finished Eagle's tattoo. I was beyond happy
with how it looked. I hoped he liked it. And I hoped I'd
get a chance to at least show him the design. I'd be gutted
if I couldn't ink it on him myself, but I had no idea if the
club would even allow him to be in the same room as me,
let alone allow me to have my hands on him. A flash of
heat went through me as I remembered him agreeing to

let me pierce his nipple—so long as I did it naked.

With a growl at myself, I tossed my pad and pen aside. There was no point in pining for something that was never going to happen. I was finding it hard enough to even sleep without his hard, warm body wrapped around mine. Spending my waking hours dreaming of him was going to send me crazy.

I carefully slipped from the bed and put on my flats before I headed out. By the time I reached the bottom of the stairs, I had to rest against the wall for a minute to catch my breath. It still hurt to take deep breaths. *Stupid fucking ribs.*

"Whoa, luv. What are you doing up and around on your own?"

I glared as Taz all but dragged me to a chair.

"Gee, I don't know. Maybe the fact I'm a grown fucking woman has something to do with it."

Bastard chuckled at me as he went and got me a bottle of water.

"Here, drink some of this, then I'll help you down to the kitchen. I assume that's where you were heading?"

The way he looked at me had me pausing. "Where is he?"

"I have no idea who you're talking about."

I went to stand so I could get in his face, but he laid a hand on my shoulder, keeping me seated.

"You know exactly who I'm talking about! I know something happened, and I know I haven't seen him in a fucking week. But no one will tell me anything! But you know, don't you?"

He lifted his hand from my shoulder and tucked my hair behind my ear. "Club business, luv. You know I can't tell you."

"Give me something. Anything."

My voice had gone whisper quiet and I winced at how desperate I sounded.

"You know how close we are to him. You know we'd never leave him unguarded."

With that he turned and left. I sat there for a full minute, waiting for my brain to jump into fucking gear. Then, with a burst of light I understood. Eagle was here. At the clubhouse. Mac and Taz would never leave him, especially if he was injured. Suddenly, I didn't feel like eating anymore. I recapped my bottle of water and made my way to the bottom of the stairs. Fuck, I just got down these bastards and now I was going to have to get back up them!

It probably took me ten minutes, and I had to stop several times, but I made it back up to the upper level. Which bedroom had Eagle used last time? Unless they lived here, the prospects didn't get their own room until after they patched in, but generally speaking, they tended to use the same one each time they stayed here. I took another drink of water before I started down the hallway. The prospect rooms were all the way in the back and I was out of breath by the time I'd made it to them. I went down there, where Eagle had stayed before, and tried the handle. Unlocked, the door swung in silently and revealed Eagle's battered body. With a quiet gasp, I stepped in and closed the door behind me.

"Oh, Eagle. What did they do to you?"

Fury at my uncle and the club rolled through me, making my body vibrate with rage. How dare they? His chest moved with his breathing but other than that, he was unnaturally still. I'd never seen him like this. Like a doll. *A broken doll.*

I crept closer, not wanting to wake him, but needing to be near him, I tried to not make a sound as I approached the bed. When I got to the side and sat on the chair that was there, his head rolled toward me. His eyes stayed shut as he slurred my name in his sleep.

"Shhh, babe. I'm here. Go back to sleep. You'll feel better when you wake."

I stroked his face until his breathing evened out again. Blinking away tears, I fled his room. Ignoring the pain of my ribs, I rushed back to my own room and got behind the solid door before I let my tears flow. I hated the Charons in that moment. I'd always loved this club, loved being a part of the Charon MC family. But now, I wished I'd never heard the name. If I wasn't a Daughter of the Club, Eagle wouldn't have been beaten for simply fucking caring about me.

Anger fueled my actions. I quickly wiped my face and went back out, easily making it down the stairs this time. The ache in my ribs was nothing compared to the righteous fury blazing in my veins. I went from room to room, looking for someone high enough up the food chain to vent my anger on. My uncle was the unfortunate one I found first.

"How fucking dare you!"

He'd been facing away from me in his office, working on something. But he rose and spun at my voice.

"What are you doing up?"

I stormed over to stand before him, wrapping an arm around my injured ribs as the pain got too much to ignore completely.

"What do you think? No one would tell me a thing, so I went to investigate myself."

His face dropped. "You went looking for Eagle. I told you to stay out of it."

"Yeah, yeah. Club business isn't my business. Well, fuck that. If this is how the man I chose is going to be treated, I'm leaving the damn club. Because he cares about me, he gets beaten to within an inch of his life? How is that fair? It's not. It's fucked up beyond belief!"

I reached out and took my uncle's right hand, examining his busted knuckles. "By the looks of it, you were the main one behind it all." I shook my head as I dropped his hand. "My father left me more than enough cash to clear my debt to the club for Silky Ink. I'll go get it for you, then I'm out of here. I'm done with this fucking club and its fucked-up politics."

I turned to leave, limping now the adrenaline from my anger had worn off.

"Silk! Wait! You can't just walk out of here like this. We're your family. We did this for you."

I turned to face him again. "For me? You think I'd want the man I love beaten up because he fucking cares about me? Because, even though you didn't tell him shit, he still saved me? Twice."

"You can't love a man you don't know, Silk. He needed to prove himself to the club, that he was worthy of you."

"What? Because I can't decide that for myself?" I shook my head again, suddenly feeling drained and tired. "I'll take Mac with me, but he's not wearing his fucking cut though. I'm serious. I'm done with this club. You'd better make sure he's been told everything you know about what you've heard from the mob, because that's why I was hurt. I might not know exactly what went on behind the scenes, but I'm fairly certain the club's fucked-up need to keep club business from prospects meant Eagle was fighting fucking blind, trying to keep me safe."

Uncle Clint opened his mouth to speak but I cut him off. "I'm done with this shit."

I left the room before he could say another word. I made it to the bar before I collapsed against the wall. Once more, Taz was there.

"Whoa, you really gotta stop pushing yourself so hard."

"Take me up to my room?"

He eyed me, then glanced over my shoulder down the hall before he replied. "Sure, luv."

He lifted me easily and carried me up the stairs.

"Want to tell me what's going on?"

"I'm leaving."

"I don't think that's a good idea, Silk. Sabella is still gunning for you."

Taz set me on the edge of my bed.

"I'm leaving here and the club. I told my uncle I'd take Mac with me, but he's not to wear his colors. You need to stay here to take care of Eagle. This is total bullshit and I'm not going to fucking sit here and take it."

Taz gave me a small smile. "You really do love him, huh?"

I rubbed a hand over the back of my neck, wincing as my ribs let me know they didn't like the idea.

"You already know the answer to that. Can you grab my bag for me? The one I had at the cabin."

He snatched it up and placed it next to me on the bed. I reached in and pulled out four rolls of cash, forty grand. I owed the club thirty-six thousand on Silky Ink, so this would more than cover it.

"Want to help a girl pack?"

"Sure, sweetheart."

With Taz helping me, I had all my personal stuff packed, and was ready to go before long. I held my cut and the cash, and Taz took my two bags, now heavy with all my things.

"Lead the way."

We'd been up here probably twenty minutes, so I knew my uncle would have called Scout in on me by now. But I wasn't going to back down. I was out of this shit for good. Hopefully, Eagle would join me once he was well enough to.

Mac

What a complete clusterfuck. It had been a predictable one, but one nonetheless frustrating. How did Bulldog think Silk was going to handle having her man fucking beaten bloody for basically no other reason than caring about her?

At least she'd agreed to take me with her. The mob was still after her ass, so if she just walked out the door she'd be dead in under a day. So, that left me standing at the bar with Scout and Bulldog, finally being told everything they knew about the fuckers after her.

"You telling me it's not only the mob after her but the Iron Hammers are on her case too? How did they know about the box?"

Scout gave me a fierce stare. "When was the last time you saw Runt?"

My body stiffened. "You shitting me? He went to them?"

"Turns out he was always one of theirs. Well, he wanted to be. Spying on us was his way of earning his colors down there. We locked those ledgers and other shit up fast, so he didn't get copies of anything, but he'd heard what we found in that box and reported it back to them."

I focused on what he wasn't telling me. "And where is Runt now?"

"Roughing up Eagle was just the entree."

Fuck. They'd beaten him, probably to death. It wasn't a huge surprise. The Charons certainly weren't one of the roughest MCs around, but they wouldn't stand for being fucked over like that either.

"Speaking of Eagle. Where does he stand with you now?"

I didn't include Taz and me in that question, but Scout knew we were a package deal.

"He handled his punishment as a Charon should. We're good. As soon as he's back on his feet, he'll get his top rocker. Maybe after that he can get Silk to quit fucking around and come back home too."

Okay, maybe he didn't get that we would stick together.

"Taz and me? Where are we left in all this?"

"You keep Silk protected, you'll get your patch soon enough. Same with Taz. Once Eagle's back on his feet, we'll cycle you and Taz on her, since I'm guessing Taz won't leave the clubhouse while Eagle's still out of it."

"Of course."

I was getting a little sick of having our top rockers held over our heads all the damn time, but considering we were still months off being here a full year, we couldn't complain too much. In any case, Silk coming down the stairs looking pale, but determined, ended our conversation.

She went directly to Scout, ignoring her uncle, and shoved her cut and four rolls of cash against his chest, forcing him to take the load before it hit the floor.

"That more than clears the debt on Silky Ink. I'm out."

"Don't do this, Silk. We're your family."

"Family does not beat the shit out of each other."

"This one does. Always has. You know that. Eagle made it through. As soon as he can stand for more than thirty fucking seconds, he'll get his top rocker. You don't need to leave."

She shook her head. "Yeah, I do. I'm not going over it all again. Bulldog can fill you in. I'm leaving."

She turned and walked toward the front door, leaving shocked silence in her wake. I'd never heard her call her uncle Bulldog before, at least not when the entire club wasn't hanging around, and by the look of stunned pain on the man's face, he hadn't either.

"Fuck me. Mac, go with her. And put her ass in a cage. She can't ride her fucking bike with busted ribs."

I spun and strode after her, Taz on my heels with her bags.

"This is one fucked-up situation, mate."

"Sure is. Sadly, it was one I saw coming. No way Silk was going to handle having Eagle worked over like that."

"I'm with her on this one. It was more the club's fault than Eagle's. They withheld vital information from him. What the fuck did they expect to happen?"

"No fucking clue, brother. But I need to catch her before she finds her fucking bike."

I could just see her riding off into the sunset like some fucking warrior princess. Then wrecking her bike because she'd jerk when her ribs jolted her with pain.

"Silk! We need to take a cage. You can't ride your bike with busted ribs!"

Thankfully, she stopped and when I got to her I took her face in my palms. "Slow down a moment and think. You know Eagle is going to come for you the second he's able to. Getting yourself killed won't help anything. Let me drive you home, and when your ribs heal enough for you to ride, I'll bring your bike to you. Okay?"

Her eyes filled with tears, but she didn't let a single one fall.

"My entire family betrayed me. The first time I've cared about a man, and they have him beaten."

"I don't suppose you got a good look at your uncle and the others? Eagle got more than a few shots in. Hell, three of the ones who went after him are in worse condition than he is and he did that after they pinned his arms down. Your man's a Marine, darlin'. He can hold his own. And he thought you were worth it. Don't make it all for nothing."

Her jaw tightened, but she didn't speak, just turned and got in the nearest vehicle. Taz dumped her bags in the trunk before saying a quick goodbye to her.

"Good luck, mate."

Yeah, I'm going to need it with the way Silk was acting. Who knew what shit she'd try to pull with this little rebellion of hers. I was fairly certain she'd want to come back to the club once she calmed down. But would she be able to push past her pride to do it?

Chapter 22

Eagle

It was a full week after my punishment before Scout finally gave me permission to leave the clubhouse. I was getting ready to head out when he'd come into my room fifteen minutes ago.

"You come to church before you leave. Be down there in half hour."

I didn't argue. I was going to see my girl today. Nothing was going to stop me. Mac was with her today—Taz and he had been taking it in turns. I grinned as I thought about how she'd thrown down for me. Silk had walked away from the only family she had, because she couldn't stand the thought that they'd hurt me. Guess that was as public a declaration as she could make about her feelings toward me. No way could Bulldog not understand that one.

Pulling on my cut, I made my way out of the room. My ribs still ached a little and my left knee didn't always bend quite right. But I was certain nothing was broken beyond repair, and I'd be all healed up in no time. I met up with Taz at the bottom of the stairs and headed down to the meeting room. We'd only been in church once before, twice if you counted the time we came here with those boxes. Prospects didn't normally get included, so yeah, I was a little nervous about what the fuck this was all about. Especially when I saw Mac sitting in the room.

"Who the fuck is watching Silk?"

The room went silent and all eyes turned to me. I didn't give a shit if I'd just broken a bunch of rules. If Silk was out there alone, I was out of here.

"Settle down. Nitro and Tiny are watching her."

Scout spoke as he walked past me, to the front of the room where he calmly sat at the center of the table. I followed Taz to sit beside Mac.

"Either of you know what this is about?"

Taz shrugged and Mac had a gleam in his eye, like he knew but wasn't going to share.

"Bastard. You fit right in here don't you? Knowing shit and not sharing it."

He laughed. "Aren't you in a peachy mood today? Thought you'd be all happy and shit that you're going to be seeing Silk soon."

"Once I see her, I'll be fucking ecstatic. Until then, I'm going to be pissed at everything that makes it so I'm not already with her."

"Wow. So this is how you're going to be from now on. Kind of glad I've been hanging out with her for most of the week, rather than you. At least she tried to pretend to be normal around me."

The bang of the hammer on the table thankfully ended that conversation.

"Short meeting this morning, as I know some of us have places we'd rather be." Bastard smirked at me. "Eagle, Mac and Taz, get your asses up here, boys."

I got to my feet first, and strolled up there. Could this really be about our patches? Finally.

"Everyone here knows what's been going on lately, so there's no need to recap it all. But we all agree, you've all more than earned your top rockers. Welcome to the Charon MC, boys. You're all officially one of us now."

I watched a little in shock, as Scout, Bulldog and Keys all squirted a ton of super glue on the back of a patch each. Bulldog came for me, spun me around and slapped the rocker across the top of my cut. Then he spun me back.

"You did good. And you've more than proven you're good enough for my girl. Your next job is to bring the stubborn woman back here, where she belongs."

He turned to grab a cut off the table, but before he could speak again, Scout broke in. "Yeah, Rose has him in the doghouse for running her off. I'm sure he'd like you to be quick about bringing her back. And you three need to go see her about getting your ink done too. Show anyone at her shop your top rocker and they'll look after you."

Bulldog handed a cut to me. "Here's her cut. We've added a patch to it. Bring her back. I miss my girl, and not just because Rose is pissed at me over it."

I held out the cut and grinned. "'Property of Eagle', I like it."

The patch was on the back, above the club insignia. A top rocker with 'Property Of' on one line and 'Eagle' underneath on the bottom rocker. Fuck, I hope she'd accept it. What if she really didn't want to come back into the club? The place had grown on me and I wanted to be a part of it.

A hard slap on my back brought my attention back to the room.

"Don't worry so much. She'll accept you, and the club. At this point, it's her pride stopping her from coming back. She knows how we work, beat downs are nothing new to her. She's just got her panties in a twist because it was you." Scout turned from me to address the room. "Let the party begin! Taz, you might even find that we've had a couple new girls join us. Try to let the others have some pussy too. You don't need it all for yourself, brother."

With a chorus of laughter, the meeting broke up and everyone made their way out. Mac was tight on my heels.

"You staying to party?"

"Not yet. I'm going to have your back until you and Silk get back here. Then, we'll party. I'm sure Taz will do enough fucking damage for all of us in the meantime."

I grinned. "I'm sure he will. Well, come on then, let's go get my girl."

I loaded Silk's cut into my saddle bag and slid onto

the seat of my Harley.

"Damn, I missed this."

I ran my hands over the bike for a second before I started her up. The rumble beneath me had me feeling instantly alive.

I was on my way to get my girl, and I might even let her do that piercing she'd wanted to do. I groaned as my cock sprung to life. Just fucking great. Now I had to ride with a fucking hard-on. Gunning the engine, I took off toward her shop. I pulled up out front, and Mac slid his bike in beside mine. Tiny was on the front door and grinned when he saw us.

"Congratulations, boys. Finally got your top rockers. Prez told me you were on your way, so I had Gabs make sure she's free for you."

Mac stayed with Tiny as I pushed through the front door into the shop, Silk's cut in my fist. Gabs was leaning against the front counter, working on a sketch. When she looked up and caught sight of me she had a gleam in her eye.

"She's back in the piercing room, getting prepped."

Heat raced over my cheeks. "How the fuck do you know about that?"

The woman shrugged. "We're roommates, and the woman talks in her sleep. A lot, lately. Have fun!"

Refusing to rise to the bait, I didn't say a word as I moved toward the back, where the closed-off piercing room was located. I didn't knock, but entered and closed the door behind me in silence. Silk was hunched over the tray of implements when I flipped the lock, the quiet sound alerting her to my presence. With a gasp, she jerked around, and the fear in her gaze hit me like a blow.

"Hey, baby. It's just me. Fuck. Don't be scared."

Fuck, I was a bastard. Of course, she'd be afraid if someone snuck up on her here where she'd been snatched before. I dropped her cut on the chair on my way over to her. She stood still with a hand over her heart.

"What are you doing here?"

I pulled her against me. "Don't you dare try to act like you don't know. Scout had me on lockdown until this morning, I got my top rocker twenty minutes ago and now I'm here to claim my woman. I promise, I came as soon as I could."

She scared the shit out of me when, for about a minute and a half, she held herself stiff and away from me. Then she softened against me and my heart started beating again. Wrapping her arms around my neck, she lifted her face to me. I didn't wait. I lowered my mouth to cover hers and drank her in. Fuck, I'd missed her so much.

Silk

Eagle was really here. This was real, and not a dream. I ran my fingers through his hair and fisted it tightly to hold him to me as he devoured my mouth. A deep moan made its way up my throat, and I loosened my hold when he pulled away a fraction.

"I thought I'd lost you and the club. It's been a week."

He cupped a palm around my face.

"Never. You'll never lose me, Silk. And the club has instructed me to bring you home. You've lost nothing. Well, except maybe a little of your pride."

Heat crept over my cheeks. "I kinda lost my temper when I saw you all beat to shit."

He gave me a lop-sided grin. "I got that impression. I wished you hadn't seen me like that, though. You weren't supposed to."

"What? So you get to see me all beaten to shit, but I can't see you when it's you all bruised up?"

I chuckled when he shook his head. "Two completely different situations, baby. And you know it." He sighed and stroked my face with his fingertips. "The club brothers are like any brothers—they solve their issues with their fists. Not that I was raised with blood brothers, but from what I've seen and experienced in the Marines and now with the Charons, beating the shit out of each other seems to be the way it goes. And it got me permission to have you, so it was totally worth it."

"Yeah, I know that. I've been watching them beat the shit out of each other for fifteen years. I guess I've never cared about anyone they've laid into before." I paused and gave him a sly smile as I pulled from his grip. "And now, here you are with a piercing appointment."

He frowned at me. "Gabs made this appointment for me without any request from me. Apparently, you talk in your sleep, baby."

"Oh, fuck." I put a hand over my mouth to muffle my laugh. "Oops."

He pulled his cut from his shoulders, and when he lifted his tight, black shirt up, my insides melted. Damn, but he really was one well-put together male.

"Strip, Silk."

He piled his clothes on the chair by the door, left there for that reason. He toed off his boots and popped the top button on his jeans before he made his way over to the piercing chair and hopped up on it.

I stood like an idiot, watching the way his muscles rippled as he moved until he cleared his throat and raised an eyebrow at me. I swallowed. Was I really going to do this? I went to double-check the door was locked before I began undressing. I was. I was totally going to pierce his nipple naked, then ride him to climax. My pussy clenched at the thought.

I turned to face him as I unclipped my bra and let it fall down my arms. His eyes had darkened with heat and he licked his lips when I slipped a thumb in each side of my panties and pulled them down. Naked as the day I was born, I padded across the tiles to him.

"So, which side?"

I pulled the wheeled table over and climbed up to straddle his waist, leaning in to lick each nipple, earning me a hiss. Fuck, how I missed his taste.

"I have no fucking idea. What side do guys normally get done?"

"Normally it's the left, or you could go with both. You know, same as me."

His hands were on the nipples in question in a flash and I shuddered over him as he expertly tugged and twisted them.

"Keep teasing me, and we'll have to fuck before you get a needle anywhere near my skin."

I leaned in and kissed him deeply until he was groaning. Then, quickly, I swung off him and grabbed a pair of gloves.

"Nope. The deal was you got some metal first, then we fuck."

I grabbed the sterile wipe and ripped the packet open.

"So, we going with the left or both?"

"Just the left, Silk."

"Baby."

He smirked. "Nope, but if you want to do the other one, we get to repeat this process some other time."

I laughed as I wiped him down. "So kinky. Now, lie still and let me work."

He stopped joking and let his body relax against the leather chair as I got the clamp and moved to start the process. My mind clicked into work mode and I forgot I was buck-ass naked as I expertly slid the needle, then the barbell through his nipple. Tossing the clamps on the tray, I picked up the ball and quickly screwed it in place.

"Done! And you didn't even flinch. Such a good little Marine."

I grabbed another wipe to clean up the area around the

new metal and moved a couple steps away to toss it in the bin when I was done. By the time I turned back, Eagle was on his feet and prowling toward me.

"Now, for the next part of the deal. Turn around and put your palms on the wall, Silk."

Fuck, the way he purred instructions had me wet. He clearly got that he'd melted my mind as he took my shoulders and turned me himself. I lifted my palms to cover my breasts on a gasp. How could I have forgotten this room had a fucking mirror wall? Normally clients liked to see their ink or metal as soon as it was done, and it had just become a part of the room so I forgot the damn thing was here. Clearly, Eagle had gotten some ideas when he saw the thing.

He pulled my hands from my breasts and pressed them against the cool mirror.

"Don't ever hide from me, Silk. I adore every inch of you."

He stepped back and peeled his jeans and boxers down his muscled legs. I rubbed my thighs together at the sight he made. He gave my butt a slap.

"Quit trying to get yourself off, baby. That's what I'm here for."

He rolled a condom down his length, then he was spreading my thighs and tilting my pelvis back.

"Watch me take you, Silk. See how fucking good we look together?"

He slid his hard cock in deep on one thrust and I threw my head back as I bit my lip to stop from crying out. The walls in this place weren't that thick. Another slap on my ass had me refocusing on the mirror.

"Eyes back on us, Silk."

His large hands gripped each of my hips, his darker skin tone standing out against my white and inked flesh. I pushed back with every thrust he made, and before long I was whimpering with how close my orgasm was. Releasing my hips, one hand trailed up to my breasts, where he plucked and teased my piercings while his other slid to my clit where he pinched down and sent me spiraling. His hand left my breast and clapped over my mouth as his thrusts turned fast and furious. His cock pulsed inside me and I clamped down on him as he sunk his teeth into my shoulder to muffle his own shout.

Warm arms wrapped around my waist as Eagle pulled me back against him. I wrapped an arm up around his neck to mess with his hair.

"I missed you, Silk. Don't ever run off like that again."

"I've missed you too, so fucking much. Don't get yourself in enough trouble to get a club beat down again, and I won't have to run off when I lose my temper."

I went to lift my other hand up but my ribs tweaked, making me wince. Eagle pulled from my body and lifted me onto the piercing chair.

"Fuck, sorry Silk. How are your ribs? The bruising is fading out nicely."

"I went to the docs the day after I left the clubhouse. They weren't broken, just bruised, so they're pretty much healed. I just can't lift that arm above my head yet. I forget that on occasion."

He pressed a chaste kiss to my lips before he moved over to the pile of clothes.

"We'd better get dressed and back to the clubhouse. There's one hell of a party going on to celebrate us three patching in, and if we don't get back soon, Mac won't get any action because Taz will have done the rounds already."

I chuckled as I slipped from the seat and began to dress. "That man has quite the appetite, from what I've heard. Someone might want to suggest to Scout the club gets more girls to keep up with him. Actually, considering how many girls he runs through, how the hell did he cope up at the cabin for so long?"

"He might like sex—a lot—but he doesn't need it. He can go without just fine, he just prefers not to. And trust me, he's been making up for his dry spell all week."

Once we were dressed, Eagle paused with a bunch of leather in his fist.

"Will you wear my patch, Silk? Walk into the club with me tonight as my old lady?"

A lump formed in my throat at how vulnerable Eagle looked in that moment. Did he really doubt how I felt for him?

I walked up and took the cut from his hands and looked it over. It was the cut I'd left with Scout, but now it had a 'Property of' top rocker and 'Eagle' on the bottom one, and on the front, just below my Daughter of the Club patch, was another smaller 'Property of Eagle' patch. A wide grin stretched my lips as I slid the leather vest on.

"Of course I will, Eagle. I always will."

He pulled me in against him and kissed me until my head spun.

"I'm going to hold you to that. Now, let's get out of here."

Taking his hand, I unlocked the door and led him out the front to be greeted by cheers and wolf whistles from Mac, Tiny, Nitro, Gabs and my other artists. Heat spread over my cheeks and I cleared my throat.

"I think we need to sound-proof the interior walls in this place."

That made everyone laugh, but I really didn't care. I was too happy to have Eagle claim me, and have my family back, to be upset about anything.

Chapter 23

Eagle

Nothing had ever felt as good as walking through the Charon MC clubhouse's front door with Silk by my side, wearing my fucking property patch. I may be fairly new to the MC world, but I still understood how fucking special it was to have a woman willing to wear a label saying she was yours for the world to see. My inner caveman was pretty pleased with himself, too.

"Oh! Claudine, you're back!"

Silk's aunt was the only one I knew that occasionally used her real name. The older woman came rushing up and pulled Silk against her for a long hug.

"Hey, Aunt Rose. Yeah, I'm back, and as an old lady."

Rose sucked in a breath before she thrust Silk away from her to take in her cut.

"Oh, honey. Congratulations! We all knew that boy would claim you as soon as he was able."

Scout came up beside me, pulling me back a little from where more of the other old ladies were gathering around Silk.

"We heard back from Sabella a little while ago. Church in five. Silk'll be fine with the other women. And the prospects are all on high alert."

I looked around and noticed that, indeed, there were a number of sober, miserable looking prospects. I couldn't help but grin a little at that. Those days were now over for me. No more being stuck on fucking guard duty without a clue why.

"Sure thing, Prez. I'll be right there."

"Good. Now, I gotta go separate Taz from the whores. That boy's gonna need his own fucking harem if he keeps this up."

Scout kept grumbling about how willing women didn't grow on trees as he made his way to the back room, where Taz was no doubt balls deep in some random club whore. I pushed my way to Silk's side and leaned down to kiss the side of her throat.

"Hey, babe, got church for a bit. You stay inside, okay?"

She turned into me, instantly ignoring all the women asking her questions.

"It's Antonio, isn't it?"

"Don't know yet. Scout just told me to get my ass in church in five, so that's what I'm doing. I'll let you know as soon as I can."

She scowled at me.

"Don't say a word, Silk. You know how this shit works. I'll always tell you what I can, as soon as I can."

I pressed my mouth against hers and kissed her till she softened. Then, with regret, I pulled away and stormed toward the meeting room, more than a little pissed I was being separated from my woman when I'd finally gotten her back. However, I wasn't stupid enough to believe this mob shit was going to go away on its own, and was glad to finally be included from the beginning.

I slipped my phone into a locker, and with a wide grin, walked into the room as a patched in Charon for the first time. It felt good. No one had mentioned a word about my beat down since the moment it was over. Clearly, it really was a clean slate type thing—for which I was glad. The beating I could handle, over analyzing the shit out of it for weeks? Not so much. Now if I could just get Silk to quit reminding me about it, I could happily pretend it had never happened.

Bulldog slapped me on the back.

"I see you got my girl to come back. Thanks, brother."

"Well, if you look at her cut, you'll see she's my girl now. But yeah, I got her back where she belongs. I think you'll find she already wanted to come back. She looked utterly miserable when I went to her. Crazy woman thought she'd lost both the club and me with that temper tantrum she threw."

He chuckled. "Well, now she's your old lady, you get to deal with those tantrums. She doesn't throw them often, but she sure as fuck makes the ones she does throw count."

I gave him a smirk. "I'll keep her in check, don't you

worry."

At that he raised his hands with a grin. "And, there are some things I don't need to hear about my niece. Come and take a seat. Let's get this shit started."

Within minutes the room was filled with men in various states of drunkenness. Seemed some started the party before the party was announced. Taz slumped in the seat next to me, stinking of sex.

"How many you gone through so far?"

With a gleam in his eye he licked his lips. "It's impolite to kiss and tell."

I scoffed. "It's impolite to screw every one of the club whores before anyone else can take a turn."

Scout banging the hammer stopped any further conversation.

"I've called church tonight because we've finally heard back from Sabella. As you all know, the bastard is still gunning for Silk. Who is now not only Bulldog's niece and a Daughter of the Club, but Eagle's old lady."

He paused as a few cheers went up. A smile tugged at my lips. I hadn't had this kind of family since I left the Marines. Sure, Taz and Mac would always be my brothers, but they were only two men. To have this entire room cheer me on for landing my girl? That was fucking special.

"We need to end this shit, so we reached out with a proposition for him. He's agreed to meet us. And by us, I mean the asshole is insisting Silk come along. Apparently, he can't trust us that she doesn't have the money, but will believe it if he hears it from her lips."

I spoke up. "He's going to try to make another grab for her."

Scout focused on me. "I think he's assuming his men will grab her before the meet. We didn't tell him we've caught and disposed of his boys yet. That'll be a nice surprise for him when we see him."

"And when is that?"

Mac was leaning forward with his elbows on his knees and a serious scowl on his face.

"Tomorrow night. Ten pm—or twenty-two hundred for you military ones—out at the old quarry. All cloak and dagger, you know—mob style."

"I'm guessing Eagle's going to be by Silk's side. Taz is a fucking excellent sniper. We have another trained sniper we can have watching over things?"

I was relieved to see a couple hands go up in response to Mac's question.

"I was thinking the same thing, Mac. We'll have four snipers set up beforehand to keep watch over the site. I want you out there, set up before nightfall. I'd love to leave Silk home but I know that girl well enough to know she'd just sneak her ass out if we tried to lock her down. Eagle, you stick to that woman of yours like glue. You hear me? Lose her again, and you won't be coming back from that beat down. Understand?"

I sat straighter and squared my shoulders. "Well, since you've actually given me all the facts this time, along with adequate back-up, it shouldn't be a problem to keep her safe."

No way was I letting him put all the blame on me. It was as much the club's fault as mine.

"Yeah, yeah. I hear ya. Right, I want at least a dozen men to go in with us. I'll need that number again to stay here and keep things tight. I want all women and children here on lockdown while this goes down. Iron Hammers are coming for us soon. Don't know when, but I don't want them trying any shit while we're dealing with Sabella. So, who's with me at the quarry?" He waited for Keys to write down names. "And who's staying here to guard our family?" Again, Keys wrote down who was staying. "Right, keep the drinking light tonight, boys. I don't want to be dealing with anyone's fucking hangovers tomorrow. And Taz? Share the whores around, yeah? Those bitches don't grow on trees and there's only so many."

Church ended with everyone ribbing Taz, who puffed out his chest and took it all in stride.

"Thinking we should have named that boy Nymph, not Taz."

Mac laughed at my comment, and didn't bother to even try to disagree.

Silk

I was glad to be back. All the old ladies welcomed me like I'd been gone for a month, not a week. They all admired my cut's new patches. No one was surprised. While Eagle was good with the hands-off thing, he wasn't so good with the eyes-off thing. Also, the fact he'd never made use of the club whores had caught everyone's attention. As much as I knew full well how the club worked, and how the men were all free to use the whores as they pleased, I was glad Eagle hadn't. I'd seen how the whores treated an old lady of a man they'd had. The bitches weren't supposed to get attached to the men. When they came on board, they were told straight-out they were there for the men to scratch an itch, nothing more. Definitely no emotions involved. However, over the years I'd seen more than one of them go after a new old lady. And honestly, I had enough shit to deal with, without having to watch my back around the clubhouse.

The men all filed out from the back room, looking serious and heading straight for their old ladies, if they had them. The others milled around the bar, a few headed to the back rooms. As soon as I caught sight of Eagle, I couldn't see anyone else. He came straight to me and wrapped his arms around me before leaning down for a kiss.

"Missed you."

I smiled and ran my fingers up his neck, into his thick hair. "You were only gone half an hour, babe."

He didn't respond, just palmed my ass and lifted me. With a chuckle, I wrapped my legs around his waist as he began walking toward the stairs. Catcalls followed us, but I didn't give a shit. Nope, I just lowered my face against my old man's throat to kiss and nibble on his slightly salty skin.

"You taste good."

I delivered one last lick up his neck before I pulled away to see where he was taking me. He headed for my room and kicked the door shut behind him as he entered. He sat on the bed and rearranged me on his lap with his palms cupping my hips, but not trying to get me naked.

"Sabella has agreed to meet with the club to sort shit out."

I tightened my grip on his hair, only releasing it when he winced.

"Sorry. What does he want?"

"Well, he wants all the money your father stole, but we ain't giving any of yours to him. He'll just have to accept the fact your father spent a huge chunk of it."

"But I still have most of the cash he left me. I can give him that."

He shook his head. "No matter how much you give him, he'll always want more. No, he doesn't need to know about the cash that was in your box. We've offered him the ledger on the N.Y. mob in exchange for leaving you and the club alone permanently. He's requested you be the one to meet him. Apparently, he doesn't trust the word of any of the club, but yours he does trust."

My shoulders slumped. "He's going to try to grab me again, isn't he?"

"Not on my watch. The meet is at twenty-two hundred tomorrow, at the old quarry. We've got four snipers who will be set up before nightfall to watch over things, then us. And there's going to be a dozen Charons with you, including Scout and Bulldog. The rest of the club is staying here. Scout's put all club family members on lockdown, just in case the Iron Hammers try anything stupid while we're dealing with this mob shit."

"Does he know about his men being killed yet?"

He shook his head. "Scout thought it would make for a nice surprise for Sabella. The bodies were wrapped and are on ice. We'll be delivering them along with the ledger. That's one hell of a message we're delivering. It should make it so he doesn't come after you again."

"Didn't Scout, Nitro and my uncle already show him it wasn't a good idea to come after me back in L.A.?"

"They roughed up some of his goons, but evidently that wasn't a clear enough message. Dead bodies are a little harder to ignore."

If I broke his fucking nose he'd remember that pretty well, too. I wondered what my chances were of getting a shot like that in on him?

"That look in your eye is scaring me. What exactly are you planning?"

I shrugged and leaned in to kiss him.

"Nothing you need to worry about, babe."

"I seriously doubt that."

But his voice sounded more than a little distracted as he ran his palms up under my shirt, lifting it over my breasts. I went to shrug out of my cut but he stopped me.

"Nope, keep the cut on. I want to fuck you while

you're wearing my property patch."

His words sent a shudder through me. He pulled the cups of my bra down so my breasts were pushed up and out toward him. My shirt bunched up above them, framing them for him. He wrapped his mouth around one already-hard nipple and swirled his tongue around the bar before tugging on it with his teeth.

"Eagle!"

He pulled the other nipple with his fingers, twisting and tugging until I was grinding against his lap and moaning.

He released me as he stood, setting me on my feet before him. I clutched at his shoulders so I didn't fall over when he dropped to his knees and pulled my pants down.

"Need to get you some skirts. This would be so much easier if all I had to do was flip up your skirt."

"How the fuck am I supposed to ride in a skirt?"

"Very carefully. Don't want the world seeing what's mine."

Before I could respond, he had his mouth on my pussy, his tongue thrust deep inside me. I spread my legs as far as I could with my pants around my ankles and earned myself a swat on the butt.

"Stand still and let me have you."

"Quit spanking my ass, Eagle! It ain't a fucking drum."

I squealed when he nipped my clit. "Keep sassing me and I'll show you just how drum-like your sweet ass can be."

Holding my lower lips apart he blew air over my sensitive clit, making my whole body vibrate with need.

"Please Eagle, stop teasing me."

He covered my mound with his mouth once more and proceeded to tongue fuck me like I'd never been before. When he moved to suckle my clit, he thrust two fingers deep, rubbing my g-spot.

"Fuck!"

I was on the edge of something huge and when he slipped those wet fingers back to rub over my asshole, my orgasm exploded from me. All I heard was ringing—all I could see were stars and blackness. It went on forever, yet not long enough.

"Fuck, Eagle."

He was still gently lapping at me when I came back to my senses, those fingers continuing to rim my asshole as I came back down. I stroked my hand into his hair, using a firm grip to pull him away from me. A shudder ran through me at the sight of his mouth and chin glossy from my climax.

"I need you to quit teasing me, and fuck me."

He turned to kiss, then nuzzle my thigh, wiping his face on me in the process.

"Ever had a cock up this fine ass of yours, Silk?"

"Nope, and it ain't happening tonight either. I need you to fill my pussy with that big cock of yours."

His eyes darkened with lust. "Fuck, I love when you talk dirty."

He rose up and spun me around so fast, I had to slap my palms against the wall to prevent myself from falling over.

"No mirror this time. Guess I'll just have to stare at your property patch here while I own your body."

Man, he was really getting off on me wearing his patch. I'd seen how the other men watched their old ladies, but I'd never seen any of them be quite this possessive. Then again, who knew what went on behind closed doors?

I tilted my ass back toward him, and with a groan, he leaned against my back, his cock sliding up between my thighs but not entering me.

"Let me take you bare, Silk. I'm clean, I haven't been with anyone but you since I got my last medical."

"I've never been with a man without a condom. I'm not on birth control."

"You got a problem having my baby?"

Fuck me, but the idea of having this man's child growing inside me had me growing even wetter.

"I take the warm rush of cream that just coated my cock means you don't have an issue with that?"

I shook my head and flexed my pelvis to slide back and forth over his now-wet cock.

"Good. I ain't ever wearing a fucking condom again."

With that he pulled back and slammed home, making both of us groan.

"So fucking tight, baby. Hold on, I can't do this slow. Need you too fucking much."

He pulled back, took my hips in his palms and began thrusting at a rapid rate, every fucking stroke hitting my g-spot and sending me higher and higher, until I was trembling with the need to come. With a final powerful stroke, Eagle slammed into me as he slipped one hand to tease my clit and the other to tug on my nipple piercing.

"Eagle!"

I screamed out his name as I came, clenching against his throbbing cock as he filled me with his seed.

The next thing I knew, we were both on the bed, Eagle's arm and leg wrapped possessively over me as he kissed up my neck and along my jawline.

"I can't believe how much I love you, Silk. I'm never going to get enough of you, of being inside you."

I trailed my hand up his arm, over his shoulder and into my hair, guiding his face to mine so I could kiss the love of my life.

"Ditto, babe."

Chapter 24

Eagle

Night had fallen hours ago, and it was time to get this shit over with. Once the snipers had called in with an all clear that we weren't walking into a fucking ambush, we all filed out of the clubhouse and saddled up to ride out. I helped Silk onto the rear of my bike. She could have taken her own bike, but she seemed to understand I needed her closer than that tonight.

Scout took the lead after a couple of prospects opened the front gates and we all followed. I was in the middle of the group, as Silk was the main focus of our protection. I didn't have the tingling down my spine to indicate things were going to go to hell, but I was still nervous. I'd have preferred to have Silk locked down with the other old ladies back at the clubhouse, but I hadn't even tried. Scout had been correct when he said she'd have just snuck out and followed us if we tried to stop her.

My woman was strong and brave, and would never sit out a fight—one of the many reasons I loved her so much. Except when the fight was with a fucking dangerous mobster, then it annoyed the shit out of me.

We all rolled in to the old quarry and parked in a line, me still in the middle, with Nitro pulling in behind us, in the cage. Fitting three frozen bodies in our saddle bags wasn't really an option.

Opposite of where we pulled up were two sleek black Escalades. The moment we turned our engines off and moved off our bikes, the doors opened and Sabella stepped free, along with five others. I figured with the fact the drivers' doors didn't open, that made it seven men with him. We had a dozen here in the open, plus the four snipers. We were as safe as we could be, given the situation. The fact none of Sabella's men were holding weapons out in the open had me relaxing a little too. By the time any one of those bastards reached a gun or knife, they'd have a bullet in their skull. *Probably more than one.*

Silk unzipped her jacket and pulled the ledger out in clear view of them.

"Ah, my dear Claudine. You are looking well. Is that for me?"

She scowled at him. "No thanks to you. Here's the ledger you were offered. Now you can leave me the fuck alone for good."

Sabella raised a single brow at her. "Really? Such language. And what of the money of mine that your father left you?"

"There wasn't any money. Just a book, handgun and a short note telling me to run away if I was with you. Be grateful Eagle was there to knock out your goon in the bank. If not for him, I'd have shot him to get away."

Sabella frowned as he tried to stare down Silk. He wouldn't spot the lie, because thanks to his stupid word choice, she hadn't really lied. That money could have been from any number of people her father had ripped off.

"About these books—it seems the FBI has gotten a hold of the one you gave me at the airport. How is that possible?"

Silk shrugged. "I haven't a clue. There was a copy of it in the box, but it's been locked up tight and no one got to it."

I held my wince in. I wasn't sure how the fuck we were going to cover up Mr. Smith's fuck-up with that one. Before I could think of anything, Scout stepped forward.

"We believe we've solved that issue. We had a rat who was reporting back to a rival club. I can only assume he got hold of the ledger at some point, at least long enough to snap a few photos of it, and passed that onto the other club."

Sabella turned his gaze from Silk to Scout and I took the opportunity to grab her hand and pull her back behind me.

"And you've dealt with your rodent infestation?"

Scout grinned in an evil way. "Of course. We actually had a few pests rear their heads recently. I think these three belong to you." He indicated to Nitro, who, along with two other men, opened up the trunk of the cage and lifted out three bodies wrapped in black plastic.

Sabella's face paled as he cussed in what I assumed was Italian when the bodies were dumped at his feet. Scout moved to stand nearly on the man's toes.

"You chose to ignore our warning back in L.A. Let me make it crystal clear for you. You come anywhere near Claudine, or anyone else involved with the Charon MC, again and you will not live to regret it. Got it?"

Sabella nodded in a jerky way that had a few of the club chuckling.

"So glad to hear it. Now, take your trash and go home. And don't try anything stupid. We have several snipers watching your every move. Wouldn't want one of them to get trigger-happy now, would we?"

I kept Silk firmly behind me until Sabella had his men load up the bodies and drive off.

"Can we move out? I don't want to risk him coming back, loaded for bear."

Scout nodded to me. "It's a plan. Let's get out of here. Nitro, hang back and cover the boys. We'll see you back at the clubhouse in half hour or we'll be back here looking for you. Understood?"

"Yes, Prez."

I'd never put Silk's helmet on so fast. I wanted to be out of this place and have her somewhere safe. In under five minutes we were ready to roll and to the roar of twelve sets of pipes we headed back to the clubhouse.

An hour later, we all sat back in church, ready to wrap

shit up for the night. Sabella hadn't tried to come back at us and had been spotted driving out of town minutes after leaving our meeting. Seemed the bastard finally learned you didn't fuck with an MC and get away with it. Before Scout could slam down the hammer, Mac indicated he wanted to speak. Dammit, didn't the man realize I needed to get back to my woman already? She was waiting for me up in our room. Yeah, we now shared her room here at the clubhouse and I was going to move into her house as soon as I could. Living full time here at the clubhouse in the prospect rooms because I had nowhere else to lay my head, was, thankfully, a thing of the past now I had claimed my woman.

Mac

All eyes were on me now, and Eagle was about to burn a hole through me with his nasty glare. But the man could wait another five fucking minutes to go ball his woman. This was important.

"What's up, brother?"

I couldn't hold in the grin at Scout calling me brother. You didn't get that honor until you were patched in.

"I've been thinking about our women. They're the club's most obvious weakness, and with what's happened to Silk recently, it's clear others aren't always going to respect that they're off limits."

I cleared my throat when Scout's beefy arms crossed

over his chest and his stare turned glacial. "Where you going with this?"

"I was going to ask about setting up some self-defense classes at the club gym. We'll gear some to men and others to women. Family gets first priority, but getting the girls in town able to take care of themselves is only going to help us keep our town safe, right?"

The tension in the room drained away and I took a deep breath. Fuck, for a second there I thought Scout was going to have me beaten for simply pointing out a fucking weakness.

"And you're able to set this shit up? Oversee it? Because I don't know shit about self-defense, other than making sure I hit hard enough the other guy doesn't get the fuck back up."

That got a few chuckles. "Yeah, I've got the knowledge. I've done my share of rounds in a cage to work with any men who want to go further with it, too."

Scout nodded and turned to face a man I'd not met personally before.

"Chip's in charge of the gym. You work with him and let us know what you need. Take your boys with you. I've seen how well Eagle can fight, and if Taz can fight half as well as he fucks, you're all set."

Even I had to laugh at that one. We'd been here for just under a fucking year and Taz already had a reputation.

"All right. Settle down. Look, we all know you're right. The days where the women were automatically off-limits are over. Especially with what we now know about what the Iron Hammers have been doing. Still haven't heard shit from them about whatever the fuck Runt told them, and we're still tracking down a fucking VCR player. Didn't want to have to buy a new one just to watch this shit, but it's looking like that's what we're going to have to fucking do." He shook his head on a huff. "We need to set up some weapons training, too. If we let it be known our old ladies are licensed to carry and know how to use that shit, that'll be good for us too."

Taz spoke up. "Let me handle that. Mac and Eagle will have the gym covered, I'm happy to help with it too. But I've already been hanging around down the gun range here in town. Old Gus gets a buzz out of having a Marine sniper hanging around, and he lets me shoot for free. I'm sure I can sort out running some female-friendly gun handling classes with him."

Scout eyed Taz in a way that had me slightly concerned for my Marine brother.

"We need to find a way to own that place. Silk's paid us out so she owns her shop clear, which we always knew would happen. That leaves us with the bike shop, storage yard, the gym and the bar. The gym doesn't bring in shit as it is. We need to start making some more green, men."

I spoke up again. "These classes will bring more people in to the gym, Scout. We spruce the place up a bit, make it female-friendly, you watch the memberships rise. Ask any large gym anywhere in the US, women are their bread and butter at the moment. We can keep the back room as is for the old boys that don't want women around. Keep them happy with their own entrance back there. It wouldn't take much to renovate it all."

I'd been in the gym a number of times. The back room was where an old ring was set up, with the old-school punching bags and other shit around it. The front rooms were used for storage and office shit. It'd be a piece of cake to clear that crap out and set it up as a modern gym. Especially using the club's manpower to get it done.

Scout stood and moved to lean against the front of the table as he continued to frown in thought. He turned to Chip. "What do you think?"

The older man shrugged. "The place is fucking dying, that's been clear for a while. Not many of the old boys still around. As much as I hate the idea of change, I can see the logic behind it. And hell, it'll certain make the scenery at work prettier to look at. So long as we keep Taz on a fucking leash, the rest of us might get some pussy out of it."

Scout shook his head on a chuckle when I stood, fists clenched with anger. "The classes we're setting up are to protect women, not to set them up to be treated like fucking whores."

"Settle down, Mac. Chip knows that. Every man here knows if they want a whore they come grab one of the ones here that know the score. Any man, club or not, that gets caught mistreating a woman in this town gets dealt with, don't you worry about that."

Taking a breath I nodded and sat my ass down.

"And just for the record, I only screw the club whores. I know how fucked up my needs are. I wouldn't ever try to force that shit on a woman that didn't know the score going in."

Taz spoke in a low voice, but it traveled, silencing the room. At least half the men here had been in some form of military service. Hell, there were two Charons I knew of that were out on deployment at the moment. War could change a man, change his needs. Roughen his edges. And sometimes what we needed to smooth that shit out wasn't what polite society could accept. It was one of the reasons I'd been so quick to jump at joining the Charons in the first place. It had nothing to do with what that bullshit FBI agent Mr. Smith was selling us. Nope, it was that an MC, a true old-school one, would be a safe place for me and my men to call home, where we wouldn't be judged for what we needed now we were on home soil again. Sure, the brothers would give us shit for those needs, like all the ribbing Taz got for his sex life, but they accepted it.

The sound of the hammer landing brought me out of my introspection.

"Done. Chip? You sort shit out with Mac and Eagle and let me know what you need. I want the gym renovations done fast. Taz? Tomorrow I want to go with you out to the range, chat with Gus and see what he wants for the place. Church is done. Get your asses out of here."

I rose slowly, feeling good about this new direction.

Setting up the gym would fill my time and give me focus. *Just the distraction I needed to keep the memories buried.* I smiled as Eagle burst out of the room, clearly in search of Silk. I was happy for him. He'd found his home. I eyed Taz as he smiled and ribbed at one of the other younger guys. The happy-go-lucky act he put on was just that. An act. I hoped he could find his place here at the club, too. And for something more than being good with his dick.

This thing with the gym would be my new beginning. My safe place where I could be who I now was. And maybe, if I was lucky, I'd find a woman who didn't mind having an overbearing, super protective caveman in her life.

If I was lucky.

Epilogue

One month later, at Silky Ink
Silk

"I still think you could have found a way to do this naked. Or topless, at least. *I'm* topless."

I gave my man an eye-roll as I snapped on a pair of gloves. We'd been living together for a month, since he'd patched in, and he was still completely insatiable. Two weeks ago, Gabs had moved out. She told me it was to give us more room, but I think it was because she was sick of trying to avoid finding us naked and at each other all over the house.

As much as I loved Gabs, I liked having the whole place to ourselves. And I'd even taken to wearing short skirts like Eagle had asked all those weeks ago. It really was simpler. Fuck, but I loved how he would just grab me, shove me up against the wall, or over the arm of the couch, flip my skirt up and fuck me.

"Sorry, babe. You need to have your shirt off so I can ink your beautiful skin. And all my gear is here at my station, and in full view of the rest of the shop, so I'm not going naked."

"We won't mind in the least if you want to strip down to do it, luv."

Eagle tensed on the chair with a growl at Taz's teasing.

"Taz, shut the fuck up before Eagle comes over there. I don't need him tensing up on me. And Gabs doesn't need you laughing while she's trying to ink you."

Gabs was doing some more work on Taz's chest. The man was going to be completely covered the way he was going. Mac, Taz and Eagle all got their club tatts done the day after the club settled shit with Sabella. Today's ink was something personal, not club related. And something I'd been working my ass off to get perfect since we were at the cabin.

I picked up the transfer and carefully placed it over Eagle's shoulder and around to his collarbone. A grin stretched my lips as I peeled the paper away, leaving the outline of the kickass eagle holding a tattered American flag in its talons that I'd drawn for him. When I'd finally shown Eagle the completed design last week I'd been beyond nervous. Naturally, he'd totally loved it. And damn, did I get fucked well that afternoon. No matter how many times I drew a tattoo up, I was always worried the client wouldn't like it. And when it came to Eagle, I really wanted him to love what I was going to ink on his skin.

"Let's get this party started."

I leaned over and gave him a kiss, groaning when he

held my face to him to take over the kiss. Within seconds, he had arousal spiraling through my body. I turned my face with a groan.

"That's not fair. I can't focus if you kiss me like that."

He ran his knuckles over my cheek before releasing his hold. "You started it, babe."

Shaking my head at his teasing, I grabbed my water bottle and took a mouthful.

"Did you want to look in the mirror at the placement? Make sure you like where I've got it sitting."

He sat up straight and turned to look in the mirrored wall at the rear of the room. When he grinned widely, my muscles relaxed. He was happy with it.

"Looks awesome, baby. Can't wait to see it all inked up."

With that, he settled back against the chair that I had set to recline nearly all the way flat.

I picked up my gun, and just like every time I started a new tatt, a buzz of excitement flowed through me. I loved my job, loved giving people a piece of art they would carry with them forever. Inking Eagle was extra special, and it was with a light heart and happy smile that I loaded up my gun with black and leaned over my man's silky-smooth skin to start the outline.

True to his Marine nature, he barely flinched as I did the outline. Even when I did the long lines that I knew felt like I was slicing razor blades through his skin, he scarcely tensed. *If only all my clients were this tough.* Over the years, I'd had people do all sorts of shit from the pain of getting a tattoo.

I paused to spray and wipe down his skin.

"You doing okay?"

"Yeah, babe. I'm good."

That he was. Damn man was good at just about everything he did. Especially in the bedroom. I paused a moment with that thought. I hadn't told him what I'd discovered this morning yet. I wondered how he'd react to the news that his sperm were apparently as hard working and determined as the rest of him.

With a smile, I got back to inking my man. I had a special plan to reveal my news. Hopefully he'd play along with it.

Eagle

I could watch Silk work for hours. Glancing at the clock, I realized I'd done just that. I'd been here all afternoon, but Silk had told me I would. The eagle she was inking on me was fucking big. It needed to be. To shrink Silk's epic artwork down to a small size would be criminal. With how it was placed on my shoulder, I couldn't see much of the tattoo, but I could see all of her—the lines of concentration, the small smile she wore the entire time she was dragging her needle over my skin. I could see I was going to be getting more ink, just so I could watch her deliver it.

I rather liked the idea of her branding me with her art.

Made our connection more permanent. Thinking about connections made me think about the ring I had in my pocket. She was wearing my patch and we were living together. And I was doing everything I could to get the woman pregnant, but we hadn't discussed marriage. I wasn't sure if she'd want it. Hell, I hadn't ever thought it was something I'd want. But when it came to Silk, I wanted every tie I could to bind her to me.

A wide smile spread over her face as she reached for her spray bottle.

"Nearly done. Can you close your eyes for a minute? I want to get it all cleaned up, then reveal it to you."

Warmth engulfed my chest. She was so fucking sweet.

"Sure, babe."

I closed my eyes and enjoyed the feel of her fingers over my skin as she sprayed the cold liquid over the fresh ink and wiped it down. I frowned when she stuck something else to my skin, just below the tattoo. What was she up to? Whatever it was, I knew she'd never do anything to hurt me so I kept my eyes shut while I tried to figure out what kind of stunt she was pulling on me. She wasn't using her tattoo gun, so whatever it was, it wasn't permanent.

"Right. Take my hand and let me help you stand. No peeking!"

I was instantly aware that the shop was now silent. Like, I could hear a pin drop silent. What the fuck had she done? I let her guide me across the floor, keeping my eyes closed, because whatever she'd done, was done now and there was no stopping it, so I might as well let her have her fun.

And I'd spank her ass for it later if she'd done something too stupid.

"Okay. Open your eyes."

Her voice sounded rough, as though she was really nervous. I blinked open my eyes and focused on myself in the mirror. The eagle looked as awesome as I knew it would, both the bird and the flag done with such skill they looked like they would come to life at any moment. I frowned at what was in an arch underneath it all.

"I'm going to be a father?"

Whoa. My head spun I turned so fast. I snatched Silk to me and held her close.

"You're pregnant, baby? For real?"

Tears filled her eyes as a grin spread across her face. "Yeah, for real. Although that part of that tattoo isn't. It's a fake. It'll wear off in a week or so. I just thought it was a cool way to tell you the news. So, you're happy?"

"Happy? I'm fucking ecstatic! You know I've wanted this. Hell, I've been at you every chance I get, hoping I'd get you knocked up."

She feigned hurt. "What? All that sex was just to make a baby?"

I held her face and gave her a deep, passionate kiss. I wished we were alone, because I wanted nothing more than to be inside my woman.

"Baby, I fuck you all the time because I can't keep my

hands off your sexy self. Getting you pregnant came in second to that. I promise."

With a chuckle she stepped back and wiped her eyes quickly.

"Um, let me cover that tatt and then we're all done."

"Not yet we aren't. Come back here, baby."

I wouldn't find a more perfect moment than this. I briefly flicked my gaze over to Gabs, who was crying, and Taz who gave me a thumbs up to do it. He and Mac had both been with me when I bought the ring.

I tugged Silk's hand until she stood back in front of me, then after quickly swiping the ring from my pocket, I dropped to one knee.

Silk gasped and put a hand over her mouth.

"Claudine Bennett, would you do me the honor of becoming my wife?"

She whimpered behind her hand and panic started to rise when tears leaked from her eyes. Surely she wouldn't turn me down? Would she?

"Of course I will! I'd love to be your wife, Colt Benally."

I slipped the ring on her finger, and before she could get a good look at it, I had her pressed close against me and my mouth on hers again. I would never, ever, get tired of kissing and loving this woman. I pulled back when Taz's whistling and commentary got quickly too much to bear.

"Taz, shut the fuck up man. You know I got sensitive hearing."

Bastard just laughed, but I didn't care. I was too busy watching my woman, my fiancé, my old lady, the mother of my child, who was cleaning over my tatt, applying cream and covering it up so we could get out of here.

"I love you so fucking much, Silk. I never thought I'd have a wife or kids of my own. You've given me everything. A home, a family."

She stopped what she was doing and cupped my face in her palms.

"And I love you, more than anything else in this world. I have no idea why you came to Bridgewater, Texas. But I'm so fucking glad you did."

Yeah, that made two of us.

Other Charon MC Books:

Book 2:
Fighting Mac

Book 3:
Chasing Taz

Book 4:
Claiming Tiny

Book 5:
Saving Scout

9 780987 627513